FOREVERLAND IS DEAD

Book Two

TONY BERTAUSKI

BERTAUSKI STARTER LIBRARY

FREE!
Click link below to get starter library.

---

bertauski.com

AUGUST

Now I lay me down to sleep,
  When I wake,
  Who will I be?

1

A rooster crows.

Over and over and over.

He wants her to wake up, to get up. But the girl is stuck in a dream where she's screaming, submerged in a cloud of fear, unable to move. Unable to see.

Everything, just gray.

She can't escape, buried beneath the snowy sleep that buzzes like the inside of an anesthetist's mask. Holding her down.

And the rooster crows.

The girl claws to escape, scratches through the cloth of sleep, follows the rooster like a beacon, a lighthouse on the rocky shoals of the living. She rises to the surface—

The seal of crusty sleep breaks.

She blinks to stay awake, to clear her sight, staring into darkness.

Her head is nestled in a pillow, covers pulled up to her chin. The gel-like mattress fits perfectly to her body. Still, her body aches.

Her eyes adjust. Forms bleed from the darkness. First, there are lines...lines scratched on a wooden wall only inches away. They are bundled in groups of five, organized in rows.

She can smell her own breath, thick and rank. A film glues the corners of her lips together. She swallows. Her tongue sticks to the roof of her mouth. Hunger growls in her stomach, perhaps expecting something now that she's awake.

"Mmmm."

She jerks her head around, sinking into the pillow. Eyes wide. She listens to her pulse.

It's a cabin.

There are more beds with lumps beneath the covers, not moving. She can't tell where the moan came from, but she hears slumbering breath.

She breathes slowly, silently, until it hurts. She tries to remember where she was before she woke, but nothing has ever existed before this moment except for fleeting dreams, like whispers of another world. She dreamed of someone else.

A boy.

The sky falling.

And screaming.

Something flutters on the back of her neck.

She runs her hand over her scalp, her hair bristling on her palm, and feels a lump. It's marble-sized and quivers beneath her touch, sending electric tingles through her head, all the way to the back of her eyeballs. She jerks her hand away. A wave of nausea fades.

She tries it again, this time starting at the crown of her head and rubbing as close as she can to the lump until the tingling warns her.

Fear balls up in her throat.

The faint sound of a helicopter is nearby, interrupted by the sound of an insistent rooster.

The girl pushes up on one elbow, waits and listens. She sits up, moving silently. Her bare feet meet a cold, wooden floor. It's brisk outside the blankets. Her bed is in the corner. With her back to the wall, a door is to her right and a window to her left.

She walks to the window.

The floor creaks, and she waits to take another step. Her reflection looks back from the dark glass like a ghost, an unreal apparition: white skin smudged with dirt. Perhaps her hair is blonde. It's definitely a buzz cut. Body odor wafts up from her long T-shirt, her legs exposed from the knees down. Outside, the jagged edges of distant mountains.

A gust of wind slams the cabin. The window crackles. The helicopter gets louder. She can't see anything in the sky, though. It's hard to see anything except her reflection. And she doesn't recognize that.

Coughing.

The girl spins around. Chills creep into her chest, fear and cold. Another girl whimpers, stifled by a sucking sound. Maybe a thumb.

There's a can on the small table in front of the window. The side has been cut out. It's fastened onto a saucer with a short candle. A box of matches next to it. She pulls one out and holds the wooden stick in her fingers, trembling. She looks around, not really seeing the back of the cabin. There could be monsters.

The girl strikes the match. The flame quivers but finds the black wick curled at the top. The tin can reflects the firelight like a lantern.

Oh my.

It's a small dormitory.

A total of six beds with a window and table between them. There are boxes beneath the beds. The tables each have a hooded candle like the one she's holding, surrounded by a variety of knickknacks.

The lumps beneath the blankets come to life, rolling over and lifting up. Their heads are shaved, each with a fuzzy crop of black or brown or blonde. Some of them rub their eyes, waking from a long sleep. One of them throws the covers over her head and whimpers.

"Who are you?" A skinny girl sits up, her skin smooth and brown. She can't be more than fourteen years old.

"Where am I?" another asks.

The girl shines the candlelight on each bed. The one in the back corner looks empty, but the rest are filled with young girls, all about the age of puberty, maybe a little older. The girl with the candle isn't sure how old she is. Her breasts are loose beneath her shirt, no bra. She's definitely past puberty. She feels older than the others but isn't sure. She can't remember her birthday or where she was born.

I don't know my name.

There has to be an adult somewhere, someone that knows where they are and how they got there.

And who they are.

She takes the candle to the front door and steps outside. The wind quickly snuffs out the flame and almost knocks the candle from her hand. The sun isn't visible, but morning light bleeds through the sky from her left. She quickly notes which way is east.

She feels the helicopter's whoop-whoop-whoop in her chest. To her right, near a barn, there are three windmills, each with big white blades spinning on a post. Grit blows into her eyes and she drops the candle to shield her face. Knee-high grass waves in a wide-open pasture.

Hooves stampede up to a five-wire fence near the windmills. A horse rears up and neighs. Two others join it, stomping around when they see her. Just past the horses, the barn looms, the doors swinging on rusty hinges that sing in protest.

One of the girls comes outside, followed by two more. They crowd together. The early morning chill has them hugging themselves, teeth chattering.

"Who are you?" one of them asks.

"Go back inside," the blonde girl says.

She looks to her left, away from the whoop-whoop-whoop of the windmills and rampaging horses, to see a big cabin built from logs like the bunkhouse.

"Hello?" the blonde calls, walking toward it.

There are no lights inside it. She steps onto the empty porch, the boards creaking under her bare feet. Some of the girls follow from a distance. The blonde cups her hands over one of the windows. It looks like a dining hall of sorts: a long wooden table with chairs on both sides and an elegant candelabrum in the center. Empty and lifeless.

Her breath fogs the glass.

There's a large garden on the other side of the building, filled with sprawling vines and rows and rows of vegetables. Compost bins are at the far end, and maybe a hundred yards past that is another cabin. Not really a cabin.

More like a two-story modern brick house.

One of the youngsters climbs onto the porch. Her hair is black, her skin dark. The other two follow. Two more are still inside the bunkhouse.

The blonde steps quickly past them. She just wants to find someone who knows what's going on. These are just kids.

Grassy stalks stab the soft bridges of her feet. She folds her arms over her chest, hunches against the chilly wind and shuffles past the garden. Near the compost bins are ten black-dotted faces of solar panels that are turned towards the east, where the sun is due to rise at any time now.

"Where you going?" someone shouts.

She doesn't know. She doesn't know where she is, how could she know where she's going? But someone does. Someone has to be in that house, and they would know. Someone knows why there's a bunkhouse of filthy girls running around in bare feet and long T-shirts in the middle of nowhere.

Someone has to.

She's halfway there when the back of her neck starts to tingle again. She's not touching it this time. It's a low vibration. It tickles at first. Makes her skin itch. She reaches up to scratch it and remembers what it felt like the last time she did that. But each step makes it worse.

Electric lines extend out from the lump, tiny bolts of lightning crawling along her jaw and the back of her head. She looks back. The girls are watching from the front porch of the dark and empty dinner house.

She starts for the brick house again. One step.

Two.

Three.

The tingling begins to sting. Tears well up in her eyes, blurring the house. She's twenty steps away from the front porch with ceiling fans and bench swings and glass tables. There's a lamp in one of the windows, illuminating the front room.

"Hello?"

She's ten steps away when her ears begin ringing. Someone will hear her. Someone will come out. Someone will tell her where she is.

Tell her who she is.

"Is anyone—"

An electric shock shoots from the lump in the back of her neck; her teeth snap together. Her jaw clenches. Black shutters drop over her eyes.

She doesn't feel the earth slam into her face.

—

2

—

Sky. Sky. Sky.

And boys.

They're laughing. One of them, his hair is brown. He has dimples when he smiles. There's a gap between his front teeth that's more endearing than goofy. He grabs her hand—

Screaming.

The look on his face.

And the sky falls, and it's over. Over.

Over—

The girl is nowhere in particular, but feels the dull grind of grit on the back of her head, the bumpy ground beneath it—

She sits up, sucking in air like she's drowning.

Sun-sting on her cheeks. She tries to open her eyes, breathing greedily. Things are a bit blurry. Her face is numb on the left side. Her bottom lip is swollen, the taste of blood.

This time, though, she remembers something. She remembers that it was cold when she awoke in a strange bed inside a bunkhouse; she remembers a dinner house and windmills. The brick house is behind her.

A few girls are on the dinner house porch. They're watching

another girl walk toward her. She swaggers along the garden, where bell peppers swing in the breeze. Her skin is pasty white, her hair jet black and shaved near the scalp. She's wearing denim jeans and a stained white shirt. Her boots are heavy.

She carries a bundle beneath her arm. She stops a few feet away and tosses a pair of jeans at the girl on the ground. Drops a pair of boots.

"Thought you might want these, Cyn," she says.

The girl on the ground squints, not sure what "sin" means. The black-haired girl smiles, sensing the confusion. It's a "been there, done that" sort of smile. She crouches down and flips the waistline of the jeans inside out, revealing a white tag and block letters.

"Cyn."

That word means nothing to her. It rings no bells, brings no memories. It's just a word.

"These were under your bed," the black-haired girl says. "At least, we figure they're yours. Everyone else had clothes under their bed, their name tagged on the inside. I'm Roc."

She holds out a clear plastic bottle.

"Water?"

Cyn doesn't hesitate, and the water spills over her lips. It washes down her throat, bringing small relief to her empty stomach. She tips it up, chugging it all. Roc holds out an apple.

"Hungry?" she asks.

Cyn takes it without a word, biting off most of one side. The sugars hit her tongue like a drug. She barely chews before swallowing and takes another bite. It's nearly gone before she looks up.

"Figured you were starving," Roc says. "Everyone is. Found a stash in the middle cabin."

The white windmills rotate in the distance, slower than before. The wind has slowed, not nearly as cold. She recalls the odd sensation on the back of her neck when she neared the brick house.

"How long have I been here?" Cyn asks.

"A while. We couldn't get near you without this going off."

Roc turns around and points at the lump. She's got one, too. And she's careful not to touch it.

Cyn remembers something electric wrapped around her face. It feels like days ago, but it was just this morning. Now the sun is overhead.

"I woke up last," Roc says. "Everyone was already outside; the sun was up. You were on the ground; we thought you were dead. The girls told me what happened, said you started wobbling when you got close to the house, did a face-plant right about there."

She points a few feet behind her.

"We tried to get you, but the lump gets strange the closer we get." Roc scratches her throat like it's starting to buzz. "There's like an invisible fence around the place. You could draw a line in the dirt right where things get weird, like we're dogs with invisible leashes."

Cyn notices the scar on Roc's throat. The raised white line slashes just below her jaw.

"How'd I get here?" Cyn asks.

"You mean outside the fence?" She lets loose a humorless smile. "The little one walked out of the brick house like nothing at all, like her leash ain't working. She got the lump, it just doesn't do anything. She says she just woke up. We were all standing around trying to figure out if you were breathing or not, and she comes out the front door and stares at us. We told her stop gawking and drag you out. She did, but you kept on sleeping. Thought you were dead, but I checked your pulse." She shrugs. "You just got knocked out."

"Where is she?" Cyn looks around. "The girl, where is she?"

"With the rest of them."

Nothing makes sense. Roc looks the same age as Cyn—sixteen or seventeen, if she had to guess. The girls, as far as she can tell, are younger. They're still on the porch, watching from a distance. She can't blame them. The brick house is spooky, even without the fence. The light is still on, but nothing moves inside.

It's almost noon. Cyn's cheeks feel sunburned, maybe a little wind-scorched, too.

"Want to tell me what the hell is going on?" Roc asks. "'Cause none of the other dipsticks have a clue."

Cyn shakes her head. "Where'd you get the food?"

"There's a stash in the dinner house, in the back room. All sorts of stuff—eggs and fruit and milk. You put that there?"

"I don't know."

"What's that mean?"

"That means I don't know."

Cyn pushes herself up, pausing until her balance is right. Roc watches her knock the dust off her bare knees. Cyn's only wearing a T-shirt and underwear that look like they've never been washed. Smell like it, too. She puts the jeans on and they fit just right. The boots are worn leather, cracked along the seams. There's a hole in the right one, but they fit. Without socks, though, they chafe.

"Maybe we should get everyone together," Cyn says. "Meet in the dinner house around the table, find out what everyone knows. See what's around here."

Roc heads back while Cyn tucks her shirt inside her jeans, flipping the waistband one more time, reading her name stitched inside. It feels strange.

Everything does.

The solar panels had raised their mechanical faces to follow the sun. The garden is mostly free of weeds. The houses all face a large, grassy meadow interspersed with swaying yellow flowers.

White-capped mountains are in the distance.

The middle of nowhere.

The girls are on the porch. Three of them stand next to the door, shoulders hunched against the slight chill. Or maybe it's fear. Their filthy shirts freshly stained, their chins glistening with the sticky juice of apples or oranges. Their eyes, though, are still hungry.

The one girl that doesn't belong is in the corner. Her blouse is clean, her shorts pressed. Her socks have little frilly edges. She leans into the railing, blonde hair hiding her eyes.

Roc tells one of the girls to fetch her an apple.

Cyn walks past the porch for a closer look at the bunkhouse. The cabins look different in the daylight. Even older than she would've guessed, like they were built with an ax. The horses gallop to the wire fence, one of them rearing up. They snort and stomp dust clouds.

The windmills stand in contrast to the dilapidated barn. Wind harvesters. That thought pops into Cyn's awareness, like she knows it's not some ordinary windmill but a wind turbine that converts kinetic energy into electricity.

Yet the barn is missing planks.

The girls watch her, all except the blonde. She's hiding in the shadows.

"Let's go inside," Cyn says.

Roc pulls the door open and lets it slam behind her. The others watch Cyn, waiting for her. She opens the door and waves them in. Cyn looks around like she's not sure if someone else will show up. The horses whinny.

The walls and furniture look like something from pioneer days, all hand-carved and primitive. A cold black woodstove is in the back, a pipe running straight up the wall, through the rafters and ceiling. But the windows are triple-pane insulated.

The girls shuffle around the table but don't sit. There are plenty of chairs—twelve of them. There are only six girls. Roc drops into the chair at the head of the table and throws her boots on it. She rips into the apple, juice dribbling from her chin.

Cyn examines the rough surface of the table and the candleholders, which appear to be iron rods crudely welded together. Wax puddles on the table. The walls are barren and the wood floor scuffed. There are two doors on the back wall, one on each side of the stove.

The girls' heads are shaved, all except the blonde. Roc's laughter breaks the silence. "You're looking at them like cattle."

Bits of apple shoot from her mouth.

"What are your names?" Cyn asks.

No one speaks. She points at the one with black hair and dark skin. Indian, maybe.

"Jen."

"That's what it says inside your pants?"

She nods.

"Okay. How about you?"

Kat's hair is bright red, her cheeks freckled. The other one is Mad.

She has black skin, tight curly hair. The blonde has found the corner again, looking for a mouse hole to climb inside.

"What about you?" Cyn asks. "What's your name?"

"Miranda." She rattles the bracelet on her right hand. She doesn't have a tag inside her designer clothes, just a fancy bracelet, her name engraved on a gold plate.

"You're the one that pulled me out of the fence."

She nods, eyes cast down.

"You woke up in the brick house. How come you were in there?"

Miranda shakes her head.

"Why doesn't the fence bother you?"

Again, she shakes her head.

"Well, what's in there?" Roc interjects.

Shrug.

"You don't know?" Cyn adds, softer.

No response.

Cyn looks over her shoulder. Roc says, "Told me she woke up in a bedroom and came down some steps, came right outside. Don't think she looked around, but how should I know? She hasn't said two words since. She ate the hell out of a can of beans, though."

Roc tosses the apple core into the corner.

"So no one knows anything?" Cyn asks. "I mean, where we are or how we got here?"

They shake their heads.

"Does anyone remember anything?" Cyn looks at Roc. She's picking her teeth. "Because I don't. I couldn't remember my name when I woke up. I don't know if we're in the United States or Russia or on another planet."

All she gets is Roc sucking on her teeth.

Cyn goes to the window. *Yet I know those are horses. I know the garden has been weeded and the wind harvesters are generating electricity. Am I dreaming?*

"I remember something," Mad says. "I remember a dream."

Cyn turns. "What was it?"

Mad describes a tropical island. She was flying over the palm trees and soaring over the ocean. She says there were boys there, like it was some sort of Neverland, only they didn't call it that.

She stops.

"Then what?" Cyn asks.

"Something happened…but…I don't remember."

The sky falls. That's what.

"What about you?" Roc points at Miranda. "You have any dreams?"

Miranda dips her shoulder. Her face is completely hidden behind her hair.

Roc rubs the scar along her chin. There's a tattoo on the inside of her right arm. The fuzzy blue lines look like a long dagger from the inside of her elbow to her wrist.

"Come over here, Miranda." Roc pats the chair next to her. "I don't bite, girl."

Cyn doesn't care about the dream. She'd rather forget it. As dire as things feel, it's better to be inside the cabin than inside the dream. The screams sounded like people were being pulled apart.

"They're hungry," Kat says.

Cyn didn't realize she was staring at the horses. They're still romping along the fence, craning their necks over the wire, but the grass is out of reach.

"How do you know?" Cyn asks.

Kat shrugs. "Isn't it obvious?"

Not to Cyn. But now that Kat said it, Cyn can tell they're anxious. Have they been without food as long as the girls? *How long have we been asleep?*

"I don't remember." Miranda is next to Roc, hugging herself.

"I'm not asking what happened before you woke up," Roc says. "What's inside the brick house, girl? Is there a phone or a computer? You know, something that could save our lives, that sort of thing?"

Cyn walks past Roc's interrogation. The kitchen is to the right of the woodstove. The door is cedar plank, but there's an electronic lock on the silver handle, one that requires a programmable keycard.

The shelves are stocked with canned goods and jars of fruits and vegetables. The food has been shoved around; empty cans lie on the floor. A half-empty bottle of water. Bruised bananas hang from a hook but are still yellow.

There are two stoves: one wood burning and the other electric. The industrial-sized refrigerator is polished silver with a pantry next to it. A nail is bent on the shelf above the sink, holding two cards on strings, each about the size of a credit card.

Cyn retrieves them. She slides one in the kitchen lock. A green light goes on and gears turn. The light turns off and the gears go back.

"I DON'T REMEMBER!"

"Don't give me that!" Roc towers over Miranda. "You walked through that house, you're not blind, you had to see something, now what's in there?"

"She's right." Cyn steps between them, kneeling down. Miranda is shaking. "If there's a phone, we could call someone."

"That's genius," Roc says.

"Let's go over there." Cyn rests her hand on Miranda's. "We'll go with you. You could be the one that saves us."

Miranda stops quivering but doesn't lift her head. Cyn pats her knee. Roc reaches over her head and yanks the chair back. Miranda has to stand to keep from falling. Cyn stands between them. She holds out one of the keycards.

"Here."

"What's this?"

"It unlocks the kitchen. If there's not a phone in the brick house, we need to start rationing food."

Roc puts the keycard around her neck. "Why?"

She doesn't look at Roc. She stares at Miranda. "Because we're going to run out."

Miranda looks up. Her eyes are blue, her face clean and free of scratches. Cheeks puffy. She lacks the gaunt tug of hunger.

Miranda waits on the front porch while Cyn and Roc lock the kitchen.

Kat, Mad, and Jen venture off the porch towards the garden. They don't want to be around Roc and she can't blame them. But they didn't ask Miranda to come. They couldn't care less about her.

She doesn't care, either.

She wouldn't hang out with them anyway. She doesn't like to mix. She's not sure what that means, but it seems to have to do with race. Blacks, Irish, and Indians—that sort of thing.

Miranda's the one quaking on the porch while they walk through the garden, but they're the dumb ones. If Cyn hadn't said something about the food, those pea-brains would've plowed through those shelves like rats led by the Dagger Queen. They wouldn't listen to Miranda. No one would. She's too small and...different.

Thank God for Cyn.

Miranda can't remember any more than the rest of them, only she didn't wake up in the bunkhouse. She saw where they woke up; it looked like a redneck cellblock that smelled like an armpit. The stink was in them and they didn't smell it. Miranda breathed through her mouth when they were in the same room.

"You ready?"

Cyn comes out of the dinner house. The shoestring is around her neck, the plastic keycard dangling between her breasts. She needs a bra. The rest of them don't.

Miranda least of all.

"Let's go see what's in the brick house." Roc puts her hand on Miranda's neck, guiding her off the porch.

Miranda breathes through her mouth.

The house is a two-story home with Old Georgetown brick, functioning shutters, and a green metal roof. The cabins look like they were built two centuries ago. The brick house, last year.

They slow at the end of the garden. Roc still has her hand on Miranda's neck, gently squeezing.

"Circle around," she says. "If we stand where the tall grass starts, we'll be able to see into the front door."

Cyn doesn't know much about the fence. The others tested it from every angle, knowing where their necks would start buzzing and how close they could get. They walk along an invisible line but only they can feel it. Feels like nothing to Miranda.

They stop twenty feet from the house. Double doors are between large windows. There's a lamp in each one, the one on the right still on.

It's no accident the house faces south, not that any of the others would know. The southern exposure allows the light inside for warmth. The other end faces north. They're protected from the winter wind by trees. Miranda doesn't know where they are, but it doesn't take a genius to know winter is cold.

She's not really sure how she knows.

"Open both doors," Roc says. "Open them real wide so we can see."

"Find the kitchen," Cyn adds. "We need all the food out of there, first thing. We don't want anything to spoil if no one's in there."

"Yeah, that's great," Roc adds, "but if there's a phone, you forget the food and start dialing 9-1-1."

Miranda wants to get away from them—she doesn't like all the attention—but the other direction doesn't feel any better. The brick house is so quiet. The lamps look like eyes, the steps like teeth. As much as she hates the attention and body odor, she remembers what the inside of the brick house smells like.

It's not body odor.

Roc pushes her.

Miranda's legs are stiff. Roc shoves her again. Miranda steps safely inside the fence. Roc can't reach her, but now she's stuck between them and the brick house. She wants to chew on her finger, bite the skin from the sides, but stops herself from that bad habit. Perhaps she'll just sit down, right there, inside the fence.

The first step is the hardest. The second one isn't much better.

The grass is worn away near the bottom step. Miranda looks down at her shoes. They aren't boots, aren't made for roughing it. These are casual flats. And she feels the pebbles through the thin soles.

She puts her foot on the first step. It feels like the house is pushing back. She wonders if that's what it feels like to the others. She doesn't want to go in there, she doesn't know why.

"Come on!" Roc says. "We're going to starve before you get there."

Miranda grabs the railing. She pulls herself up—a high-pitched scream.

It's somewhere toward the dinner house. Cyn and Roc turn toward it. Miranda backs off. The girls aren't in the garden. Cyn starts walking, careful to stay outside the fence. It's hard to tell where it's coming from.

They hear it again. This time, two girls are screaming.

Cyn starts running. Roc follows, but she goes straight through the garden, plowing a path through the rows and snapping plants off at the base. Miranda is all alone, one foot on the bottom step. The lamps stare at her—one on, one off—like the house is winking.

Or got punched out.

She leaves the safety of the fence and runs around the garden. Right now, the pack is safer than the unknown. The screams are coming from the trees.

3

Jen stumbles out of the woods before she falls. She scrambles to her feet.

Roc is there first, rushing to the trees. More screaming. Kat and Mad come out a little farther down. Cyn puts her arms around Jen. She clings to her. Her chest heaves with sobs.

"What is it? What happened?" Cyn says.

Kat and Mad fall behind Cyn. Their arms and faces are scratched and bleeding. Mad hides her face.

"Settle down, settle down." Cyn peels Jen off of her, brushing away tear-streaked grime. Long welts line her face. "What happened?"

"We were..." Jen swallows a sob, taking a deep breath. "We were just looking around. Mad saw it first and then...then I saw it, too."

Mad's still hiding her face.

"What is it?" Cyn asks. Neither of them answer. She looks at Kat.

"I didn't see anything. I hauled ass when Jen started screaming. There's a little path in there, but we cut through the trees; limbs tore us up."

"Where is it?"

"Go down a bit; you'll see the opening. Mad's the one that found it—"

"I'm not going back there." Mad's shaking her head.

"Me neither," Jen adds.

The girls sit closely, huddling behind Cyn. Miranda stands several feet away. They're watching the trees. Limbs begin cracking. Cyn creeps closer, her heart thumping.

Something rushes through the thicket.

Cyn backs up, arms out, like a mother fencing off her cubs.

Roc jumps out, wiping spiderwebs off her head and arms, spitting.

"What's in there?" Cyn asks.

"There ain't a trail, I can tell you that. But something's back there. Something dead."

"Down there." Jen points at the bunkhouse. "You'll see down there."

There are black plastic cisterns on the back of the bunkhouse and the dinner house. They're as tall as the roof and are connected to gutters to collect rainwater. Each must contain thousands of gallons. There are no windows on the back of either cabin, but there's a door on the bunkhouse, right between the cisterns.

Cyn wanders over, warily looking at the trees and back to the girls. There's a narrow path starting at the bunkhouse door that cuts to an opening.

Cyn's guts feel twisted, her eyes unblinking. She points at the opening and Jen nods. Cyn ducks under a low-hanging branch and enters the cool shade. Branches have been cut away. A dirt path swings around the tree trunks and, up ahead, turns to the right.

Roc breathes loudly behind her.

Cyn pauses, looks and listens. The wind rustles the tops of the trees, but the air is dead beneath it. She reaches the turn and stops. The smell hits her. Something foul, something spoiled. It's not a skunk. More like road kill baking on summer asphalt. She leans around the corner and pulls a branch down.

Twenty feet away, right where the path turns, there's something on the ground. Tan and ragged.

Cyn takes a step and waits for it to move. Deep down, she knows it won't. *Pants. Those are tan pants.*

Two legs lie across the path, both mired in dirt and dried blood. There's only one shoe. The other foot is bare, the sole caked with mud.

"It's a body." Cyn says it louder than she intended to.

Roc looks over her shoulder. "Told you."

Cyn covers her face with the bottom of her shirt. Roc does the same. The smell penetrates the fabric. Even when she holds her breath, she still feels it.

The torso is off the path, buried in the undergrowth. The pants are shredded on the back side, exposing muscles and tissues. Looks like the work of scavengers. Hopefully, long gone.

They'll be back.

Cyn stops short of the body. The odor saturates her face. A knot swells in her throat. She blinks away the tears and tries to hold her breath again. Vertigo spins in her head, but she wants to make sure.

An adult.

The woman is heavyset, facedown in the weeds. Her hair gray and matted. The shirt has been clawed away, the bra strap still intact. The flesh isn't.

"The hell happened?" Roc asks.

"I don't know. Wolves, maybe."

Maybe.

"Think we need to bury her?" Roc asks. "Keep the wolves away?"

Cyn is thinking the same thing, but she doesn't want to touch that body to roll it into a hole even if they dig it right next to her.

"Let's leave it," she says. "Keep the girls out of here for a while. No one comes down this path, not until we're sure it's safe."

Roc is already backtracking.

Cyn kneels down for a closer look. She dry-heaves once and pinches her nose. If there was more than an apple in her stomach, she would lose it, but she's not coming back anytime soon. She wants to be sure she's not missing anything. Perhaps if she sees the face, it will remind her of someone. Maybe jog loose a memory, provide a clue.

But there's nothing familiar. Not the clothing or the body or the hair. And she's not about to roll her over to see the face. She's certain it's beyond recognition.

There's something in her hand. Cyn pokes it with a stick, but the fingers are stiff. Looks like a plastic bag.

Cyn backs away. She'll come back much later to investigate.

Or maybe never.

—

4

—

Miranda doesn't sleep much that first night.

There's an open bunk in the back. The clothes in the box are her size, but they're filthy. She sleeps in the clothes she's wearing. They're dusty, but at least they don't smell like wet animal.

She's the first one in bed. There's no way she's going back into the brick house, even if there's clean clothes and a soft bed in there. She just wants to go to sleep, wants to wake up from this dream. Because it has to be a dream.

The other girls wander into the bunkhouse once it's dark. Miranda peeks from under the covers, just a sliver of an opening. They look drunk, sort of staggering to their beds and getting undressed, eyes half shut. They're breathing heavily, softly snoring.

Somewhere out there, a wolf howls. It sounds like outside the cabin. Others join. It's getting hard to breathe beneath the blanket, but she's not about to look. She's trying not to think about an animal getting inside.

They're probably coming back for the body.

She didn't follow Cyn and Roc into the woods. She stayed back. She wanted to run, but then she would've been all by herself, so she waited outside the trees. She never saw anything, but she caught a whiff.

Cyn didn't talk about it, but Roc did. She said it was an old woman, half-eaten. Said the head had been gnawed off and the spine stuck out like a chewed corncob.

Miranda didn't believe her, but still...she tries not to think about it.

She doesn't fall asleep until the wolves finish howling. But then, in the middle of the night, someone gets up and goes out the back door. Miranda figures someone's going to pee.

She has to pee, too, but decides to hold it. Doesn't matter if those wolves stopped howling, they could still be out there. The bathroom is a little outhouse near the trees. She doesn't know what's worse: walking outside at night or peeing in that bathroom.

It's a tie.

Half an hour later, the girl comes back. She must've delivered a number two.

Even grosser.

5

Not day.
Nor night.
Endless gray. Forever and ever.
It cannot be grasped.
Cannot be let go.

Cyn tears at the fog. It slips between her fingers, yet clings to her skin. She tries to swim, tries to run, tries to do anything but be there.

She hears them cry. The boys are out there. They're crying for help. The rooster crows.

Sleep is like death, bottomless and heavy. Her head is a rock sunk into the pillow; her body gently cradled in the gel-like mattress. Feels like she's hovering in its embrace. Cyn opens her eyes and stares at the lines carved in the wall. She can't remember getting into bed.

They fed the horses and chickens before sunset. The girls wanted to pet the horses. Kat knew what food they ate and how much. The barn had a feed room with tack and barrels of oats.

They straightened up the kitchen. Dinner was pickles and boiled potatoes. The brick house sat in the distant dark, one eye lit on the front porch.

They went to bed, but she doesn't remember doing it.

Cyn quietly sits up. Her feet hurt like she'd been walking barefoot. She doesn't recall taking off her boots. She's wearing the same T-shirt. The smell of death clings to it like smoke. Or perhaps that's the dead body still staining her sinuses.

She reaches under the bed and slides out a box. She digs blindly through a stack of shirts, finds a pair of socks near the bottom and something else. Something leather.

It's curved at the bottom with a smooth, cold handle. There's not enough light to see, but she knows what it is. She lights the candle. Buck knife.

She unsnaps the latch and slides it out of the leather case. The blade is silver, heavy. She flicks the end and listens to it ring. The edge is sharp, but the tip is dull.

The lines on the wall.

Are those days? Has she been marking how long she's been there? There are so many. She pulls the bed from the wall, the legs grinding. The lines go all the way to the floor.

More than a year.

Cyn snuffs the candle out and gets on her knees. She reaches under the bed, feeling one of the boards that support the mattress. She unsnaps it one more time and reaches over the bed, gouging a line in the wall.

A new row begins.

There are plenty of tools in the barn, but no buckets. A dozen eggs fit in the cradle of Cyn's shirt. It's more than they'll eat, but she wasn't going to leave the eggs to rot. The cisterns stand like black sentinels drinking from the roof. There's a door to the kitchen on the outside of the dinner house.

Cyn slides the keycard into the slot and listens for the gears to turn before pushing it open. She flips the light switch, turns on the griddle, and looks for butter.

There's a list of daily chores tacked to the refrigerator. She puts it in her back pocket. The refrigerator is stocked with milk, fruit, and dried strips of meat. The meat could be from a hunt—there's probably elk and deer—but milk and fruit? Oranges don't grow where there are snowcapped mountains. Someone had to bring those.

They'll be back.

No butter in the fridge. There's a cabinet below the sink but no food, just hundreds of plastic bags containing clear liquid. They look like IV bags. The shelves on the door contain brown bottles of peroxide and iodine.

Medicine, good.

She grabs one of the IV bags. No label. Maybe medicine or nutrients. If things get desperate, they might be drinking them.

Half the eggs get burned.

Mad finds a tub of lard and turns the heat down, salvaging the other eggs. Cyn scrapes the blackened bits onto a plate. They each get two eggs and a banana. Cyn's eggs look like they were cooked with a hammer.

They eat in silence.

Kat's the first to finish, licking her plate. She starts scraping the inside of the banana peel. Miranda picks at her food, pushing the crispy parts to the edge. Roc pinches them off her plate. Miranda doesn't complain.

Grit gusts against the windows. It sounds cold.

Roc takes her plate to the kitchen and returns with a jar of preserved apples. The top pops. She dips two fingers inside like chopsticks.

"We need to start rationing," Cyn says.

"There's enough food for months," Roc says.

"We might be here longer."

"I don't plan on being here that long."

"Where you going?"

"Out there." Roc points at the front door. "I'm not waiting around to die; I'll hit the hills and take my chances."

"That's not smart. Grizzlies are out there."

"How do you know?" She plucks out another apple.

"We're in the mountains. This looks like Wyoming or Montana. Either way, bears live here."

"She's right," Kat adds. "This is the wilderness. You won't survive two nights out there. Plus, we're at the end of summer. That means it's going to get colder."

"And we need to conserve food." Cyn reaches for the jar.

Roc slides it away. "Maybe I'm Daniel Boone."

"You don't know who you are." Cyn looks around the table. "None of us do. And until we know more, we need to work together. We need to survive until someone finds us."

"That's your plan? Hang around until someone finds us?"

"Look, oranges and apples don't grow here, someone brought them. Someone built these cabins."

Roc laughs. "Maybe the dead lady did."

"That's not funny!" Miranda stands up. Her chair falls over.

Her chest heaves, fists clenched at her sides. Her lip starts trembling and she crosses her arms, turning her back.

The wind hurls another gust of sand.

"Look," Cyn says, "there's a lot we don't know. We don't know anything, really. We have to play it safe. We need to conserve food. We have to eat to survive, and that means staying hungry, eating little. We need to make it last."

"Maybe the world ended, is that what you're saying?" Roc says.

"First, we need to survive. So would you put the lid back on that jar and put it away?"

Roc wipes her chin, staring at Cyn. They're all watching.

"How about this?" She lifts the jar as if to make a toast. "We go ahead and divvy this up since it's already open. After that, we tighten the screws. I promise."

Roc doesn't wait. She walks around the table, giving everyone a portion. The pieces plop onto the plates, cinnamon syrup spilling over the plump slices. Cyn watches the keycard dangle from her neck.

The girls pause, but their appetites take over. They clear their plates and slurp up the syrup. They don't look at Cyn. She doesn't eat the fat chunks mellowing in a puddle of sugar water, even though her stomach fights her. Roc drops her boots on the table while running her finger inside the jar.

"I found this." Cyn pulls the paper from her back pocket. "It's a chore list. I think we need to start doing it."

She spreads it on the table.

"It makes sense, seems like things we should be doing." No one objects. "Someone needs to be in charge of the garden, like weeding and harvesting. Who knows how much longer that stuff will grow; we need to get as much food out of the garden as we can. We've got at least one empty jar to fill."

Roc licks the rim.

Jen raises her hand. "I'll do it."

"Then there's the barn, and feeding the horses and chickens—"

"I'll do that." Kat stands up.

"Okay, good. I saw tools in there, so you and Jen can get that figured out. Someone also needs to manage the kitchen, clean stuff, and plan the meals, do all the cooking—that sort of thing. Mad?"

She nods.

"That leaves chopping wood." Cyn drops her finger on the chore list. "There's a stack on the other side of the barn. I think we need to stock up all the wood we can. If we're here all winter, we'll need to keep the stoves burning. I don't think the bunkhouse will stay warm enough without a fire. We have to plan for the worst, start searching for dead wood or fallen trees. There are axes and wheelbarrows in the shed."

Cyn looks at them.

"Stay off the path in back. We'll just leave the body alone for now."

It gets quiet. Time slows.

They're all wishing Cyn didn't remind them.

"What do you think happened?" Jen asks.

"I don't know." Cyn shrugs. "We just have to survive. We have to hope."

"What about her?" Roc slides the empty jar in Miranda's direction. "What's she going to do?"

Miranda remains distant. She grabs a lock of hair from behind her ear and puts it in her mouth. She hasn't touched her preserved apples.

"She'll have to do what none of us can."

The others don't say anything, either.

Cyn takes her plate to the kitchen and eats the apples. She rinses her plate. Roc drops her plate in the sink, still chewing. Miranda is already on the front porch, her plate still on the table.

The apples gone.

$$\overline{\mathbf{6}}$$

"I don't want to do this," Miranda says.

"Who the hell wants to do any of this?" Roc snaps.

Miranda looks at the meadow and the faraway trees, the mountains beyond. She thinks about running, not turning back, just going and going and getting as far away from this place as she can. The wolves are out there. Bears, too.

Maybe that's safer.

"Look." Cyn touches her shoulder. "We've got to know what's in the brick house. We need to know if there's a phone or a computer. And if there's not, we need food."

She gently squeezes.

"You're the only one that can do it."

Miranda looks at the wooden planks. She nods and starts for the brick house without them. She doesn't like to be touched, even if Cyn is the nice one.

The lamp in the window is still on. Miranda's legs begin to lock up as she nears the fence.

"Go on." Roc shoves her. "We ain't got all day."

Miranda trips ahead and stops. She's inside the fence and Roc can't touch her. Stuck between two rocks—the brick house and the Dagger Queen—she pauses.

Anger balls up in her belly. If she was big enough, she could drag that bitch through the fence and watch her go unconscious. But Miranda's a waif. A fairy compared to Roc.

A skinny little Barbie.

"Come on, let's go!" Roc claps. "Everyone's working and you're standing."

"Take it slow, Miranda," Cyn says. "One step at a time. Open the door, look inside, and go in, nice and easy. No one's going to hurt you, we're right here. Go on."

Like they can do anything if something happens.

She pulls herself up the steps with the help of the railing. The floorboards are painted. There are glass tables and rocking chairs at both ends. One of the tables has a tall glass on it, half-full of diluted tea.

There are twin doors. Miranda drops her hand on one of the brass knobs. The hinges creak. She decides to push both doors open.

The smell hits her.

It's dull and rotten, sticking to the back of her throat, clinging to her tongue like gluey vapor. It's the smell from the woods.

"What is it?" Cyn asks.

"It smells. Bad."

"Smell ain't going to hurt you," Roc says.

"Cover your face." Cyn demonstrates with her shirt. "Breathe through your shirt."

Miranda does that. It helps.

The first step inside makes her dizzy. It's not so much the odor, more like déjà vu, that strange sense she's been here, done that. She braces herself against the doorjamb. Roc's voice is distant. Miranda's ears are ringing.

The front room is immaculate, the couches pristine. The coffee tables are arranged with magazines and framed photos of the mountains and trees. Elk grazing in the meadow. There's a TV set in a cherry hutch and a grandfather clock ticking in the corner.

No computer, though.

No phone.

There's a hallway down the center of the house with a metal door at the end. Everything is homey and nice: there's crown molding, the wood floor looks polished, and the lamps have frilly lace on the shades. But the door at the end of the hall looks thick and heavy.

The staircase is halfway down on the right. That's where she came down only a day earlier. Seems like forever. She didn't pay much attention to the house then. Too consumed with what was going on outside. Now she wishes she had looked around. Then she wouldn't have to be doing this.

All the doors along the way are closed. *Thank God.*

The odor, though, gets worse. It seems to be clinging to her clothes. She'll smell worse than body odor. She continues, one step at a time, just like Cyn told her. There are frames on the wall, photos of grandmothers and grandchildren. Sometimes they're photographed out in the meadow or on the porch of the dinner house. There's another one in the woods next to a small cabin.

Miranda swallows a lump.

She stops for a moment, pulling a deep breath through her shirt, closing her eyes. She feels funny. Maybe she's hyperventilating.

She should probably open a few doors, look for a phone. Roc and Cyn are watching, expecting her to do something. She gets halfway down the hall. The stairwell is to the right, but there's an open door to the left. It's the kitchen.

There's a sink below a window that overlooks the garden. Jen is on her knees, plucking peppers and storing them in the bottom of her shirt.

All the cabinets are closed and the island countertop wiped off. The sink is empty. There's no sign of a phone. There's a door to the right. Miranda reaches out with her free hand, tears building on the rims of her eyelids. She rests her hand on the knob, suddenly battling thoughts of dead bodies stacked inside and tumbling down when she opens it.

She stifles a sob and her hand slips from her face. The swampish odor wafts inside her head. She bends over. A tear splashes onto the linoleum.

She has to take something out there, something that will satisfy them. Miranda closes her eyes, and before her thoughts seize her arm, she yanks the door open—

Food.

Lots of it. Cans of beans, beets, corn, beans—a culinary treasure chest. The shelves are deep and loaded, enough to feed them all winter.

There's a hamper on the floor. She holds her breath and lets go of her shirt so she can scoop the contents of one of the bottom shelves into the plastic hamper with the crook of her arm. She dry-heaves once.

She drags the hamper across the floor, backing into the hallway with the food in tow. She feels dizzy again. The smell has worked its way past her throat and into her esophagus, staining her senses.

But she keeps going, despite the tears... She closes her eyes, backing out of the hallway and into the front room. She backpedals until she feels the cool breeze and the sun. She steps off the porch, the hamper banging on the steps and cans falling out.

She keeps going.

One foot after another.

Until she backs into something soft. Arms wrap around her.

"You did it." Cyn has her.

Miranda collapses. The tears, this time, are different.

She never wants to go in there again.

7

"This is good stuff." Mad holds up a can of black beans. "Everything on our shelves is generic, but this is brand name. Is there more?"

"Miranda said the entire pantry is stocked," Cyn added.

"Where is she?" Mad asks.

"Puking." Roc's laughter sputters.

Cyn walks away from the back corner of the dinner house. The outside door to the kitchen faces the garden and brick house. Mad slides the hamper inside and starts stacking the goods. Roc follows her, pulling out random items and setting them to the side.

"Get all that inventoried," Cyn says. "I want a list of all the food we have in stock."

"You an accountant now?" Roc says.

"We've got to plan our meals, know what we have. Then we'll know how long it'll last."

"There's a crapload in the brick house, you said so yourself."

"We won't know how much until we get it. Until then, we work with what we have."

Jen arrives from the garden, a pile of green peppers cradled in her shirt. She puts them in the sink. "We're going to eat like queens tonight," she says.

"No, we're not," Cyn says. "We're only going to eat what we need."

"Well, these peppers aren't going to last forever."

"They'll be just fine for a couple of weeks. We prioritize what needs to be eaten first. We'll eat what comes out of the garden until the cold gets here." Cyn looks at the sky like the color tells the season. "After that, we start on canned goods."

Roc's pile is two cans high. Cyn grabs the can of cherries, the pie-filling kind. Roc drops her hand on Cyn's wrist. "What're you doing?"

"Helping."

"I've got a system here; you're messing with it." The dagger tattoo ripples. "Why don't you start writing stuff down?"

"Your cans are out of order. They need to be organized with the others."

"They will. I'm just looking, seeing what we've got. No need to be getting your hands on everything."

Roc stares. She doesn't let go until Cyn looks away.

"Look at this." Jen digs to the bottom of the hamper. "Soap."

Cyn had forgotten what clean smelled like. She's afraid to take the soap, nervous that if she gets clean, she'll just be more aware of the filth. Maybe it's better to just wallow in it.

At least for now.

Miranda comes around the cistern, head down, hair in her face.

"You all right?" Cyn pushes the hair away. Her skin is clammy, the color sort of yellowish.

"Well, look who's here." Roc peeks out of the kitchen. "Don't tell me you fed your breakfast to the outhouse. That's a waste. Give her a demerit, Cyn."

"You need some water?" Cyn doesn't wait for her to answer and whispers to Mad to bring a cup.

"What'd you see in there?" Roc says.

"Give her a second," Cyn interrupts.

"She's had twenty minutes. What'd you see in there, Shiny?"

Miranda hides her right foot behind her left. The shoes are scuffed but still reflective. She can't hide them both; instead, she backs up.

Mad hands a plastic cup to Cyn. "Here, have a sip. You don't want to dehydrate."

Miranda holds the cup with both hands. She takes a drink.

"Look, I know you're traumatized." Roc steps outside, getting between Miranda and Cyn. "It's a big, scary house, but we could use a little help here."

"I brought the food," she mutters.

"Yeah, thanks. But boiled yams ain't going to call for help. Did you even look around?"

Miranda shuffles her left foot behind her right.

"Give her some space." Cyn gently grabs Roc's elbow. She pulls away, eyebrows wedged together. "Just give her a minute to think. Go count the food—she's not going anywhere."

Roc continues staring. She doesn't want to do what Cyn says, but she does it anyway. The cans slam together. Mad and Jen stand back.

"Something's dead in there." Miranda doesn't look up.

"Did you see it?"

"I could smell it."

"Where was it coming from?"

She shakes her head. "The doors were all closed."

"Was it coming from upstairs? Downstairs?"

"Downstairs. I think."

There's a dead body in the woods; no surprise there's one in the brick house, too. Cyn feels sad for the old women. She knows she shouldn't, because they were apparently living in luxury and the girls in filth, but she doesn't like to hear that people are dead.

"What else did you see?" Cyn asks. "Besides the kitchen."

The cup is shaking in Miranda's hands. "It just looked like a nice house. The front room has a television and coffee tables with magazines. It was all very clean. The davenports aren't faded—"

"The hell is a davenport?" Roc asks.

"It's a couch," Cyn answers. "What about a phone or a laptop or tablet? Did you see anything electronic besides the TV?"

She shakes her head.

"Did you open any doors?"

The water lightly splashes inside the cup. Cyn takes it before she gets wet.

Metal cans tumble across the kitchen floor.

"You didn't even look." Roc comes out again. "You just went straight to the kitchen and didn't even—"

"I looked!" Miranda screeches. "There's no phone, all right! There's no one to call. It's just a house with no one in there but a dead body, all right?"

"Yeah, a house *you* woke up in. A house only you can go in. You didn't look around, Shiny. You walked your little white ass in there and clicked your heels, hoping you'd be back in Kansas when you opened your eyes. And when that didn't happen, you grabbed some food. Well, good for you, you're a hero. We should all kiss your ass that we'll starve to death in three months instead of two."

"I looked."

"No, you didn't. You didn't go upstairs, you didn't open a single damn door. You didn't look, Shiny."

"Don't call me that." Miranda wraps her arms around herself, rocking.

Roc goes inside the kitchen. A can of green beans ricochets off the sink and rolls out the door. Mad and Jen get out of the way. More cans crash. Cyn reaches out, but Miranda jerks away. She bows her head, quivering. Her sobs are silent thumps inside her throat.

"You're going back in there." Roc comes out and points a can at Miranda, the label hanging. "You're going back in that big-ass house and opening those doors, and you're going to find out what the hell is in there—"

"NO!"

Miranda runs.

Roc swipes at her. Cyn flinches, wanting to stop Roc from chasing her, but she doesn't have to. Instead, Roc rears back and throws the can. The label shears off, flapping to the ground. The can misses, wide left. It rolls into the tall grass.

"You need to go get that," Cyn says.

"Yeah, I'll get it when that little bitch goes back in the house."

"She's scared."

"Who isn't?"

Roc watches Miranda sprint deep into the meadow, swallowed by swards of wildflowers and grasses, disappearing on the other side of the slope. For a second, Roc tenses. She might give chase. Cyn would have to stop her if she did. She couldn't let her go after Miranda. She's just a little girl. And their only hope.

But then Roc kicks an errant can toward the garden and curses. She stomps around back, out of sight.

Mad and Jen start cleaning up.

Cyn considers going out there. If she goes too far, if she doesn't come back, she's a goner.

She'll never survive the night.

8

The wind harvesters lift her out of dead sleep. That's what sleep feels like: death. Cyn lies beneath her warm blankets, listening to the *chop-chop* of the wind harvesters and the soft breathing of her bunkmates.

The last thing she remembers is eating. If she concentrates, she recalls walking through the grass, her hand on the door...

And then gray.

Something's out there. Something's coming.

Someone.

It's just a dream, but it's not the random images of dreams. She feels like she's somewhere else when she sleeps. Somewhere, but nowhere. It makes no sense.

She reaches under the bed without letting the cold air inside the covers; rolling over, she scores another line on the wall.

Day three.

She tries not to look at the endless bundles that are stacked like sticks below her puny new lines, too many to count.

Cyn slides the box out from under the bed, blindly pulling out a second heavy sweatshirt and jeans. She pauses for a moment, bracing for the morning chill.

The boots feel like reinforced cardboard. It'll take several steps to loosen them up. The soles bang against the wood planks. She walks to the back door and sees the lump beneath the covers of the last bed on the right, blonde hair splayed on the pillow.

She made it.

Cyn smiles. Miranda must've snuck in when they were asleep. Good.

She runs to the dinner house. The wind smacks her, grit biting her cheek. The egg collection will have to wait. The dinner house creaks. Cyn considers firing up the woodstove, but doesn't want to waste wood. She has no idea how much wood it's going to take to survive the winter.

Cyn rubs her hands for warmth. The scent of fresh vegetables instantaneously reaches deep inside her. She's tempted to sneak a bell pepper, maybe one that's half rotten, one they wouldn't likely use. No one would know.

She distracts her senses while she waits for Mad and starts taking inventory of food. Black beans, garbanzos, corn, and tomatoes on the top shelf. More of the same on the second shelf. Canned fruit is on the third shelf, with a gap on the far right.

No cherries.

Cherries.

She shifts the cans around to fill the hole. She'll bring it up at breakfast, see if anyone has anything to say. Maybe making everyone aware that she's watching will put a stop to it.

Tap-tap-tap.

Cyn jumps. The pencil rattles on the floor.

The sound on the outside door is small. She opens it. Miranda is outside, her arms wrapped around herself. Her clothes are smudged with dirt and grass stains.

She's shivering. "Sorry."

"For what?"

Miranda looks down, still shaking. She doesn't have to say anything else. Cyn knows she feels bad about not going back into the brick house. She's their only hope to see what's in there. But she's so meek. So scared.

She goes back to the inventory. Cyn gets down to the bottom shelf with Miranda watching her, grateful there are no more gaps to hide.

"Can I help?" Miranda asks.

The dinner house groans against the wind. "You can get the eggs."

"I don't know how."

"It ain't hard. You just go in the coop and pick them up and bring them in here."

Cyn fires up the griddle. Mad should be waking up soon. Miranda stands next to the door, shuffling her feet. She's not asking to help so she can really help; she's just asking to be polite. Or maybe she's waiting for Cyn to help.

"Look." Cyn pulls plates out of the cupboard. "I didn't make you go back in the brick house yesterday, but things have got to change. You can help out. Those shoes ain't made for working, but we ain't got the luxury to do what we want, understand? It's cold out there and maybe you're scared of chickens, but those eggs need collecting."

The door shuts. Miranda's gone.

Maybe she thought Cyn would take care of her, protect her. Well, maybe so, but that doesn't mean she's going to hang around while everyone else carries their weight.

Cyn eyes the shelf with the missing can of cherries.

There are enough problems already.

$$9$$

The clouds roll over the sky like a lead blanket, blotting out the sun for a week. Rain leaks from the dreary sky, the wind throwing it against the buildings like pellets. The wind harvesters churn ceaselessly.

Miranda stands inside the barn. The doors are wide open, but the wind and rain can't reach her. The cold, however, always finds its way in.

She looks puffy, wearing three sweatshirts. If there were more, she'd be wearing them, too. She doesn't care that they're stained and slightly damp, or that they smell like mold. The barn smells better. If she hand-washes them with water from the cisterns, they'll never dry. She'll never be warm.

She shivers beneath layers of grimy cotton.

Filthy. Just like them.

Jen and Mad spend their time in the dinner house. The kitchen is clean and orderly. The cans are stacked in straight lines and the inventory posted. They found a pack of playing cards in the back of the pantry. Sometimes Kat joins them.

They never ask Miranda.

Roc hardly ever leaves the bunkhouse. Except to eat.

And steal.

Miranda hears her leave the bunkhouse at night when everyone is sleeping. Miranda hears the back door open, hears her come back thirty minutes later. No one seems to care that she's stealing.

Cyn doesn't.

She's out in the meadow. Despite the bitter rain, she paces across the open field, counting her steps. If she's not chopping wood, she's out there. Doesn't say what she's doing. No one really talks about what they're doing. Not anymore.

"Chickens need fed." Kat drops two steel buckets on the dirt floor.

Miranda leans over, looking inside: seeds mixed with food scraps from the garden. The wire handles are cold. She carries them through the breezeway and braces for the weather as she steps outside. Mud sloshes beneath her rubber boots. No more shiny shoes. Kat lets her use the work boots as long as she helps with the animals. It's the price she pays to keep her feet dry.

The chickens come out squabbling. Miranda quickly heaves the contents through the wire fence, a pathetic attempt to spread the food, but she's not going inside. Chickens freak her out, the way they peck. She's afraid one will pluck out her eye. Chickens can do that, they can fight.

She runs back to the barn.

"Wash them out," Kat says before Miranda can put the buckets down.

She knows, but she wouldn't have cleaned them and Kat knows that, too. The water from the cistern is cold—always cold. She dries them with a damp towel, her hands stiff and slow.

There's a horse in the breezeway when she's done. He jerks his head in her direction, nostrils exhaling like exhaust. Kat puts a brush in her hand.

"Brush Blackjack while I tend to his hooves."

"How do you know his name?"

"I don't."

Kat's got a dingy rag tied over her head, covering her red hair. Probably full of lice. She digs through a plastic toolbox.

The horse's coat is matted in patches, what Kat calls rain rot. She minds not to get behind him, in case he kicks. "He can snap your bones," Kat had told her.

Kat begins digging into the bottom of the front left hoof with a tool.

"Doesn't that hurt?" Miranda asks.

"Keeps the thrush out."

"But it doesn't hurt?"

"Not any more than if you cut your hair."

Kat reaches for a pair of long-handled pliers that pinch off the end of the hoof like nail clippers.

"How do you know how to do all this?"

Kat shrugs. "Thinking about it don't do you no good. Like Cyn says, we got to survive until we figure something out."

Her dialect had changed. She sounds so country.

"How come everyone gets to be good at something? You got horses, Mad's a cook, and Jen does the garden."

"And Roc does the stealing."

Kat drops the hoof and goes to the other side. Miranda looks down the breezeway, hoping no one is around. She walks a safe distance from Blackjack's rear end and starts stroking his right flank. Kat digs the packed dirt out of another hoof.

"You know about that?" Miranda says.

"Don't take a genius."

"I thought I was the only one that heard her getting up at night."

"I don't know anything about that, but I see her hanging around the kitchen when no one else is around. She's got that key around her neck, what do you think she's doing?"

"Why don't you say something?"

"Like that's going to do anything."

"Tell Cyn."

Kat snorts while reaching for the hoof trimmers. "Cyn can't do anything. I mean, she's trying to be a leader and everything, but what's she going to do about Roc? Seriously."

The rain patters louder on the barn roof. Cyn's still out in the meadow with a sheet of plastic over her head. She looks lost.

"What about me?" Miranda runs the brush through the horse's tail. "What am I good at?"

Kat stifles another laugh.

"What?"

"I ain't going to say."

"Go ahead. I can take it."

Kat finishes filing the hoof and stands up. Straight-faced, she says, "Ain't it obvious?"

Miranda shakes her head.

"You're nice enough and I appreciate the help, but I think there's something missing in you. Something fake. You're a beauty queen."

Miranda picks the long hairs from the brush. She tries not to let her lips flutter. "That's mean."

"You asked."

Kat taps the horse's back leg and gets to work on the next hoof. Miranda drops the brush into the bucket. She doesn't feel much like helping anymore, even though it proves Kat's point.

She's a beauty queen.

The rain sounds like falling rocks.

$$—$$

10

$$—$$

The pencil isn't working.

The paper is limp in Cyn's hand. She can't hold the sheet of plastic up and write without the rain falling on her notes. Maybe she'll just walk to the east end of the meadow and make observations; she doesn't necessarily have to write everything down. So far, there's nothing but trees and grass.

She'd already determined that the house and cabins faced south and the trees were approximately six hundred feet away if she walked straight out of the dinner house. If she went west, the land rolls for quite a while—maybe miles—before the next dense stand of trees. It'll take a full-day excursion to explore that. Once she gets a feel for the surrounding area, they'll do that. The only thing left to explore is the trees behind the cabins.

Where the body lies.

Cyn studies her notes where she's sketched the outline of the meadow. She puts the point of the pencil in the middle, about where she's standing, and twists back and forth to mark where she's starting when the hard rain comes, hitting like cold bullets, running down the plastic, marring the world around her.

She runs for it.

The puddles seep through the holes in her boots. She splashes a path straight for the bunkhouse, smelling smoke. She rushes inside. The bunkhouse is warm and dry. *Warm?*

One of the beds is only a few feet away from the stove, the seams glowing.

Cyn strips off the wettest layers of sweatshirts and wrings them out near the door. Her feet slap across the floor. She sits as close to the stove as possible, hands out. Heat is welcome. She drags the blanket off of her bed and strips the rest of her clothes off, the fleece rough on her skin.

"Cold as a witch's tit." Roc's head appears from the bed.

"I'm going to need help cutting more wood," Cyn says.

Roc settles back inside her blankets. They sit in silence, absorbing the heat. Cyn doesn't move. She can't put those clothes on. It'll take hours for them to dry.

"You having dreams?" Roc's voice is muffled. "About the gray?"

Cyn doesn't answer.

"You see the lumps coming for us?"

A shiver runs through her. *We're having the same dream.*

"Someone's coming," Roc says.

"Don't say that. It's just a dream."

"That we're all having. I talked to the others; they saw it, too. Someone is coming out of the fog, coming to save us."

"We don't know that."

"I do. And I ain't freezing my ass off while all this wood sits out there."

"Bad idea."

Roc wraps the blanket around her face. Her lips glisten. Cyn smells peaches.

She doesn't say anything.

"When the weather breaks, we're going to start exploring what's out there. I've mapped the surroundings, but it's time to go farther out. I'm planning a day-long hike in two directions, far enough out that we'll be back by sunset."

"Good luck," Roc says.

"You're going, too."

The covers slide up Roc's face, leaving a sly eye peeking out.

Cyn scoots closer to the stove. Her skin is hot, but her bones are still frigid. She puts her head inside the blanket teepee, breathing the warm, rank body odor.

Welcome to the cold, she thinks. *Here to stay*.

11

"Miranda!" Mad waves her hand in front of Miranda's face. "Yoo-hoo, girl. You going to eat, or do I need to feed your breakfast to the chickens?"

Miranda looks at the plate in Mad's hands. "Thank you," she mutters.

All the girls are sitting and waiting, spoons in their hands. Everyone is there except Roc. Once Miranda sits, they dig in. That's Cyn's new rule: eat together, like a family.

Except Roc. No one seems to mind.

A dysfunctional family.

Cyn is at the head of the table, fingers steepled in front of her. She watches the others eat. Eggs and hominy. And prunes so slimy they race past the tongue and down her throat before Miranda can properly swallow. She doesn't want to taste them.

"This sucks." Mad looks at the cold woodstove.

"This all sucks," Cyn adds. "But we've got to save the wood for the real cold."

Cyn promises not to light another fire. Roc lit the one yesterday. *No more*, Cyn promised herself.

"As soon as the weather breaks, we're hiking into the countryside.

I've got some routes planned to get as far out as possible and be back before sunset. Maybe there's a trail out there or a sign of civilization."

The wind blows, and the roof crackles in protest, reminding them how cruel the weather is.

"What if it never breaks?" Kat asks.

The door slams open. Roc throws a square of wet plastic onto the floor and stomps mud into the floorboards. "Started without me?"

Miranda hunches over her bowl even though it's empty. She feels Roc's shadow pass over her. The kitchen lock beeps. Roc slides the keycard out and puts it around her neck.

Cyn stares ahead.

Roc makes just as much noise coming back, grabbing the chair next to Miranda. A poison slick of fear coats her stomach. She hides within her blonde locks.

"That's not what we're eating," Cyn says.

Roc pops the top off an extra-large can of baked beans. She dumps them into a pile and shovels in two spoonfuls. "Well, you shouldn't have started without me."

Mad walks loudly to the kitchen, using Cyn's key to open the door.

"She seems pissed," Roc says around a fourth spoonful.

"Give her your keycard," Cyn says. "She's running the kitchen; you don't need it."

"Give her yours."

"I'm first up every morning, getting things ready. Mad needs access."

"Yeah, well, I'm making sure no one is thieving."

"And who's watching you?" Kat says.

Roc stops chewing. Lowers the spoon. She glares from beneath her hooded eyes.

"You better watch your mouth."

"I'm keeping an eye on Mad," Cyn interrupts. "There's nothing to worry about. It'll go easier if she's got the key, Roc."

Roc hunkers over the plate, pushing the final bites with her dirty fingers. Every last bean eaten. She drops her heavy hands on the table and exhales, looking around.

"It's food you're worried about?" she asks.

"We're conserving."

"Well, I know where there's more. How about you, Shiny?"

A rancid flavor crawls into Miranda's throat. She feels Roc's weight lean closer, smells her musky odor. Cold beans on her breath.

"You know where we can get some food?" Roc kicks the back leg of Miranda's chair.

"Stop," Cyn says.

"Stop what? Stop getting more food? I thought that's what this was about—getting food. Make up your mind, fearless leader. You want food or not? Because if you do—and I think we all do—I know where to get it."

Roc slaps the tabletop. The dishes rattle.

Miranda squeaks.

"I don't want food, Shiny. I want...the hell...out of here!"

"STOP!" Cyn's chair tips over. She hangs on to the table's edge. "Stop threatening her, Roc. She'll go inside when she's ready. There's probably nothing in there but food that's not going anywhere. We've got to focus on conserving what we've got."

Roc hovers in place. A fearful shiver trickles down Miranda's neck.

"Whatever you girls want." Roc tosses her plate in the middle of the table. "Call me when you've had enough of this crap."

"We're splitting wood after cleanup," Cyn says.

"Good. We need some."

"You're helping."

Roc shakes the water off the plastic, drapes it over her head, and leaves the door open. The rain patters on the front porch.

They sit quietly. Kat is the first one up. They begin clearing off the table. Cyn is still standing, eyes cast down.

She never finishes breakfast.

—

12

—

Miranda snuggles up in bed, warm and smoky.

Roc started a fire that afternoon and no one said anything. Not even Cyn. They spread their wet clothes on chairs. The fire was wrong, but they were warm.

Roc did nothing but take.

Miranda feels the decay of cowardice in her backbone.

They all do.

When the back door clicks shut sometime in the night, she comes out of her sweet slumber. She has learned to ignore the nightly raids while everyone slept. Everyone else slept right through it. Miranda could stop her, but not by herself. But if they all come together, if they're all sufficiently pissed off, if they all taste the foulness of their cowardice, they'll rise up together.

Miranda can do that. She can bring them together.

If she can wedge a few slivers of wood between the door and the doorjamb, Roc will be locked out. She'll have to pound on the door to get back inside, waking everyone up. And if they don't wake up, she'll stay out there in the rain.

Maybe she won't survive. That's how nature works.

She quickly finds three long slivers that are thick on one end, like custom-made shims. She starts for the door—

Something's not right.

Roc's bed isn't empty.

It has to be her. Who else would do that?

There's a pile of clothing in the center of the cabin, like someone had undressed, stepped out of stiff jeans, and tossed shirts and socks next to them.

Her ears prick to attention, primed to grab any sound out of the ordinary. She walks softly, stopping each time a board creaks. Miranda squats low to the floor and grabs the pants, but it's too dark to read the tag inside the waistline.

She goes from bed to bed, all of them occupied except one. The one to the right of the front door. The blanket is turned back, a dirty sheet exposed. Lines carved into the wall.

Miranda covers her mouth.

She runs to the bed and pats the covers like Cyn must be in there somewhere. She has to be. She can't be the one. She just can't.

Miranda runs to all the beds, no longer concerned about noise or who might return from the midnight run, because it can't be Cyn. She identifies them all and they're all there, sleeping soundly.

All except Cyn.

Miranda rubs her face, pinches her arm. She has to be dreaming. There has to be an explanation, has to be a reason.

She's not a thief. Can't be.

Miranda looks out the window. The dinner house looms. Nothing moves. No ghosts. No Cyn. She considers going out there, but what's she going to do if she runs into her in the middle of the night while everyone else is sleeping? What good will it do?

Instead, she crawls into bed, hiding beneath the heavy blanket. Staring at the crackling stove. Listening to the bunkhouse resist the rain. She doesn't move.

Until the doorknob turns.

Her heartbeat thumps in her ear against the pillowcase. In her throat. Miranda nearly closes her eyes, peeking through a crack. She spies the form walking slowly past her bed and around the stove.

The fuzz on Cyn's head is orange in the stove's glow. Her clothes drip water onto the floor. She strips them off, slapping them over a chair until she's completely naked, her hair matching the hue of her pubic hair. Despite the orange glow of the fire, her skin is pale as moonlight.

The body of a mature woman.

Cyn pulls one of the dry sweatshirts off of a chair and wipes down. She rubs the scruff on her head. Her ribs push from beneath her skin, her pelvis knifing out.

She dresses in the center of the bunkhouse. Miranda pushes down the blanket, observing her sluggish, mechanical movements. Watches her put the finishing touches on a perfect crime. When everyone else is dead asleep, she can do what she wants.

But Miranda's not like them.

Now she knows.

Cyn climbs into bed and doesn't move. Miranda's skin crawls. So exposed. So betrayed. Cyn pretends to be one person, but she's another beneath the surface. She's a thief and no one knows it. At least Roc is honest about her darkness. *It's the wolf you don't see that's dangerous.*

Miranda lies awake for most of the night. As the embers die and the bunkhouse cools, cold penetrates the walls and slithers beneath her covers. It's a different kind of cold, one that a woodstove can't cure.

Before morning, she crawls out of bed. She's tired of being scared and hungry. Tired of the cold.

She has to act now, while they're all still asleep.

—

13

—

Cyn notches another line.

She doesn't count them, just sees the bundles. Funny how minutes become hours, hours become days... *Will it become years?*

The dream hasn't changed. Something is in the gray, but it doesn't mean someone is coming for them. Dreams are thoughts, not reality.

Cyn plucks her clothes from the chair around a cold stove, still damp. She pulls her boots out from under the bed. She stitched the holes in her socks, but they won't last. They already have the color of chocolate.

Her feet are caked with mud. She needs to do a better job of washing them, especially before getting into bed. A bad case of jungle rot will only make things worse.

The wind harvesters are relatively quiet. The patter of rain is gone. She runs to the dinner house, her stiff boots squeaking. Cyn gets an old-fashioned coffee percolator set up. There might be enough coffee to brew for another couple weeks. No one else drinks it. *Coffee is for adults.*

Enjoy it while it lasts.

She checks the shelves while the percolator burps. Everything is in order. No gaps, nothing shuffled around or apparently missing. That's good. Cyn will update the inventory list after breakfast.

The coffee is strong. The caffeine surges into her head, clearing out the cobwebs. She holds the mug with both hands, the steam warming the tip of her nose. She'll collect the eggs when she's finished.

Cyn stands at the window, occasionally sipping, watching the sky lighten over the trees. The brick house is brighter. The windows are lit, like another lamp has been turned on.

Something's changed.

She almost drops the mug, coffee splashing on her chin.

In a second-floor window, a shadow passes.

SEPTEMBER

Biting the hand that feeds.
Blaming the one that bleeds.

14

"Cyn!"

Cyn looks up with a log in one hand, the ax leaning against her leg. Jen's running alongside the trees, waving as she approaches the barn.

"She's come out!" Jen's shouting.

Cyn drops the ax and sticks her hand in a bucket of frigid water, cooling the blisters. Sweat tracks down the sides of her face even though she can see her breath.

The brick house is still lit up. All the lights have been on since Miranda disappeared. They haven't seen her in days and thought she was dead. Cyn saw a shadow pass by a window from time to time. The girls had seen her ghost.

Cyn walks through the garden; several rows have nearly defoliated to the soil, weeds already crawling over their withered leaves, rain resting on the waxy surfaces. Drizzle drifts down in tiny droplets.

The girls are in front of the brick house.

"What's going on?" Cyn asks.

"You ain't going to believe this," Kat says. "Beauty Queen dumped a whole bag of winter clothes for us. We're talking coats and pants, socks and shoes. We're set for winter, boss."

Jen holds up a sweater. "So long smelly rags, hello Versace!"

It's a travel bag, something a hockey player would lug onto a bus if he were hauling designer gear for women. The girls pull out sweaters and coats, shoving them back to the bottom in search of something better, thicker, and warmer.

"Take it to the bunkhouse, keep it from getting wet. And take inventory of what's in there, see what we've got."

Roc snorts. Inventory doesn't exist in her world.

"I've got something for you, Cyn." Jen holds up a white sweater, white pearls attached evenly across the front. "Match your hair."

Cyn laughs. She wouldn't mind getting all dressed up, but there's a time and place for that. It isn't now.

They drag the oversized luggage through the grass, giggling. *It's like Christmas. In Hell.*

Roc hasn't moved off the fence that is clearly defined by the trampled grass. Her arms are stiff, each hand latched onto the opposite bicep. She's staring at the door, which is slightly ajar.

Is that music?

String instruments moan in concert. At first she thought it was the wind but, no, it's violins and cellos calling out long, mournful tones. Cyn hadn't spent much time near the brick house since Miranda had gone in.

Roc hardly left.

Cyn pulls a square plastic sheet out of her back pocket and unfolds it over her head. The rain tracks off the edges. It's dripping from Roc's furrowed brow.

"Want under?" Cyn lifts the corner of the plastic.

Roc's eyes set deeper.

"That winter gear is nice."

"Can't eat it," Roc says.

"What she doing?"

There's a loud *bang* somewhere deep inside the house. Cyn stands on her toes, as if four inches will give her a better vantage point to see through the windows. A few steps in either direction doesn't help.

Something is sliding. The door opens. Candlelight flickers against the walls. Classical music bellows.

Miranda backs out with something behind her. Her hair is radiant, pinned above her ears. The jeans are new. The coat, too. And the outdoor Merrell hiking shoes—those look new.

She looks up at the gray and dimming sky, pulling the fuzzy-edged hood over her head.

"Jesus," Roc mutters.

Miranda pulls a travel bag out of the house. It thumps down the steps, scratching the wet grass. She stops a few feet from the fence line, the tall grass on the inside. She goes back to the porch and fetches a bamboo stick with a plastic hook attached to the end.

"Use this." Still not looking at either of them, she offers them the bamboo. "Drag it across the fence. I stuck rain gear in there if you want to put it on."

"Princess," Roc says.

Cyn hooks the handle of the travel bag, sliding it well past the fence. There are shoes and boots, tons of socks and rain slickers. Roc ignores the one Cyn holds up. Rain drips from her chin and brows, eyes dark and deep.

Cyn shimmies into a green poncho and throws the hood on. The material sticks to her skin.

"Thank you."

"I'll send out food tomorrow, once I get it sorted."

"What you mean is pick out the best food and give us the rest," Roc says.

Miranda pulls at the strings dangling from the hood.

"I thought you were scared?" Cyn says.

"Not so bad."

"Find any phones?"

"No."

"You checked all the rooms?"

"Yes."

"Even the one with the dead body?" Roc adds.

Miranda's lips twitch. She flicks a dark glance at Roc. "If there was a phone, don't you think I'd call someone?"

"So you haven't checked them all?" Roc says.

Miranda holds her glare and turns to Cyn. "I can wash the clothes and dry them when you need it."

"There's a washer and drier?" Cyn asks.

"It's like a regular house. Looks like six or seven people lived here."

"What for?" Cyn asks.

Miranda shakes her head.

"Isn't it obvious?" Roc says. "What else do rich people have to do with their money besides build a house in the middle of nowhere? Huh?"

Roc leans on the bamboo stick.

"Probably too noisy in the city to hear Mozart. And all those poor people get in the way, too. That's why we're out here, right, Shiny? We're here to chop wood and weed the damn garden. We're in the servant quarters, getting the horses ready and serving up meals. We're slaves, Cyn."

Roc elbows her in the ribs.

"They got a shower in there?" Roc pokes the ground with the stick. "Hot water? You got that, too? I know you do because that hair is shining under that hood, girl."

Miranda dips her head.

"Probably have a toilet to tinkle in, too. You tinkle, right? We piss, you tinkle. And you sure as hell don't fart. You fart, Cyn?"

"Why are you doing this?" Cyn says.

"How are you going to wash those clothes for us? I mean, if we can't get in there to do it, how are you going to figure it out, Shiny? While you're sitting in the hot tub, filing your nails—"

"I gave you clothes!" Miranda shouts. "I'll give you food! Can't you have an ounce of appreciation?" Miranda shakes her fingers as if she were pinching a walnut. *Just an ounce.* "It's not my fault you're out there and I'm in here. Why are you blaming me?"

The bamboo squeaks in Roc's twisting hands. "Because tonight, when I go to bed hungry and dirty and cold, I'll know you're in there curled up on the couch with vanilla-scented candles. And I can't take that."

"You wanted me in here."

"Now I want you out."

"I didn't have to share anything, you know. I could stay in here until you're all cold and dead, when you've all cheated each other out of food and clothing."

Roc shifts her weight. Her hands grip the end of the stick like a bat. Miranda is too close to the fence. Roc turns as if she's going to walk away, fed up with the injustice, disgusted with looking at a clean and comfortable young girl who is providing them with clothes and food.

The stick settles on her shoulder, both hands still firmly grasping the end. She plants her right foot, the bamboo levels out and begins to arc—

Cyn strikes out with rigid fingers, catching the tendon in Roc's elbow.

Roc's left hand opens. The bamboo cane falters in her right hand. She loses momentum, accidentally striking Cyn across the back instead of cracking Miranda on the side of the head.

Roc is stunned.

It all happened so fast. It would've been easy to knock Shiny out, drag her across the fence line. Her lips thin out. The bamboo cane lands softly in the grass. She grabs two fistfuls of Cyn's poncho.

"Touch me again, I'll throw you into the fence."

Rain spits off her lips, spattering Cyn's face.

"This time you'll never wake up, bitch."

Roc throws her close to the fence. Cyn feels it in her neck.

"And if I even see you again," she says, pointing at Miranda, "I'll throw a rock through every window. You'd better hope that fence stays up."

Roc walks off. Her form blends into the rain and gray dusk. She goes inside the dinner house through the kitchen door. Cyn will have to correct the inventory in the morning.

"Thank you, Miranda." She zips up the bag.

Miranda nods. She goes inside, closing the door behind her.

Cyn lugs the bag through the rain, the strap cutting into weeping blisters.

$$\overline{}$$

15

$$\overline{}$$

Miranda presses against the door, mouthing the lyrics to Carl Orff's "O Fortuna". The words are Latin, but she knows them. The poem of fate and tragedy. The string instruments draw her out of her body, out of this world, away from these feelings.

The music is her source of sanity, masking the haunting sounds in the house. It smothers her thoughts, transforms her emotions. Allows her the strength to stay inside the brick house. Without it, she'd be out there, with them.

And she can't do that.

Not now.

Miranda's hands tremble over her lips, brush the hair from her face. She cups them over her mouth, trying to slow her breathing. She's hyperventilating.

Why does the Dagger Queen have to be such an ungrateful, ragged bitch? Miranda went through every bedroom, searched every closet just so they wouldn't freeze. The two downstairs bedrooms are the largest, but there are four more upstairs. She doesn't go up there at night, not anymore. Too many strange sounds.

She spent days picking out clothing that will fit them, coats to keep them warm. They think they'll survive a real winter in those dirty rags? If they want to live, they need Miranda.

Why do I have to suffer?

"O Fortuna" ends with a flurry of applause, followed by "Ode to Joy".

She peeks between her fingers, staring down the end of the hall. The one room she hasn't explored. The room with the smell. It took every bit of Miranda's courage for her to climb the stairs during the day, but there wasn't enough courage in the universe to open the metal door.

If she hadn't found the shelf of candles, she's not sure how long she would've lasted. It takes six Yankee Candles of evergreen, vanilla, and apple-cinnamon to battle the odor. *Smells like the Gingerbread Man's corpse.*

Miranda crawls into the kitchen, candles on the counters, and leans against the industrial-sized refrigerator to the left. Her breathing has slowed. She lets Beethoven finish "Ode to Joy" before eating something.

16

Cyn isn't the first one awake.

Kat is stoking the fire. Jen and Mad sit cross-legged, sorting through clothes. It looks like they just struck gold. Cyn curls up beneath the blankets. The windows are dark. Rain patters the roof. The rooster is quiet.

Jen snatches a fuzzy sweater from the pile, holding it up to her chest. "Liz Claiborne. You like?"

"The fuzzy collar will drive you nuts," Mad says.

"But what will the boys think?"

Mad's laughter is punctuated with a snort. The first time she's ever done that. Maybe only the third time she's laughed.

There's a stack of clothing next to Cyn's bed. It's like Santa brought sweatshirts and coats and balled-up socks. On the bottom, thick and puffy, are tan coveralls.

"Those are yours," Jen says. "We thought you could use them when you explore the countryside."

"It's cold out there," Mad adds. "Plus, you're not getting new boots."

"Nothing's going to fit *your* paddles, Cyn," Jen says. "Unless Miranda finds snowshoes."

The girls laugh. Cyn joins them. She's got wide feet for a girl.

Her body odor wafts out, permanently stained and eternally damp from the sheets. Cyn shucks her clothing, dropping each piece at the foot of the bed. Her soft, warm skin contracts in the frigid air.

"Whoa!" Mad hides her face. "Decency, girl!"

Kat stares, smiling. "Panties in there. On the bottom."

Cyn never thought she'd be excited about underwear, but denim has about rubbed her parts raw. She craves cotton. The fabric snugs against her hips and feels nice between her legs. She pulls a padded sports bra over her head and quickly puts a new Ralph Lauren on.

Lastly, she steps into the Carhartt coveralls. It's all baggy, but so warm, so comforting, like a mother's embrace. Exactly what she needs.

Thank you.

The stove throws orange light against the walls. Shadows stretch over the floor. Jen struts to the front door.

"You like?"

She's wearing jeans cuffed at the bottom with sequins stapled to the outer seams and a cardigan that hangs to her knees. The girls clap. She stops at the front door and turns, lips pouty, and catwalks to the stove. Kat puts her fingers in her mouth and a whistle splits the bunkhouse.

"Shut the hell up!" Roc flops over in bed.

They look at the lump in the corner bed and stifle their laughter.

"Let's grab some breakfast," Cyn says. "I'll get the eggs."

17

A gust of wind splashes against the window. The brick house creaks under the assault.

Miranda takes the sweet honeysuckle candle into the bedroom to the left of the kitchen. *Adagio for Strings* plays in the front room. She sits at the desk and sorts through the tubes of lipstick and lotions, humming along with the music, imagining the conductor's steely glare and fluid hands.

The upper desk drawer is full of office supplies. The second drawer is a mess of papers and envelopes. There's a box at the bottom. She pulls an oversized pair of binoculars out of it.

Mighty powerful ones.

She steps to the window, lifts them to her eyes, and scrolls the middle dial. The wind harvester comes into focus. Kat is pulling on the barn door. The hinge must be damaged; the door only gets halfway closed before the wind snatches it back. Cyn helps push while Kat gets the latch into place. They run for cover.

Binoculars just armed Miranda in the battle against boredom.

She puts them on the bed, digs through the middle drawer for more treasure, and strikes gold again. This time, a fat manila envelope full of photographs. They're old and scratched, bent at the corners, mostly shots of the ocean, yachts, beach houses. The sorts of things wealthy people photograph.

The bottom drawer is mostly junk. A few more photos and a box of necklaces. She starts to shut it when she notices a leather-bound notebook, scuffed and tied with an elastic band, at the very bottom.

The pages are rough-cut. The script is beautifully written in blue ink. She flips the pages, captivated by the handwriting. The words are a work of art.

There's no name inside the cover. The line on the first page reads

They call this place the Fountain of Youth. I call it Hell.

Miranda sits on the bed, flipping through the pages. No dates or page numbers, just line after line of lovely script.

Everything arrived. Some of my possessions, though, were sent back. Not enough room, I was told. Perhaps they're right. There really isn't a need to make this place a home. But I'll be here until the end, so forgive me if I want it to feel like home.

Until the end? Is this a place for dying? Miranda adjusts the pillows and leans back. She reads more, but it quickly becomes mundane. Three pages on learning to saddle a horse isn't riveting. Still nothing about why they're here.

Miranda begins speed-reading.

Until...

My girl arrived.

Miranda sits up. She adjusts the journal to catch the waning sunlight.

My husband is completely opposed to her. But she's so much like me in my younger years, when I was hardheaded and tough. He just wouldn't understand. I can't sponsor someone I can't relate to, and she's perfect. I understand his reluctance, though. She's a risk.

In fact, she's dangerous.

Her background is quite alarming, but she's the perfect candidate. If she weren't, they wouldn't allow me to sponsor her.

I didn't greet her when she arrived. I was supposed to; that's what all the sponsors did—they met their girls when they arrived. I just wanted to see her from afar. She just reminds me so much of myself, it's quite distressing.

Her hair—it's just like my hair when I was that age. I can't quite believe my luck.

There's a space. As if the journal skips a few days. Maybe weeks.

They're scared of her. That's good. My husband had no idea of just how frightening I could be when I was growing up. Nothing got between me and what I wanted. She exhibits the same attributes.

Sweet Jesus, I like that.

I know that she's capable of getting what she wants. A trained fighter. Perhaps a murderer. She grew up in the roughest parts of the city; she did what she had to do to survive. I respect that.

And I look forward to seeing just what she can do. After all, I wouldn't be here if I hadn't done the same.

Miranda drops the journal onto her lap and looks at the photos on the desk. She spreads them out on the bed. It looks like vacation photos, water and sand and boats. But there's one. It looks recent. This one isn't on a tropical island; this one has snowcapped mountains in the back and open meadows. It features a group of old women dressed like ranchers.

Six of them. Four wear cowboy hats. They have their arms around each other, grinning and laughing. Four of them have gray hair, one of them has dyed brown hair.

The sixth has black hair. Jet black.

My girl has been very disruptive, although I would disagree. She's demonstrating amazing leadership qualities. She picked out the toughest of the bunch and asserted her dominance. It was quick and decisive.

I watched her from my bedroom, how my girl took her behind the cabin. How she took her down in a split second, with minimal effort. It was exciting, if

I'm honest. To see someone with that much power, that much aggression. She would've killed her if she had to. That's not what I want, but I like having that as an option. I like knowing that others' lives are at my discretion.

I must admit that I was a little nervous that she would go too far, but she's smart. And that's why I sponsored her. She knows exactly how hard to push.

I think I will introduce myself to her soon. We will get along very well, I believe. She needs some guidance. If she continues, she'll discover why she's here.

Sweet Jesus, that would not be acceptable.

Miranda drops the book.

She pushes the photos around. If it wasn't clear already, it is now. The girls will need more than warm clothing to survive.

—
18
—

The wind hurls a gust of rain against the dinner house like a bucket of water. Jen and Kat race along the garden, hiding from the weather beneath their hoods. They grab onto the handle of a bag. They lug it like it's a dead body, having to stop halfway to adjust their grip.

The garden is a sopping mess. The roots have drowned. The landscape is an eternal shelf of misery. If Cyn is waiting for the weather to break before she escapes, she'll be here too long. Maybe this is always the way it is. Maybe clear skies are rare.

The wind hurls the front door open. Kat grabs it while Jen drags the sack inside. There's a zipper down the length of the brown plastic bag. Cyn has never seen a body bag, but the sack could pass for one. She doesn't say anything, doesn't want to put that thought in the girls' heads. No one wants to believe there are body bags in the brick house.

"Oh my God. My boots are filled with ice water." Jen sits down and pries her rubber boot off. Her socks splatter the floor with water. "I swear to God, there's a gallon in here."

"I done told you, tuck the boots inside the pants." Kat peels her jacket off.

"No, you didn't."

"Did so."

Mad comes out of the kitchen and they slide the bag in front of the hot stove. Cyn looks away while the zipper is drawn to the bottom.

Just in case it is a body bag.

Mad plants her hands on her hips. "I thought she was sending food?"

"You got something against warm clothes?" Kat says.

"What good are they if we starve?"

"Maybe we can eat the gloves." Jen holds up fur-lined leather gloves. "Looks like rabbit skin on the inside."

For the third time in a week, they unload Gucci and Ralph Lauren. Jen pulls out a full-length fur.

"Oh my God. It's so soft."

"Take that off," Kat says. "You look like an idiot."

The bag is nearly empty. Cyn starts sorting the gear into piles.

"Looks like this one's for you, Cyn." Kat lifts up a North Face coat.

"Why me?"

"Got your name on it." Kat flicks a white piece of paper folded and pinned to the front. "Says to meet Miranda up at the brick house, she wants to talk."

"Secret meeting, huh?" Jen says. "Better hope Roc doesn't find out."

Cyn takes the coat and looks inside as if there might be more. She slides her arms inside, zipping up the front. It fits wonderfully.

"Nothing secret," she says. "You can come if you want."

"Pass."

"I'll watch from the window," Mad adds.

Cyn puts on the rain gear while the girls continue sorting, discovering another load of insulated socks. She's watertight when she leaves. All except for boots. Still, nothing fits.

Miranda unfurls a red and white umbrella. The black rubbers are up to her knees. She stops a few feet from the matted grass, where the invisible fence still works.

Cyn has the hood pulled over her eyes, standing in a shallow puddle. "Why haven't you sent food?"

"It's coming, I promise." She sniffs, glancing behind Cyn. "I'm just sorting through the inventory, that's all. There's a lot."

Cyn doesn't blink. "We're hungry, Miranda."

"We all are."

"Are we?" She tips her head.

Another glance behind Cyn. "I'm scared that everyone is in danger."

Miranda reaches inside her coat and pulls out the leather book. She looks around, steps over to the fence, and hands it to Cyn.

"What's this?" Raindrops spatter the cover.

"A diary."

Cyn quickly stashes it inside her coat before the pages swell.

"Most of it is just regular, everyday stuff—riding horses and hiking. If you ask me, it's like this place is some sort of dude ranch for old, rich women, like one last thing for them to do. I think they move here; I think they're sick. They end up dying out here."

"What about us?"

"They sponsor us, but that's all it really says. Like we're a bunch of poor kids they bring out here to save, maybe bring us closer to nature. I don't know."

"You're not poor, Miranda. You never were."

"You don't know that. Maybe they're training us to be better, maybe that's why I'm in here. Maybe I graduated and moved into the brick house and all the rest of you will, too."

She had never considered that until just then.

Cyn nods, but not in agreement. "Why are you giving me the book?"

"The lady that wrote all that," Miranda says, looking around, "sponsored Roc, and she talks a little bit about her. Says she's from the street, that she's dangerous."

"I figured that out."

"She killed someone."

Cyn nods again. Now she looks behind her, like something might be crawling through the weeds. "That's what it says in the book?"

Miranda nods. "In so many words. I just thought you should know that she's more than just a bully. I think she's a murderer that someone wanted to rehabilitate. I think those things in our necks are to protect the old women from us."

"Why doesn't yours work?"

Miranda rubs her neck. "Like I said, maybe I passed a test and they turned it off. It doesn't say."

"Anything else?"

"Just don't let her see the book."

"She can't get to you, Miranda. You're safe in there."

"I'm not worried about me. She starts reading that, and who knows what she'll do. Maybe she'll start stealing food right in front of you."

Miranda doesn't look away this time. She wants to see a reaction. Cyn doesn't blink.

"I'll keep it safe. Let me know if you find anything else."

"I will."

"You've searched the rest of the house, right?"

Miranda sniffs and doesn't answer.

"Because we're cold and hungry, Miranda. You're warm and full and clean. The least you can do is open all the doors. I don't want to be out here for months and find out a phone is behind a big, scary door."

Miranda turns without another word. She makes it to the porch, flapping the water off of the umbrella. Her hand is on the doorknob.

"Thanks for the clothes," Cyn says. "I'm exploring tomorrow, no matter what. The coats and stuff will make all the difference."

Miranda looks at Cyn's rotten boots. There's nothing she can do about that. She kicks off her boots and goes inside, where the air is warm and dry.

Bach's Toccata and Fugue plays ominously. She kneels down and taps the stereo to skip that song. The foreboding pipe organ cuts off, leading into the soothing sounds of Pachelbel's Canon in D Major. She basks in the uplifting tones, imagining lakes of glass and open fields with laughing children.

$$\overline{}$$

19

$$\overline{}$$

Cyn hoists the backpack off the bed. Her back sags under the weight of clothing, a tent, and a sleeping bag. Her knife is stashed near the bottom, next to a leather-bound journal.

"You sure about this?" Jen helps Cyn adjust the straps.

"First thing in the morning."

"What if it's raining?"

"Then it's raining."

The backpack is surprisingly balanced. Cyn walks around the bunkhouse, her bare feet slapping the boards. She bends over to pick up a wet sock that's fallen off a chair near the stove, just to see how it feels.

She locks her thumbs beneath the straps.

"Here." Jen twists wires around the buckle, a slim strip of dangling aluminum. "I made it."

"What is it?"

"Good luck."

"I'm heading straight south, uphill to find a vantage point. I figure I'll be able to see into the valley in all directions after a half-day hike. I'll be back before nightfall."

"You're taking a lot of food for a day hike," Roc mutters from bed.

"Something goes wrong, I may have to camp."

"We should vote on it."

"You can come." Cyn pulls her arms out and lets the backpack bounce on her bed. "I can pack enough for two."

"You don't know what's out there." Kat sits backward in a chair, leaning toward the stove. "You should be taking one of the horses."

"I don't know how to ride."

"I can teach you."

"We don't have time."

"It's a bad idea, Cyn."

"Surviving isn't enough."

Roc pops her head out of the covers. "I thought that was the whole point of starving ourselves—to survive long enough for someone to find us."

Cyn points at the marks on the wall. "I got tired of that."

"So now you're rushing out to die?"

"Who says we're not an experiment, that maybe we'll wake up again and not remember anything, like it's the first day?" She yanks the bed away from the wall, exposing all the marks. "Maybe we'll wake up tomorrow and the whole wall will be filled because all we're doing is lying in bed and waiting."

"I hope so. Then I won't remember how miserable I am now."

"You'll still be miserable."

"I won't remember it," Roc says.

"I don't want to fill the wall, that's all I'm saying."

"Maybe you need to run these things by us, stop making all the decisions on your own."

The windows are dark. Night has descended. Cyn already feels the weight on her eyes. The girls do, too, making their way to bed. Kat throws a few more logs on the fire before crawling under the covers.

Cyn strips off her pants and socks, stuffing them beneath the covers where they'll be warm in the morning. She takes the keycard from around her neck, crosses the room, and presses it into Mad's hand.

"Take care of that," she whispers.

Mad puts it around her neck and tucks it inside her shirt. Cyn pats her shoulder. She should have the keycard, especially if Cyn doesn't return.

Soft snores are already drifting up from the bunks.

Cyn pulls the blankets over her shoulder and snuggles into her pillow. She begins to drift off, carrying a guilty weight with her. She'll be leaving the girls alone with Roc. But she'll be back. She won't abandon them. Even if the girl in Miranda's journal is real, Roc is more interested in sleeping and eating.

The girls won't get in the way of that.

20

The last cracker.

Miranda shakes out the crumbs and licks them off her palm. It's past midnight and she's still hungry. The food for the girls is almost loaded and ready, just a few more items to think about. She's got to be careful. Can't give away too much.

The photos from the bedroom are scattered on the coffee table. She pushes them around like playing cards, endless tropical scenes that make her feel colder.

Hell.

That's what the woman wrote in the leather-bound journal about this place, like she didn't want to be here. *Why did she come here? She's got all those boats and houses and she comes out here until the end?*

Miranda's stomach whines. She takes the binoculars to the window. It's something to do, to help her forget about food. There's not much to see at this hour, but there's nothing else to do. The day is a better time for spying. She spotted Jen inside the dinner house, picking her nose and wiping it under the table.

She scans the horizon, looking for a wolf or a marauding grizzly bear. Maybe she'll spot a truck or an airplane—wouldn't that be nice? She'd be the one to save them, laugh right in the Dagger Queen's face.

Sometimes she catches Roc sneaking into the kitchen when the others aren't around. She hasn't seen her at night, though. Not yet. What's she going to do if she does see her? Tell the others? They already know and do nothing. How long will it be before Roc just steals right in front of them?

If Miranda had a gun, she could make things right. Problems go away in a hurry when someone has a bigger stick. Miranda would do it, too. Why not? She's the runt. A gun would level the playing field.

Time for a little payback.

Something moves.

Miranda's heart thumps. "Our Father, Who art in Heaven, hallowed be Thy Name..."

The prayer leaps to her lips like a talisman. She aims the binoculars at the garden. *The kitchen is open!*

There's no light, but the door is clearly open. The shelves are easy to see in the moonlight. She turns the knob, watching the open doorway—

Someone comes out.

Cyn's skin is bluish-white. Her legs are bare from her pointy hips down to her naked feet. She's wearing panties and a T-shirt and it's freezing. She must be carrying the keycard. Cyn closes the door and heads around the back of the dinner house.

Miranda keeps the binoculars trained on her.

Cyn doesn't turn toward the bunkhouse. Miranda fumbles the binoculars, losing sight of her. She presses them against her eyes, refocusing, scanning. *Where'd she go?*

There. Right there near the trees.

Miranda races to the kitchen for a better vantage point. Her pale skin flashes in the shadows.

She almost drops the binoculars this time.

"Our Father..."

Cyn just went down the dead-body path.

21

The rooster.

Cyn rises from sleep, her head still in the clouds, listening to the wind harvesters thump and the rain patter. She hooks the clothes at the bottom of the bed with her foot and dresses without breaking the warm seal of the blankets. Her feet are sore.

She sits up and inspects the scratches on the soles and the dirt around her ankles. Doesn't notice the smell anymore. Mud flakes on the floor. She doubles up on socks.

The sole is breaking away on one of her leather boots. It won't last ten more miles. The old boots probably can't make it to the chicken coop and back. She could duct tape it, but a new pair of L.L. Bean duck boots is under her bed.

Cyn shoves her feet inside and laces up. The soles rap the wood planks. They're damn snug, but dry. She rolls the pant legs over them and tosses the old leather boots under the bed.

The knife is already packed, so she uses the edge of her candleholder to make a thin scratch on the wall. The girls snore on.

Outside, the sky is a colorless tarp. Rain taps the hood of her coat. The windows in the brick house are lit. Cyn fantasizes Miranda will wave from the front porch, tell her she found something, anything, so she doesn't have to hike.

False hope brings false suffering.

She takes her first step. Due south.

<hr>

Her feet already ache.

There was a dense stretch of forest at about the half-mile mark, but it didn't last long. It's hard climbing after that, mostly hills with boulders and grassy clumps in between conifers. There's easier ground if she goes around, but she stays on a southern course. It'll be easier to map, and she won't get lost.

The sun is a hazy circle. Cyn unzips her coat, letting in the cool air. She doesn't want to break a sweat. Too late for that.

She takes a swallow of water. If she can reach the next summit, she'll have a look around, stop for a snack. She hoists the backpack and grinds ahead.

She hasn't been at it long and her legs are weak. Hopefully, she'll find a second wind by noon when she turns back. Maybe she'll glimpse a column of smoke before that, or a road or town. Something.

So far, nothing but God's country.

The back of her right foot is on fire. She limps along, taking easier paths that put her slightly off course. She stops often to correct her path. Her breathing falls into rhythm with her stride, head down. One step at a time.

One after another.

Her head feels light. There's a buzziness behind her eyes. She's breathing heavily, maybe the air is thinning. She can't dehydrate, not out here.

There's a large boulder at the summit next to a dead tree. If she can make that, she'll rest. She'll eat. She's been hiking for an hour, maybe longer. Each step forward is another step back.

She figures she's about a mile out from the cabins when she reaches the top. Cyn throws the bag down, collapsing against the stone. The aluminum strip dances around. She's winded, can't catch her breath. So dizzy. *So thin.* The sensation is sort of like a fence, but slightly different. Not so much in the neck, more in the gut.

She chews a bite of jerky and leans her head against the boulder. The tree, its gnarly trunk long dead, the bark flaked off and blown away, exposing the smooth weathered grain beneath, is wedged inside a fracture, as if it broke the stone but couldn't survive.

To her right, far to the west, is a large lake. The water is glassy and blue. It looks like a day or two away. Where there's water, there are animals. People, too. To the east, open valley.

She peels off her right boot. The heel of her sock is soaked red, a hole worn through the outer sock. She strips them off. The skin is stripped off her Achilles. What was she thinking, hiking in brand-new boots?

Stupid. Head back before things get worse.

She leans her head back, working on the last strip of jerky, staring down the slope. It'd be nice if the rest of the trail were that easy. The grassy hill goes down a mile or so to a line of trees. May as well go back, there's nothing but grass and rocks, a scraggly tree here and there. Unless there's someone in a hole, she's not going to find anything.

She washes the jerky down with a swallow of water and chases that with the yams. A nap would be nice. Kick the boots off and rest an hour or two. She'd still be back by lunch.

Even though she already ate it.

The aluminum strip rattles against the backpack. Her eyes get heavy, but she's not going to do it. There's work to be done back at the cabin. And she'll need to treat the sores on the backs of her feet.

She hoists the backpack.

At the bottom of the slope, there's an opening. A peculiar one. All these trees and just a blank opening. If she had binoculars, she could see if it's anything. It would take half an hour to get down there.

But it's so cleanly open. So clear-cut.

Cyn drops the backpack by the rock. It'll go faster without the weight, and she'll return to get it, anyway. It'll be easier on her feet. She considers hoofing it barefoot, but forces her boot back on, wincing.

Cyn half-steps her way down the slope, focused more on the topography than the destination. The buzzy, good feeling in her stomach dissipates as she descends, replaced with fatigue. She stops halfway, shading her eyes.

Looks like an opening.

A bit farther down the hill, she sees a pair of depressions coming out of the trees and fading into the patchy grass. Tracks.

She hobbles along a little too quickly for comfort, but she's going downhill. The impact on her heels burns; she's paying no attention to the increasing lightness in her head.

The buzzing in her neck.

The numbness in her fingers.

Cyn trots to the opening, more sure than ever that those are tracks. Someone drives through here! Maybe they deliver supplies along this route. Maybe someone lives nearby, or this is a hunting road.

It's something.

Has to be.

Cyn reaches the shade of the tall spruce when darkness falls on her. She leans back, but her momentum carries her forward.

She can't stop.

She tumbles into the clearing, recognizing the warning too late, remembering the sensation rattling along her neck, reaching around her face.

Dragging her into darkness.

Two miles from the cabins, Cyn passes through another fence.

22

Cyn stares down. She's looking at something, seems like she should know what they are.

Ah, yes. My feet.

She wiggles her toes, scratching at the bed of pine needles. Pine needles that are gray and grainy.

The world is gray.

No black.

No white.

Just every shade of gray in a pixelated world.

The air is heavy, pressing all around. Her arm moves in a strangely slow manner, like animation trying to catch up with real time. She wiggles her fingers, dirt packed under her nails, as close to black as anything around her.

She's breathing sand.

I'm in the dream. In the gray.

She doesn't recall the needles below her feet, though. Not in the dream. She reaches out, running her fingers through the branches that suddenly appear from the fog, prickly, short needles that poke her numbly.

She doesn't remember how she got here, only sees the light ahead.

She follows the path. Trees on both sides, branches crisscrossing over-head. The dense light is closer.

An opening.

Her hands out, she quickly steps ahead, almost running, as if there's something on the other side—

She skids to a halt. Her foot slips, hanging over the edge where the ground ends.

A sheer drop-off. No bottom. Just fog.

Never-ending gray.

The trees continue to her left and right, growing up to the ledge, where they, too, fade into the gray. *Do they go on forever? Or does the gray consume them?*

Cyn kicks a rock and watches it silently evaporate into the mist. Gone.

The distant nowhere of homogenous gray swirls.

Voices are distant.

Too distant to understand. Close enough to recognize.

Like children on playgrounds.

She reaches out, as if fairies will poke their heads out. The particles of gray begin to shimmer. A low thrumming bass rattles somewhere out there like thunder, reaching inside to shake her intestines. She feels something.

Something coming.

Stalking her.

It's coming!

She turns, steps—

Like a wave swelling from the deepest part of the ocean, something curls over her, driving her to the ground—

Color.

The world lights up with color.

There are paisley flowers on the walls and a soft comforter beneath her arms. The sun shines brightly in her eyes. She covers her face, recognizing the bare light bulb in the ceiling fixture.

"You're a bad girl."

He's heavyset, standing in a doorway. His head is closely shaved. Black and white whiskers cover his face.

He unbuckles his belt and slides it from the loops. Cyn pushes back on the bed and grabs a pillow. The man folds the belt over and snaps it. She squeals.

He grins. "You deserve this."

The belt stings the tops of her toes. She crawls back, hiding behind the pillow. He snatches her foot before she can yank it away. Grips her ankle like a vise.

She hears the zipper.

Feels the full weight of the man. His chest in her face. The smell of his armpit. He uses his knees to open her legs. She feels so small.

So young.

She feels the pressure as he pushes inside her. Like a pipe.

"You deserve this." He thrusts.

She tears.

Screams into the hand cupped over her mouth.

The gray moves in and she's back in the woods.

She scuffles across the soft needles, back into the world without color. Her eyes wide with panic, afraid to look down, afraid to see a red stain spreading between her legs.

A memory.

Her stepfather had done that to her in a trailer outside Cleveland. He raped her for years…until she left. She wasn't old enough to go out on her own, but she was smart enough to leave.

Why do I remember that now? Where the hell am I?

It's coming back.

She feels it rumbling like electricity, a storm stampeding from out there, a battering ram plunging forward. She starts to get up and begins to run deeper into the trees, away from the cliff—

Asphalt scuffs her cheek. Something drips and echoes.

Her face is fat and numb. Her body like wood. There's pressure in her arm.

"You did it," someone whispers. His voice echoes. "You killed her."

Somebody weeps.

Footsteps splash away.

Cyn bats open her eyes, heavy like coins. She wants to run, too. She can't feel anything. Her chest rises and falls involuntarily. She wants it to stop. There's something bad, something rotten inside her. She wants to flush it out, to get away.

For it all to end.

She moves her arm, the pressure spikes at her elbow.

A syringe. A needle filled with red. Stuck in a bulging vein.

She just can't get away—

Cyn sobs into the ground. The memory is a dead weight on her chest. She starts crawling away from the memories. Away from her life. I don't want to remember, I don't want to know! Stop this...please, stop.

The needles begin to thin. She feels a clump of grass.

She's beneath an underpass—

Running from the police—

Swings her fist, her knuckles meeting the soft flesh of collapsing nose—

It's so hard to crawl.

The memories pile into her, filling her like liquid metal, sluggish in her veins. Heavy on her heart.

Cyn closes her eyes.

She crawls deeper into the trees, further away.

Clutching more grass, fewer needles. Hand over hand, like pulling out of a hole. She feels a breeze. The wet tickle of grass on her cheeks.

Her legs are dead.

She rolls onto her back. The gray turns to black. And stars sparkle. The moon brightly smiles in a clear night sky.

Cyn lies on the slope, the trees below her.

She made it out of the clearing. It's not an escape, just another fence. Another nightmare.

But the entire day has passed. Night has arrived.

She doesn't attempt to get up. Sleep, as it always does, arrives like a hammer. She hears herself whimpering, fearing not the wolf's howl, but her return to the gray.

23

Miranda sits back, binoculars up. Her eyes ache, but she continues to scan the horizon, a landscape void of life beyond trees and grass. The snowy mountains pale in the setting sun's dying light, appearing after so many days behind gray skies.

Cyn has been gone all day.

The girls have been outside. Jen cleaned out the garden, harvesting the last of the vegetables. Kat's in the barn, Mad is in the kitchen. And Roc came to eat.

But no Cyn.

It's getting late.

Candlelight flickers inside the dinner house. Miranda turns the binoculars to one of the windows, adjusting the focus. She sees Jen with a plate in front of her. She bows her head for a moment before scooping up food with her spoon.

Dinner is over in less than a minute.

Jen licks the plate. Miranda imagines the others are doing the same. The girls move past the windows, wiping the table and gathering the plates. Except Roc.

She goes back to bed.

Miranda slices off a piece of cheese she found in the back of the pantry. She was eating it with crackers earlier, but she needs to save those. There are only four boxes left. She figures if she eats ten a day, they'll last four months. It's been hard holding back. Sometimes she wonders if it's easier to have nothing.

Miranda lifts the binoculars again.

Kat and Jen are on the front porch, looking at the horizon. A candle warmly lights their faces. Miranda adjusts her focus across the meadow to the sparse trees on the hillside. Cyn has been plundering the kitchen, but if she doesn't return, things will get worse.

Our Father, Who Art in Heaven...

Roc returns to the dinner house.

Kat and Jen step aside. She nudges them, not bothering to say a word. Not bothering to look to the horizon.

Miranda tastes something bitter in the back of her throat. She grinds her teeth, wishing the binoculars were attached to a weapon.

Roc walks through the dinner house, passing both windows on her way to the kitchen. Kat and Jen are watching her through the windows in the front. Several minutes pass.

The kitchen door bursts open.

Roc stomps through the garden, dragging one of the empty travel bags behind her. Mad watches from the kitchen. Kat and Jen come around the front. Roc points at them, obscenities streaming out in all directions, no one spared.

Bile rises in Miranda's throat.

The big bad wolf is coming.

Miranda crawls off the couch, staying close to the floor so that Roc won't see her. She leans against the front door and pulls her legs against her chest. There's a box in the hallway half-full of food. She keeps filling it, plans every day to put it in the front yard, but every day she pulls items back out and swaps them with others.

Sometimes she eats them.

She just can't decide. Once her food is gone, she'll have to leave. They just don't understand.

The front window rattles. Miranda jerks toward the sound.

"The hoarding ends now, Shiny!" Roc shouts. "Time to share or time to burn."

Miranda squeezes her legs tighter. She swears she heard her say "blow your house down".

"I know what you're doing in there. I know you're sitting around eating all the food. I'm not letting that happen. Get out here."

The window rattles with debris again.

"Now!"

Miranda lowers her head. Roc is throwing something at the window. She'll keep throwing it unless she goes out there. Miranda squeezes her legs until her arms hurt. The back of her head thumps on the door.

She messes up her hair, pulling her shirt out. She stands, her legs cold and weak.

Pebbles pepper the front of the house.

Miranda puts her hand on the doorknob, turns and pulls.

The door cracks open.

Roc stands on the fence line. Staring.

"Fill it up." She tosses the bag onto the steps. "I'm not playing."

"It's almost ready. There's not as much food in here as I thought."

"Liar."

"I'll bring it out tomorrow. I promise."

"You'll bring it out now."

Miranda looks back. "It's not ready."

Roc bends over and picks gravel from the dirt. "You're a greedy pig."

"Stop it. It's not my fault."

"Shower all you want, but you can't wash the pig off. A pig smells like a pig." Roc sniffs. "I can smell you from here."

"That's not true."

She tosses a pebble. It plinks off the door. "Like a pig in slop."

Miranda almost closes the door. She doesn't stink. If she does, it's because the house smells. If she does, it's because there's something dead, but it'll wash off. If she could come outside, it would wear off. But she's stuck.

The Dagger Queen.

Another pebble hits the door and bounces across the porch.

"You should behave yourself." Miranda yanks the door open. "You need to learn manners; you are acting like a spoiled brat. You! You're the brat! I come inside the house and I give you all the clothes and you stand out there calling me names, throwing rocks at me... Have you no appreciation? No scruples?"

"Who the hell do you think you are?" Roc pokes at the rocks in her hand.

"You're the bully, Roc. You are. I know more about you than you do. I read something about you. I read that you're trouble. That you're dangerous."

Miranda glances at Kat and Jen, who are standing not far away.

"You're stealing from them. You're going to hurt them. And when they're starving and you're not, I'll be safe in here. I'll keep my food; otherwise you'll take it all from me like you'll take it all from them. I'm not the pig. You are."

Miranda steps onto the porch. The fence protects her—she knows this. But the step is an act of bravery, of defiance. And Roc knows it.

She's not hiding anymore.

"I'll tear you apart," Roc says.

"You're scum."

Miranda goes back inside and closes the door. She's not shaking. Roc is a thief and now they all know it. And until they do something about it, she's not giving them her food. And if Cyn doesn't return, they never will.

Miranda's not selfish. She's smart.

"You're dead!" Roc shouts. "When I get to you, you're dead!"

Gravel scatters against the house.

Miranda smiles. She hit her good, where it counts. Right on the pride. Her anger is fully lit. It hurts and this gives her pleasure.

Miranda looks out the west window. Kat, Jen, and Mad are watching from a distance. Roc might take it out on them.

What have I done?

Boom.

Miranda jumps, a squeal popping out of her. Something thumps the door and rolls on the porch.

"The party's over, Shiny!"

Roc pushes the tall grass around, searching for something larger.

The pleasurable confidence leaches away from Miranda, leaving twisted, toxic fear in the pit of her stomach.

She can't get in here. She can't get to me.

And she has to sleep. The sun has dipped below the mountains. Darkness is near. They'll fall asleep like they do every night. No one will wake up until morning, no matter what. She just has to survive this and then Miranda could do something. She can end this.

Permanently.

It's Roc or us. If it wasn't for Roc, Miranda would be out there with the girls. It's Roc's fault. All her fault. If Miranda gets through this, she can sneak out at night, smother her with a pillow. Put a knife in her throat, a stick through her eye—

"You're dead, bitch!"

Roc heaves a stone, this one purple and angular. The size of a softball. Miranda instinctually leaps away from the window—

The window spiderwebs into a thousand lines. But it doesn't break.

SHHHHHT-THOOM.

SHHHHHT-THOOM.

SHHHHHT-THOOM.

Metal shutters slide in front of the windows. The room dims as light is cut off from the outside one window at a time. Dust trickles from the ceiling as shutters bang closed over the upstairs windows.

Miranda falls against the door and hides her eyes.

Roc's voice is muffled. Distant.

Another stone bangs harmlessly off the shutter to the right of the door. A distant curse punctuates it. Miranda crawls away from the door and curls up in the middle of the floor, listening to shot after shot land harmlessly against the house.

Classical music plays softly.

Something is beeping in the back of the house. An alarm is going off, a steady, even droning. A mechanical warning.

The metal door is cracked open.

A red light is flashing.

24

The brick house is a tomb.

And each time the back room beeps, a nail is driven deeper into its lid, shutting it tighter. Darker.

Miranda feels the weight of the shutters sealing in the sound, shutting out the light. She tries to open the front door. She raps on the windows. She's safely entombed, away from danger. Roc will never hurt her.

But she's haunted by thoughts.

The beeps bounce around the walls, driving deep inside her head. She presses pillows to her ears, buries her head beneath couch cushions and blankets. Still, it's out there.

The incessant warning.

She heaves a candle at the metal door. "Shut up!"

The door eases back. The crack widens. And the alarm seeps out louder. Fiercer.

Miranda weeps with her ears covered. Hours go by, trapped with her worst fear. There's no avoiding it.

The back room is calling.

Exhausted, she turns off the music. She stands in the hallway, red light pulsing. Each beep perfectly spaced, exactly pitched.

"You win," she whispers.

Miranda wipes her face. A wave of serenity passes through her. No more avoiding it. Hate it, but embrace it.

She takes a step. Then another.

Her fingers against the door, she pushes it open.

Unbelievable.

A chuckle rattles her throat. She shakes her head. Ten feet, straight ahead, there is another metal door.

But in between, there's a room. The flashing and beeping are coming from her right. Miranda takes a half step forward, peering slowly inside. A countertop runs along the right wall with several monitors mounted above it, computers below. All the screens are blank except for the largest one in the corner. A red square blinks in time with the beeping.

The smell is not any worse. Whatever is dead, she tells herself, is behind the next door. Relief rises again with a trace of dread.

Another door.

There are chairs along the clean countertops. The computers have flashing green lights, indicating hibernation.

She looks to her left before entering.

The furnace and hot water heater are in the corners. Generators and battery banks, all stacked and wired: power storage for the solar panels and wind harvesters. With all the computers, the power consumption must be considerable. Three wind harvesters still seem like a lot, but some could be backups in case of failure.

Or whatever's behind the next door.

Miranda flips the light switch and goes to the large monitor.

BREACH. The word flashes over and over.

Roc had shattered the window and activated the security system. And if she can't turn it off, she'll go insane and may never escape.

She touches the spacebar on the keyboard—

It stops.

The screen sputters to life. A program opens. An interface scrolls with numbers and words, nothing that makes any sense. She's afraid to click anything that might start the alarm again. Besides, Roc is probably still stalking the brick house; it's better to keep the windows covered up for now. Despite the claustrophobia.

The computer below the counter whirs. The other computers answer the call, spinning awake, green lights flickering.

The generators kick on. All the monitors light up.

Miranda backs up.

Images appear on a dozen screens. The far left monitor displays a view from the front porch. Evidently floodlights have been activated, illuminating far out into the meadow.

The monitor flickers to another view, this one overlooking the garden. Several seconds later, it goes to the back of the house, eventually cycling around to the front.

The other monitors are glowing with eerie green light.

Night vision.

The inside of the dinner house and the kitchen are displayed in infrared. There's another monitor showing the inside of the bunkhouse, the views focusing on each of the beds. Four beds are filled. The fifth bed—the one tucked in the corner—is Miranda's.

The sixth is also empty. *Cyn.*

Miranda watches it cycle through again. She'll never survive out there. Not in this weather.

Not in the wild.

The next monitor illuminates views from another building. At first, she thinks it's the barn. But there's no pasture, no fence. And none of the other buildings are around. Just trees.

It's in the woods!

No one really goes back there. Three of the views are just trees, but the fourth shines brightly on a path leading up to it. Miranda leans closer; something is at the end where the path turns sharply.

A ghostly chill passes through her. *That's a leg.*

The dead body. It's there. That's the body down the path. None of the girls have ever gone past it to discover the cabin in the woods. The four views—presumably from four different cameras—are frightening. But the fifth one is shocking.

Miranda jumps back, covering her mouth to hold back panic. Tension holds her eyes wide, and her jaw clamps shut.

An old woman.

She's inside a tiny room, lying on some sort of hospital bed. She stares at the image, a ghostly green visage of a comatose old woman. And then it's back to the trees.

Miranda watches the cycle. The path. The body. The woman again.

Suddenly, the brick house feels much less like a tomb and more like a fortress. The last place she wants to be is outside. Something's in the trees.

The generators kick off.

All the monitors go green. The floodlights must have turned off to conserve power. The cameras switch to infrared.

She glances at the unopened door. The last frontier. Her last hurdle of fear. She's had enough, though. The adrenaline is wearing off. Exhaustion takes its place.

Miranda goes to the couch and curls up beneath the blankets, still hearing the beeping in her head. She falls asleep.

Much later, the generators start up.

Miranda lifts her head, staring at the clock. It's almost one o'clock in the morning.

The candles have burned out. The hallway appears brightly lit. Maybe the floodlights have turned on, but she doesn't care. Miranda closes her eyes and goes back to dreaming.

Dreaming that final door leads to oceans and beaches and yachts.

$$\overline{}$$

25

$$\overline{}$$

Cyn hangs in that place between sleep and wakefulness, disconnected from her thoughts and body. She's rudely yanked into the world by fiery spikes deep in her feet.

Ceiling. Wall.

Daylight shines through a window, late morning.

She's wearing her coat, boots, and stocking cap in her bed beneath the covers. Sweat soaks through her thermals and cotton shirts.

Her memories are fragmented and cluttered, like a junk drawer dumped onto the floor, each piece unrelated to the next. Each piece broken.

Something inside her had died.

She throws the blanket off, her joints stiff. There's a full-blown fire in her boots. Slowly, she slides her legs off of the mattress, placing them gently on the floor. Her pulse slams in her heels, her feet swollen and snug inside the rubber.

She doesn't think, just reaches down and pries off the right one, ignoring the slivers of pain that bore through her heel and into her thigh.

She stifles a scream. Her breathing is shallow, rapid. Awareness hangs tenuously on each breath. She opens her eyes.

The sock is red. The back of it completely worn away, revealing scorched tissue, red and angry, as if a belt sander had been laid on her heel.

She wedges her finger under the sock, hand quivering, and peels it away. It sticks on the floor. The cool planks bring little relief.

Ten more breaths and off comes the left one, not as bad as the right. The sock not as red.

She waits until her pulse stops hammering in her heels. Now that her feet are out, the pain recedes and they swell without constriction.

I walked through the night.

That's how she got back to the bunkhouse; she trekked through the midnight hours until she crawled back in bed. There's no memory of it. Like every night, there's only falling asleep and waking in the morning.

She didn't expect this.

She didn't expect to sleepwalk to the bunkhouse. It would've been better to sleep on the hillside than mangle her feet. Infection could be the end.

Her backpack isn't in the bunkhouse. It must be out there, on the hilltop next to the split boulder and dead tree, where the slope leads to the trees where there's an opening and tracks and...

And memories.

That's why she feels dead inside. She remembered her past in that place, the memories forced inside her. A past she wants to forget.

She stands, welcoming the pain to blot out thoughts, erase the guilt and rot and ugliness. She has to stay present, be in the here and now, not there.

First, she must tend her wounds.

She knows where to find medicine.

"You're up... Oh my God!" Mad shouts, stepping out of the kitchen.

Cyn hobbles past the dinner table. Mad gets out of the way, staring at bloody streaks, the shiny wounds on her heels. Cyn falls onto the stepstool next to the sink and lets out a troubled breath. Pain crawls through her legs and into her stomach.

"We thought you were a goner." Mad reaches into the pantry. "When you didn't come back last night, I didn't think we'd ever see you again. You must've walked all night."

She's holding a white metal box, staring at Cyn's feet.

"How'd you do it?"

"I don't remember." Cyn takes the box from Mad.

"That came with Miranda's last batch of clothes. There's ointment and gauze and enough wrap that you can get those covered." Mad bends over, grimacing. "Those get infected, you'll be in a world of hurt."

The box is filled with small amounts of iodine and triple antibiotic and other low-dose pain meds. She'll go through all of those before it's over. Cyn opens the medicine cabinet beneath the sink and looks at the brown bottles with pills. She's not sure what they're for or how much to take. *Last resort*, she decides. *If I start a fever.*

She begins to close it. "What the hell happened?" she blurts.

Mad steps back. Cyn's tone is direct. *Harsh.*

"This thing was full, but now there's a bunch missing." Cyn pulls out a clear plastic bag. "Where are they going?"

"I don't know. I don't use them. I don't even know what they are."

Cyn doesn't know, either. But they're missing. And the shelves of food are half empty. They shouldn't be, not by her estimates. She looks at Mad.

Mad shrugs and looks away.

"Where is she?"

"Up at the brick house, I think." Mad takes the keycard off of her neck. "Here's your key."

"Keep it."

Cyn slides an empty pail from under the sink. "Fill this."

Mad brings her fresh water. She helps clean the blood from her feet. Cyn winces when she comes near the wound. Mad doesn't stop. She cleans it, scrubbing away the dirt and dead skin. She applies the iodine and triple antibiotic. Cyn does the wrapping, though. She weaves the ACE bandage over and under each foot until they're fully wrapped.

She tests her weight. It's manageable.

She opens the kitchen door. There's a small fire on the other side of the garden, near the brick house. The windows are all covered with metal shutters, like a fortress under siege.

Cyn doesn't ask. Barefoot, she walks outside. Her gait is slow and methodical.

<hr>

"Glad you're back." Jen stands in the garden. "I didn't want to wake you…"

Cyn doesn't answer. Eyes ahead.

Roc stacks wood on the growing fire at the fence line. There are smoldering branches on the porch. She squats down, rubbing her hands.

Cyn stops several feet behind her. Adrenaline numbs the pain, lubricates her joints, and pumps into her arms and back.

Roc feels someone watching and turns around. "Believe this? Bitch is hiding in a bomb shelter. I'm going to smoke her ass out."

She returns to rubbing her hands.

"Nice shoes," she adds.

"Give me your key."

Roc pretends not to hear. She looks over her shoulder, eyeing Cyn's stance. The calm expression.

"You find a bunch of bravo berries on your vision quest?"

"The key." Cyn holds out her hand.

"Not happening." Roc laughs, shaking her head. Her hand moves to a branch.

"Last chance." Cyn removes her sweater and wraps it around her forearm. "The key, Roc. And it goes easy."

Roc stands, thick branch in hand, the opposite end glowing embers. "You're about to make the mistake of a very short life."

"Come on," Jen says. "Don't do this. It's hard enough out here."

"Back up." Cyn points to where Kat and Mad are watching near the edge of the garden. "This is going to happen quickly."

"I'm going to set you on fire." Roc circles around, getting her back away from the fence. "Throw you on the porch and burn the little piggy's house down. You won't go to waste, Cyn. You'll smoke out the little princess; then I'll have fun with her. Take my time."

She grips the branch like a smoking club.

"I'm tired of playing nice," she says. "We're in the bush where the alpha dog eats."

Cyn watches her eyes, keeping her peripheral vision on the branch, and adjusts her stance as Roc circles. She stays loose, hands open.

Fingers twitching.

"You ready?" Roc fakes a swing.

Cyn remains relaxed.

Roc smiles, laughs. Her grip strengthens, forearms tense. She stops walking sideways and pauses for a moment.

Reaches back for the big swing—

Cyn shoots.

She doesn't feel the bite in her heels when she launches her shoulder into Roc's midsection. The branch comes down on the back of her thigh, but the collision with the ground knocks it out of Roc's hand.

Cyn throws her leg over Roc, mounting her, keeping her head buried against her collarbone. Roc curses, throwing weak punches into the side of her head. Cyn reaches up without exposing her face, interfering with the strikes while she hooks her heels around Roc's legs.

Pain is irrelevant.

She's patient, tightening her grip each time Roc bucks. Every twist allows Cyn to gain more control, immobilizing Roc with a full-body clench. She doesn't know how she's doing it. Maybe it's the memories. Maybe, out there in the gray, something downloaded into her psyche.

This is who I am.

Roc growls. Tries to pull her hair. Her strength drains quickly. She throws glancing blows off Cyn's shoulders with no leverage, no power. Cyn remains clenched.

Waiting.

Roc goes limp, struggling to catch her breath. Resignation sinks in. She's helpless, back to the ground.

Now she strikes.

It's quick and surgical. She pops up just enough to bring her elbow into the side of Roc's head before hunching over again to ride out Roc's short burst of fury. Once exhausted, Cyn lands another elbow, this one slicing from the left, gashing open her scalp.

Blood drains into her ear.

Confusion glazes her eyes. Concussion symptoms already in effect. Two more elbows and Cyn sits up, heels hooked.

Blood is smeared across Roc's forehead, pooling around her eye. Cyn's knuckles crack against her jaw. Another hook from the left. Roc's head limply rotates, blood streaming from a hole in her lower lip.

"Stop!" Jen shouts. "That's enough!"

Cyn sits upright, all of her weight bearing down. She's hardly winded. Roc gasps for air, head rolling back and forth, a distant gaze, no focus.

Jen pulls at her, cheeks glistening with tears. "You're going to kill her."

"Get back."

Roc shakes her head, spittle building at the corners of her mouth, struggling to breathe.

Cyn gets up. The burn on the backs of her legs throbs worse than her heels. She paces around the gurgling mess and yanks the keycard from around her neck.

She turns around, facing the meadow, looping the keycard over her head. She grinds her teeth, hardening against the soft emotions rising in her throat.

Roc spits blood.

"I don't know where we are," Cyn says, "but two miles out there is another fence."

She rests her hands on her hips, turning to the others.

"Do you know what that means? Do you?"

She waits.

"It means we're never escaping."

"Why?" Jen asks.

Cyn doesn't answer because it's obvious. They all know; they just don't want to say it. There's a fence surrounding the hills, an enormous dome over this world like some science experiment. Only they can't see the gods' microscopes or what they're looking at. Or what they're doing to them.

She knows one thing they don't, though: bad things are beyond the fence.

"I don't know why we're here, but I know this." Cyn points at Roc. "You're poison."

Roc attempts to sit up. The tip of her tongue pokes around her lower lip, assessing the damage.

"You have two choices." Cyn holds up two fingers. "One, we tie you to your bed and feed you like a cripple. You don't ever leave it. You understand?"

She looks at the girls. They're still speechless.

"If you don't like that, you're banished from this camp. You go out there on your own. We give you enough gear and food to last a couple days, but you never show your face here again. If you do, I'll throw you through the fence and you'll sleep forever. You understand this?"

"Cyn, don't say that," Jen says.

"She would've killed you, Jen! She was trying to kill Miranda, and she's eating all the food and contributing nothing. You know it—all of you know it. She was going to end us. I'll do the same to her." Her eyes are so relaxed, so convincing. "I won't hesitate."

Jen covers her mouth, her voice muffled by her fingers. Mad puts her arm around her. Kat watches impassively.

"We'll vote." Cyn holds up two fingers. "I vote number two."

Roc pushes up on her elbows. Head down.

"Kat?" Cyn says.

There's a long pause. Kat stares at Roc. "Two."

Cyn points at Jen. She shakes her head, refusing to answer.

"Mad?"

Roc turns a hard stare, focus finally returning with vengeance. The cook looks at the ground, then back at her.

"I can't do it, Cyn."

Cyn nods. Roc spits at her feet, flecking the bandages with blood. The backs of her feet are already soaked with her own.

"Get up." Cyn waves her to stand. "You try anything and I knock you. Now get up."

Roc takes her time moving to her knees, slowly standing. Her shoulders slump. Cyn puts her finger on her chest and begins pushing. Roc backs up a step, slapping her hand away.

Cyn points. "Keep stepping."

Roc steps backwards, glaring beneath furrowed brows. Cyn shadows her steps until she feels the fence in her neck. Roc stops.

Jen is sobbing.

"You've stolen food. You do nothing to help us survive—"

"I helped pull you out of the fence on day one."

"You tried to burn down the brick house. You're nothing but a threat, and you don't deserve to stay. But you can thank those two you won't freeze tonight in the wild."

"Kiss my ass."

"Step backwards."

Cyn is within striking distance, dangerously close, daring her to do something. Roc doesn't take the bait, the last of her dignity falling away.

"Step back or get knocked back."

They stare.

The battle is over.

Roc steps across the fence line. Her eyes roll back as the fence lights up the knot in her neck. She collapses, unconscious. Cyn stands at her feet, close enough that her vertebrae shiver.

"Get something to bind her," she says.

Jen's sobs fade.

The leather-bound book spoke of a dangerous girl.

It wasn't Roc.

OCTOBER

I dreamed a dream,
    And it was you.

—

26

—

Cyn chops wood until her feet are numb. She keeps them heavily wrapped, but it'll be weeks before she can wear boots. She doesn't mind the cold. It soothes the wounds. She changes the bandages frequently, keeping them clean.

Her knuckles ache. Gripping the ax for hours at a time doesn't help, but they need wood. And she needs something to do. She refuses to sit still.

If she does nothing, she thinks. She remembers.

The brick house is still locked tight, with no word from Miranda. Roc occupies the bunkhouse, and she'd rather not be near her. Cyn walks her to the outhouse. She doesn't trust the others.

Be easier if Roc was dead.

No other way to put it. She's a threat, a waste of food. If she loosens her bindings, if she catches Cyn by surprise, the others will pay dearly. Cyn is comfortable with the idea of killing her. She could do it. She could cut her throat, this she knows.

And she hates that. She hates that she could do it. Hates that she wants to.

Hates that she remembers.

She doesn't like the memories. They feel foreign and wrong. She'd gotten used to a fresh start, even if it was a miserable one. Now she's dragging the past with her, each step heavier than the last.

Even when she doesn't think, the gray dream returns at night to find her. She walks to the edge, the trees rustling behind her. She trembles, fearing what will come out of the fog, what heinous memory will force itself upon her. She stands frozen, toes over the ledge.

Trembling.

She wakes as if someone has their hands around her throat, as if she's drowning. It takes all her effort to force down the sobs. The backpack is still on the hill with her knife. She reaches under the mattress for a spoon and puts a light scratch on the wall.

Marks another day.

Another day she hasn't died.

Do we die?

———

Mad is the last one to sit down for breakfast.

They bow their heads, allowing a moment of silence before plowing through eggs and pinto beans. Breakfast doesn't last long. Hunger doesn't go far away. They scrape their plates, listening to the wind.

Cyn grips the edge of the table, staring at her plate while the others wipe their mouths and lick their fingers. The scabs are thick on her knuckles, the tendons popping up as she squeezes harder.

It's been days. No one asks about the trek; they don't want to know what happened to her, why she returned... *different*.

They hardly talk to her.

But she can't hold it in. Closing her eyes, her tongue won't work. Her lips clamp shut.

Mad scoots her chair out from the table.

"I remember who I am."

Silence.

Mad sits back down. Cyn doesn't look up. She can't, not yet. But she started. Something she hasn't been able to do yet.

"How you know that?" Kat asks.

Nervous energy constricts around her chest. She stands too quickly, knocking her chair over. The girls are staring.

Waiting.

Cyn paces back and forth, searching for the courage she had only moments ago, courage that has drained into a pool of quivering fear. Strange how easy it was to destroy Roc, how helpless she feels faced with emotions.

Memories.

She stops at the window, the glass cold. The brick house is shuttered and quiet.

"The fence that's out there—it's different than the one around the brick house. When I fell into it, I just started remembering...things."

Long pause. "How did you get out?" Kat asks.

"I crawled out." Cyn shakes her head. "At least I think I did; it's all a little cloudy."

There's nervous shuffling. But she's stuck again. She wishes she'd never started talking about this, just wishes they would eat and clean up and chop wood and go to sleep. Keep it simple. No need to dredge up these—

"I want to remember," Jen says.

"No," Cyn says. "No, you don't. You don't want to remember. I wish I could put the memories back in the gray. Wish I could forget them."

"Memories don't make you who you are," Kat says.

Cyn steadies her hands on the windowsill so the girls don't see them shaking.

"But memories tell you what you've done."

Something drifts over the garden. Snowflakes are falling. Cyn feels them inside her, cold and drifting.

What the hell is this place?

"We've got names, too," Kat says. "How can we go forward if we don't look back?"

"What if the memories drag you down?" Cyn says to the window. "Trap you in your past?"

"I'll take my chances."

"Really?"

"Better than this. You said so yourself just before you hiked off. You said it's better to take a chance, to explore, than sit around waiting to die. You said that, Cyn. You regretting it?"

Cyn presses her forehead to the cold window, snow spitting on the ground and resting on the brown grass. She involuntarily claws the windowsill. She can't fight this, not the way she beat Roc.

Can't hide from it, either.

Her throat knots up. The sadness just won't go down this time.

"You want to remember?" she asks.

They agree.

"I was raped," she says. "My stepfather did it until I was ten. What if that happened to you? You want to remember that?"

She closes her eyes, swallowing.

"That's not your fault," Jen says.

"That ain't you now," Kat says. "I know you, Cyn. You ain't memories."

"But they're in me now. I did bad things—you saw what I did out there." She points to the garden. "I remember what I've done. I'm no better than Roc."

"Yeah, you are."

"And neither are any of you." Warmth dissipates. "You're just as bad, and that's why you're here. That's why we're all here. This is Hell, and we're paying for what we've done."

"You don't know that," Jen says. "You don't know that."

"Those memories might not even be real," Kat says. "Maybe they're not even yours."

"You think I can just remember to fight and do that to Roc? No, that was me out there, and you know it."

"None of this makes any sense. This whole place is playing tricks on us; maybe those things you think you remember are fake. They're just thoughts."

"No. They're real."

"Yeah, and you know what? I don't care," Mad says. "You came back and saved us from Roc, so if you're some evil demon, then I'm on your side. We need you."

Cyn shakes her head. Her heart is beating in her throat now.

"I want to remember," Kat says. "It ain't your decision to make, either. If you think those memories are real, then I want to know. I want to understand. Even if bad things happened to me, they're still part of me."

"Me too," Mad says.

"Me too," Jen adds.

Cyn nods at nothing in particular. She licks her lips, which are suddenly dry. Her hands are no longer shaking. She stares out the window again. Snow is already dusting the ground and the brick house's roof.

"When I can wear boots again, we'll go out there. You can get your memories. Just remember what I said: you don't want them."

Another long pause. The chairs slide out; plates scratch across the table. Mad begins cleaning up in the kitchen. Kat goes out the front door.

And the snow continues.

—

27

—

Steam rises from the bowl.

Miranda blows across the broth, mouthwatering. She made herself wait until late in the afternoon to have lunch. She's been eating five meals every day, and it's time for some self-control.

Down to three meals. Plus two snacks.

She wraps a blanket over her shoulders and continues to blow on the soup. The monitors are blank. Several cups and wrappers are scattered on the countertop. She sits in the chair, careful not to spill the soup. She taps the spacebar, lighting up the monitors.

She navigates the main screen while the soup cools. The first pop-up box asks: Deactivate Security?

The cursor moves over YES and stops on NO.

Click.

It's easier that way.

Since the brick house was shuttered, the girls stopped asking for food. They don't know if she would open the door or not. And now that she's learned to work the cameras, being inside the brick house is almost as good as being out there.

Without actually being out there.

The bunkhouse shows up on the big monitor. It's empty except for the bed in the back corner. No one hangs around the bunkhouse anymore, not with Roc tied up. Miranda missed what happened, just woke up and Roc was cursing from her bed and Cyn was out back chopping wood.

Miranda scrolls the mouse-wheel and the view zooms in on Roc. *Asleep again.* Mouth open. The swelling has gone down, but that front tooth is definitely brown, killed at the root.

If only I could've seen that.

At some point, Mad will drop some food within reaching distance. Roc already looks gaunt.

Miranda slurps a spoonful and cycles through the cameras. The dinner house is empty. Kat is in the barn, shoveling crap out of the stall. *I don't miss that.* The unmistakable thumping of an axe is near the barn.

Cyn is swinging it. That's all she does. Her feet are wrapped in thick wads of cloth that often hang off the ends of her toes like loose socks. Miranda isn't sure why she's doing that, especially with an inch of snow everywhere.

The garden is dead, so Jen helps drag wood out of the woods and stacks it after Cyn has split it into stove-size chunks. They'll have enough to burn for three winters.

Miranda eats a few bites of soup and clicks over to the last camera view.

The old woman.

Not as shocking as the first time, but still creepy. Sometimes there's a blanket over her, sometimes she appears to have adjusted her weight, but she's always lying down, eyes closed. She must be awake sometimes, but Miranda never sees it.

For a while she thought the old woman might be in the very back room, behind the locked door. But she decided against that. The old woman isn't dead. Her nostrils flare, her chest moves up and down. Very much alive, very much asleep.

She's in the woods, in a small cabin. No doubt. She wants to tell the girls, but then they'd ask for food. Miranda likes things the way they are. Besides, the old woman is out there.

Miranda is safe.

She slides the bowl onto the desktop and goes to the kitchen. She counts out ten crackers, heats up a cup of tea, and returns to the back room. The monitors are now cycling through the views of the countryside. She doesn't need the binoculars anymore; the cameras have excellent zooming capacity as well as night vision. She could see gnats humping on a log if she wanted.

She crushes up half the crackers, stirs them into the broth, and eats them before they're too soft. She's scooping out the noodles—

Something moves.

She taps the keyboard, backing up to the last view.

There.

There's an unnatural color in the meadow. In a landscape of browns and greens, something bright red and yellow is approaching.

She scrolls the wheel.

Zooms in.

Can't be.

She's hallucinating, has to be. Maybe the tea has peyote or the crackers are laced with LSD or—

"Cyn!" Jen's voice calls from behind the barn.

She sees it, too.

—

28

—

The thin layer of snow is more sloppy than frozen. Cyn's feet slosh in mud. She can't feel much. She'll go inside, warm up. Just one more swing.

She's said that ten times. *One more swing.*

With the log balanced and pointing at the sky, she swings—

"Cyn!" Jen shouts.

The axe ricochets, burying the blade in the ground.

"Look!"

Cyn wipes her eyes, the sweat smudging the landscape. Something's in the barren meadow, like wildflowers. She lets go of the axe and continues walking and wiping.

Kat comes out of the barn, dropping the brush in the snow.

Jen is running.

Cyn blinks her vision into focus. She's not sure what she's seeing. It can't be. It just can't...

She starts running, too.

Her legs are like cold stumps. She feels the skin splitting on her heels but powers through the pain, into the meadow, toward the brightly clothed people staggering across the field.

One of them collapses. The other stumbles forward aimlessly, falling to his knees.

Jen drops down next to the man on the ground, putting her arm around him. Cyn puts her hands on her knees, ignoring the pain cutting through her feet, biting deep into her bones.

She touches the old man on the ground.

They're real.

Jen turns him over, putting his head in her lap. His receding gray hair exposes most of his scalp. His cheeks are pale, lips blue. Teeth chattering uncontrollably.

"Get him into the bunkhouse," Cyn says. "Wrap him in blankets."

He's dressed for the beach: a bright red shirt with yellow flowers, white shorts smudged with dirt. His arms and legs are covered in scratches, the worst on the top of his head, blood trickling down to his chin. They sit him up. The old man doesn't see anything. He's staring off into nothing, just trying to breathe.

"We're picking you up," Jen says. "Can you help?"

He doesn't respond. Kat and Jen wrestle him to his feet and heave his arms over their shoulders. He flops along with them, his breath heaving in and out.

Cyn leans over the teenage boy. He's taller than her, about her age, and isn't dressed any better than the old man: just a T-shirt, shorts, and flip-flops.

"Can you walk?" she asks.

He's staring at the ground, mouth hanging open. Daydreaming. Or so far into pain, he's receded to the safety in his mind.

"Come on." Cyn hooks her arms under his armpits. He doesn't help and she can't lift him.

"Hey!" She slaps him. "Wake up!"

It shocks him back to the present moment. His shaggy hair falls over his eyes, but he looks at her, sees her. His cheeks are rosy.

"You hear?" she asks. "You need to stand and walk, you understand?"

He nods once.

Cyn lifts again and up he comes. His legs are scratched like the old man's; big toe split open, the nail missing. *How did they survive?*

She puts his arm over her shoulder, more for guidance than support, not sure if she's helping him walk or he's helping her. Kat and Jen are picking up the old man, who's stumbled face-first into the ground.

Eventually, they get inside.

"Take these." Mad holds two white pills in her palm. "There aren't many left."

Cyn works up enough spit to swallow them dry. Her heels are screaming all the way to the top of her head. She rests on the edge of her bed, keeping the weight off her feet.

Two beds have been pushed in front of the stove, which is stocked with flaming logs. The old man and boy hunker beneath the blankets, still dressed in dirty, wet beachwear. No one wanted to undress them.

Kat and Jen watch them shiver.

More mouths to feed.

Cyn calculates the number of weeks these two just took out of their stock. If they stay, they might not make it through winter. Then again, maybe these two know something.

Something that will get them out of here.

"Put them in the same bed for the night," Cyn says.

"They barely fit," Jen says.

"It's our wood, our food, and our beds. None of us are sleeping on the floor."

"But that's mean—they're hurt. I'll sleep on the floor. Let them be comfortable."

"No, you're not sleeping on the floor. They'll be fine."

"They'll share body heat," Kat adds. "That's what men did in the Civil War—slept together. Hell, the old man needs it."

The old man rolls back and forth, moaning. Jen pulls the covers back over his shoulder. The scratch over his head is caked with dried blood. He needs to be cleaned up, but at least he's not bleeding.

"I wish something would make sense," Cyn mutters.

"Why start now?" Kat says. "I'm just getting used to it."

"We need to find them clothes for tomorrow. If they survive the night."

"You want to move them into the same bed now?" Kat asks.

"After dinner."

Kat tosses another log onto the fire. The old man starts rambling again. Jen kneels next him and puts her hand on his forehead, her face etched with concern.

"Don't..." he mutters. "Don't leave us out here."

"We won't." Jen strokes his head. "You're safe now. It's all right."

A moan rattles his throat. More angry than pained. "I paid good money, damn you."

Jen looks up, confused.

"Delirious," Kat says. "His brain probably froze."

"I'm staying," Jen says. "Can someone bring dinner to me? Maybe they'll want to eat, too. Are you hungry?"

The old man remains quiet.

The boy's eyes are still unfocused, like he sleeps without closing them.

"They're from the dream," Roc says from her bed.

The girls look at Cyn. She doesn't say anything. She remembers the dream they've all been having, the one where someone's coming out of the fog. She also remembers falling into the fence, hearing the voices beyond the cliff, like speeding apparitions on a carnival ride.

She has the same thought: that there are people out there.

But that's a dream.

And two men just walked into their lives dressed for the beach.

29

The old man and boy eat chicken noodle soup for breakfast, spilling broth down their Christian Dior sweaters and furry Forzieri coats. The old man is still shaking.

They don't talk, just eat. The boy mechanically lifts the spoon to his mouth like he's running on autopilot, his body programmed to eat, methodically moving the spoon in timed increments.

The old man, however, looks around after each bite, studying what he sees. He doesn't look at the girls, as if he's already figured them out. He's just trying to figure out where the hell he is.

He lifts the bowl to slurp out the last of the noodles and wipes his mouth with the back of his hand.

"My name," he says, "is Mr. Williams."

"If you want to stay, you'll have to pull your weight," Cyn says.

"Cyn!" Jen glares at her. "Mr. Williams, we're just happy you're feeling better. My name is Jen."

"Yes. This here is Sid." He pats the boy on the shoulder. Sid keeps eating, one spoonful at a time. "Do the rest of you want to tell me your names?"

Mad and Kat respond. Cyn only stares.

"How about you?" he asks.

Cyn nods. Finally relents. "Cyn."

"Yes."

His eyebrows rise. They're bushy, unwieldy and wild. He looks around the room, out the window.

"Sufficiently unpleasant here."

"You were expecting a beach?" Cyn says.

"Hoping, I suppose."

"What's that supposed to mean?"

Sid appears stuck, his spoon dipped in the soup. Mr. Williams nudges him. He begins eating again.

"There something wrong with him?" Cyn asks.

"It's been a long trip. He's still...adjusting." He looks out the window. "Tell me a little bit about this place."

Mad comes out of the kitchen and slides a bowl in front of Mr. Williams. Steam rises from the soup. "That's enough food," Cyn says.

Mr. Williams avoids looking at her. He takes a moment and looks up when his expression has softened. Smiles again.

"If you're annoyed," Cyn says, "you're welcome to give back the clothing and be on your way."

"Not at all, my dear." His smile is wide enough to expose a gold molar.

Cyn's back stiffens. She bites her words.

"My apologies," he says. "Please, tell me about where we are and what you've been doing here."

The girls look at each other. Cyn doesn't know why she's so tense. She's afraid she'll snap at him. Perhaps it's watching them eat their food, the way he's looking around, judging the room.

"We don't remember," Jen finally says. "We just woke up here. We don't know...anything."

Cyn stares at Jen, getting her attention. *No more.*

"I see," he says.

"What does that mean?" Cyn says.

"Thank you for your generosity." He takes Sid's bowl, pouring the remains into his bowl. "I see you all are very hungry, and we don't want to be an imposition. Or eat food we haven't earned."

He stands up, holding the chair for support. Sid stands so that Mr. Williams can hold on to his shoulder.

"Let an old man rest, if you don't mind. So that I may gather my thoughts. Come along, Sidney."

Sid leads the way, still wearing flip-flops. Socks cover his bloodied and bruised feet. The old man stops him at the door.

"Would you mind if we rested in separate beds?" Mr. Williams asks. "There's not much room in one bed."

"During the day." Cyn folds her arms. "Not at night."

Mr. Williams's teeth are straight. His smile, hollow.

30

Miranda watches the girls bring the men into the bunkhouse. They sleep in separate beds next to the stove until night; then the girls shove the younger one in the same bed with the old man. They barely fit, but they seem too exhausted to care.

She zooms the camera, but their faces are buried in the blankets. They hardly move.

Miranda wakes the next morning in the back room, curled up on the office chair and wrapped in a blanket. The bunkhouse is empty except for Roc, who is waiting for someone to bring her breakfast.

Miranda doesn't bother with breakfast or tea. She flips through the cameras and finds everyone except Roc in the dinner house. The men are dressed like women. They were dressed like cruise-ship tourists before that. *How did they even survive?*

The boy is strange. He's skinny and tall, would be cute if he wasn't so zombie-ish. She zooms in on his face. He's yet to really look at anything. Hasn't smiled or frowned or anything. Not even sure if he knows he's hungry and cold.

The old man, though, he's sizing things up. He doesn't react to Cyn being a bitch. He's looking around, learning who's in charge. He's not biting the hand that's feeding him.

But he looks familiar.

He says his name is Mr. Williams, but that's no help. The boy's name is Sid, but she's never seen him before. She's positive. They go back to the bunkhouse. Mr. Williams has Sid push a bed in front of the stove and climbs into it. Sid goes to the corner where Miranda slept and lies on top of the covers, staring at the rafters.

She focuses on the old man. *Where have I seen him?*

She flips back to the dinner house, listening to the girls argue. Cyn is adamant about survival. They don't know these people, they could be dangerous, there's only so much food. Jen just wants to help.

Miranda prepares a cup of green tea, stirring in a dollop of honey. She paces the hallway while steeping the bag. She listens to a piece composed by Richard Strauss, closing her eyes and letting her thoughts fall into the music's flow.

Vacation clothes.

She puts down the teacup.

There's hardly space on the coffee table. She stacks empty plates and pushes trash onto the floor, but it's not there. She goes to the bedroom next to the kitchen.

The photographs are scattered on the bedspread. She pushes them around, sorting through images of oceans and beaches and boats. She picks up the photo of a couple standing on a balcony, the sharp line of the ocean behind them.

More hair, fewer wrinkles.

She takes it to the back room and holds it up to the monitor.

—

31

—

Cyn falls on the footstool. The walk from the bunkhouse to the kitchen has become a long one. She stopped chopping wood and now spends more time next to a stove, but still, her feet hurt.

Especially in the morning.

She unwraps the dirty bandages. The wounds are red and weepy. She's resorted to folding clean patches to cover her heels, wrapping them with strips of cloth ripped from T-shirts.

We need clean clothes.

The brick house is still shuttered and quiet. Not a crack of light penetrates the shielded windows. No sound, no movement.

Is she even alive?

"I don't like the way that looks." Mad leans into the kitchen.

"I don't like a lot of things."

She's used half the ointment and nearly all the bandages. There won't be much left if someone else gets hurt. Cyn opens the cabinet beneath the sink, picks up one of the brown bottles, and shakes it. Pills rattle inside.

"Don't know what's in there," Cyn says. "It could be poison."

"That gets infected, it won't matter."

"How many should I take?"

Mad shakes her head. "Hell, I don't know."

Cyn pops the top and dumps several capsules into her palm. They're blue and white. *Why don't they have labels?*

"No." She snaps the lid back on and puts the bottle away. "I'm holding off."

Mad nods. She's not sure she should take the pills, either. Downing a bunch of unknown pills isn't great advice. At least not yet. She goes back out to the dinner room and returns with tree branches.

"Use these," she says.

Crude branches are tied with twine, with handles about halfway down. Wide braces are fastened on top to fit beneath her underarms, and a wide bottom is formed to keep the branches from sinking into the soft earth.

"Jen put them together," Mad says. "These, too."

She tosses a pair of boots on the floor. The backs are cut out.

"They're not waterproof, but at least you won't go barefoot."

Cyn holds them up. She laughs.

"Told her you'd be pissed."

"They're brilliant."

"Okay. I was wrong."

Cyn stands, balancing with the sticks under her arms. They're not the most comfortable support, but with a T-shirt or two wrapped around the tops, they might be all right. Mad's right: an infection is the end. There's no CVS, no Doc in the Box to wipe out a blood disease.

Game over.

Mad kicks the cabinet door with her toe. Cyn pokes one of the crutches in the opening, bouncing it back open.

"More of those bags are missing."

"Forgot about those," Mad says. "How many?"

"You serious? This thing was half full."

Mad leans over. "I'm not taking them. Honest."

They're definitely missing, no doubt about it, no need to get an exact count.

Point is, who's taking them?

"Here." Cyn yanks the drawer open next to the stove and pulls out a pen. She breaks it in half and hands the ink-filled tube to Mad. "Cut that with scissors, smear it on the handle. Blue fingers are guilty."

Mad stares at the tube. *A good pen wasted.*

She digs a pair of scissors out and begins to lay the trap.

Cyn sits down on the footstool, spreading a layer of salve on her heels while Mad smears the inside of the handle.

"Good morning, girls."

Cyn nearly jumps off the stool. Mr. Williams pokes his head inside the kitchen. She didn't hear the front door open. He smiles with all of his crooked teeth. His cheeks are fleshy, not pale. His eyes clear, not glassy. And he has ditched the frilly Christian Dior coat.

"Feeling better?" Mad stands, ink on her fingers.

"Your soup is a miracle worker, Ms. Mad." A gold cap twinkles. He tugs on the collar of his coat. "I'm a Ralph Lauren man. Makes all the difference. How are the ankles?"

"Beautiful."

"How did you hurt them, if I may ask?"

"Too much walking." She makes the final wraps and tapes the cloth in place. "How did you get so chipper?"

"Sleep works wonders."

Again, the gold cap.

"Ms. Cyn, I'd like to request your assistance in a tour of your camp. I'd like to know exactly how Sid and I might contribute. The last thing we want to do is become leeches. You've been so kind. That is, if you're up to it."

Cyn looks at Mad. She shrugs.

Clearly, he knows who's running the camp.

"Where's Sid?"

"Resting." His expression is slack. "Can we talk?"

He doesn't wait, going out the front door and standing on the porch. Cyn gingerly slides her foot into the altered boot. It hurts going in, but the opening along the back keeps the pressure off. She pushes up on the crutches.

"Keep an eye on us," Cyn says. "Just in case."

Mad watches from the front door. Cyn hobbles out with the old man to the meadow.

The sky is a thin slate of gray, bleaching the sun like tissue paper. The wind harvesters barely turn.

Cyn rests on the crutches, pointing out the houses, the barn, the garden, and everything they've done since waking up. She leaves out the hike, something he doesn't need to know.

"The girl you have tied in the bunkhouse," Mr. Williams says. "She was assaulted?"

"She's trouble."

"I see."

"You don't belong here." Cyn looks at his summer loafers. "Where'd you come from?"

"Hmm." He locks his hands behind his back, lips mincing on thoughts. "Did you realize those wind turbines and solar panels generate enough power to run ten or twenty houses?"

"Not ours." Cyn points a crutch at the bunkhouse. "No heat, no lights. Just the kitchen."

"And the brick house?" he asks.

"I don't know what's in there."

"You don't know?" He lifts his eyebrows. Inquisitive, but not really.

"There's an invisible line around it, something we can't go past."

"What happens if you do?"

"A thing in our neck." She bends her head, exposing the lump. "It knocks us out."

"You mean like this?"

He has one, too.

"Yeah. Like that. Why do you have one?"

All he says is, "Hmm. Is there anyone inside the brick house?"

"Miranda's in there."

"I see."

"Do you know something?" Cyn turns to face him. He's far too calm for someone that was nearly an icicle a few days earlier.

"I suppose," he says, turning with his hands still behind his back, surveying the grounds like a land developer, an eye for value. "But is that all? Is that everything around here, or is there more?"

She wants to poke him with the crutch, double him over so he gets to the point. A few days ago they could've left him for dead, now he's looking left and right with his bottom lip plumped out like he owns the place.

"There's a dead body," she blurts.

The eyebrows rise. "Sounds interesting."

"You see it, you answer my questions. All of them."

"I'll answer all your questions, Ms. Cyn. Undoubtedly. But I am very intrigued by a dead body. If you're up for it, perhaps we could see it now?"

"In the woods."

"Very well."

<hr>

Mr. Williams isn't shocked. And it's beyond gross. The stink has waned, but the sight of the deflated clothes and discolored flesh is almost too much for Cyn.

She stops halfway down the path, letting him go the rest alone. He shuffles along like he's out for a Sunday stroll, a speed bump up ahead.

At first, he bends over with his hands on his waist, studying the lower torso. He crosses over and does the same with the upper. Then he takes a knee and pokes the skull with a stick.

She almost vomits.

"The only older woman, you say?" he asks.

Cyn moans.

"Do you know her?"

She shakes her head. "You?"

He drops the stick and stands. "The wolves have eaten well."

Cyn turns around, leaning heavily on the crutches. A knot the size of a softball has formed in her stomach.

"Have you gone beyond?" he asks.

She takes a moment before looking. He's pointing over his shoulder. She shakes her head.

"Down the path?" he asks. "You've been here all this time and haven't ventured beyond the body?"

"We're a little freaked out."

He waves his arm. "She was going somewhere; let's take a look. Come on, she hasn't moved in weeks. You'll be all right."

Cyn pivots. She holds her breath, sliding her crutches along the wet snow until she reaches the body. She tries not to look but notices the flesh is mostly bone. The fingers, like leathery sticks, are clenched around a clear plastic bag.

Like the bags in the cabinet.

She follows Mr. Williams.

His hands are in his pockets; she swears he's humming. The path bends left and then right, weaving deeper into the forest. She's not sure how far he wants to go, but her arms are aching. This path could go on forever. She's about to turn around, to call ahead, when he stops.

And she sees it.

A dark alcove in the trees. And a small cabin covered in leafless vines and silver lichen. It's not much bigger than a closet, ten feet by ten feet at the most. Mr. Williams waits for her. She leans on the crutches.

"You didn't know this was back here?"

She shakes her head.

"Well, someone does."

He points at the tracks in the snow leading from the front door. Someone has been in and out—many times.

A cold chill rises in Cyn's stomach.

Someone has been watching them. Have they been coming out at night? Are they hiding?

Mr. Williams walks up to the door. Cyn follows—

"Oh!" She stops.

Puts her hand to her neck. The tingling wraps around her face; darkness threatens her vision.

"What's wrong?" he asks.

Cyn backs up slowly. First one step, then two. She rests on the crutches until the feeling goes away.

"There's a fence around it."

He's immune, like Miranda.

He smiles and tries the door handle. It's locked. He twists it up and down, but it refuses to open and looks plenty thick to resist persuasion. There are no windows to peek through. Mr. Williams walks around the right corner. A few minutes later, he comes around the other side, dragging his fingers along the wall, looking up and down, like he's expecting a secret door to open.

None do.

He locks his hands behind his back and stares at the front door. "I'd like to speak with Ms. Miranda," he says without turning.

"Tell me what you know. Why were you in beach clothes? What is this place?"

He turns. One eyebrow raised. "None of this is what you think it is."

"Tell me. You said you'd answer all my questions."

"I will, Ms. Cyn. I promise. But first, I need to know a few things before explaining our strange arrival. Trust me, it will benefit all of us if I understand everything before explaining."

Cyn squeezes the crutches, clenching her teeth.

He faces the cabin, teetering on the balls of his feet. She doesn't stop him from walking past her.

32

Miranda hasn't slept much.

She spends most of her time watching the old man, even when he's sleeping. At first, he and the boy slept like they were dead, lying in bed all day, only getting up to eat.

Cyn still makes them sleep in the same bed at night. Miranda thinks it's rather cruel. The men are sick. One of the girls could make a bed in front of the stove. The way they sleep, they'd never know the difference between a mattress and a plank floor.

Miranda has been so consumed with the monitors, she stopped playing music days ago. She moves only between the kitchen, bathroom, and back room, her obsession blotting out fear.

He knows something.

It's the way he looks around, studying his surroundings, taking it in, digesting it. Sometimes she catches him nodding, affirming some thought or feeling, and then hiding behind a smile.

Finally, he's ready to talk. That's what Miranda thinks. He's been biding his time and now he's feeling better, ready to make a move.

He gets out of bed and sorts through a pile of clothes, switching out some of the things the girls put on him when he was too weak to dress himself. He instructs the boy to remain in bed. The boy does as he's told, curled beneath a fleece blanket, doing what he does: staring and drooling.

Ignoring Roc's pleas for help.

The old man goes into the kitchen. He thanks Cyn for her gratitude because he knows she's in charge. She couldn't care less. Cyn doesn't stand, doesn't make eye contact, just sits there with the permanent scowl.

Miranda turns up the sound, but they don't say much in the kitchen. Cyn and the old man go out to the meadow, where Miranda can't hear. And she can't read lips. They're pointing around the camp. Cyn must be giving him an update about how they woke up and what they found.

Miranda feels a cold sensation crawl up her back when Cyn points at the brick house.

She pulls her legs onto the chair. The old man nods as Cyn explains how Miranda's hiding from them, denying them food, telling him lies about her.

They finally look away. They walk around the buildings, toward the woods. Toward the path.

Miranda reaches out, tapping keys and directing the mouse, changing the views. She loses them in the trees. She flips back and forth, finally finding the view from the little cabin in the woods.

The old man walks along the path with a slight hitch in his step. He stops and surveys the front of the cabin, looking left and right. Cyn hobbles not far behind.

The old man comes up to the front door and, without hesitating, turns the knob. It doesn't open. He's adamant, twisting in both directions and pulling with both hands like perhaps the hinges are rusty.

Cyn suddenly backs up.

The old man turns around. She explains something. Miranda turns up the sound. She rubs the back of her neck. The old man isn't distracted. He walks around the east corner of the building, looking up and down, as if a secret crevice might reveal itself.

Miranda punches a key. The old woman is on the monitor.

The old man and Cyn's voices are muffled, but they're out there, right outside the small building.

The old woman is still motionless, but in a slightly different position than the last time. The pillows have been rearranged beneath her head, and a different blanket covers her. She's sure of it. Last time it was a brown fleece blanket, but now there's one with woven Native American patterns. But she's still asleep, her chest gently rising and falling.

Her gray hair is pulled off her face, kinky strays poking in different directions. It's too dark to tell how old she is. Old enough.

The voices are gone.

Miranda switches the view outside the cabin. No one is there. She cycles through the outside cameras and finally sees the old man crossing the dead garden.

<hr>

"Ms. Miranda?" He raps on the shutter over the front door.

Miranda wraps the blanket more tightly around herself, sinking into the chair.

"My name is Mr. Williams. I'd like to talk with you."

She jumps out of the chair before fear holds her down, and paces back and forth, mumbling. Looks down the hallway. It feels so much longer, so much darker.

"Ms. Miranda?"

Rap, rap, rap.

Miranda takes a long breath. She tiptoes through the house, listening to his gruff and muffled voice call her name. She leans against the door, careful not to bump it or scratch it.

She feels his knuckles through the protective shield.

"I know this is all very confusing," he says, "but we have a lot to talk about. Perhaps you could open one of the shutters?"

It's been so long since she's seen daylight with her own eyes, not the camera's eye.

She slinks to the back room, dropping the blanket near the kitchen. She taps the spacebar, activating the main monitor. The cursor speeds across the screen and centers over the same question it asks every time.

Deactivate security?

The cursor hovers over YES.

She looks to the other monitors. The brick house camera is focused on Cyn standing beyond the fence, leaning on sticks. *She'll know I've been hiding. She'll be pissed.*

She releases the mouse like a hot coal.

"Ms. Miranda?"

Miranda switches the view on one of the smaller monitors to the front porch, swinging it around to focus on the old man. He has a slight hunch near his shoulders. His hair is wispy around the crown.

He knocks again. Turns his head.

Looks right at the camera.

He knows!

He drops his hand to his side, still looking. A nod of resignation. Perhaps a brief smile.

"Perhaps she's trapped." He turns to Cyn. "We need to find a way to communicate. Maybe there's a crack in one of the shutters; I can slide a note inside for her to see."

He looks at the camera again.

"She needs to know she can trust me. That I can help."

They walk back to the dinner house. One slowed by injury, the other by age. Miranda watches them go through the front door and sees them sit down at the dinner table. But she doesn't switch the view to look and listen.

Instead, she runs to the kitchen.

She begins hiding food around the house.

33

Sleet pecks the windows.

Cyn's breath curls in column after white column, each fading into nothing. The stove is lifeless.

Pain greets her. *Good morning.*

Her heels throb. Each pulse pushes pins into her legs. She pulls the covers up to her chin, closing her eyes, wishing it away. But it doesn't. Nothing goes away, no matter how many times she asks.

The girls are waking. The bed in the far corner is missing. Cyn lies still, hoping her heels will forget she's awake. She scratches another day on the wall, ignoring the endless lines behind it. They are her challenge, each line a brick in a wall that she's building up to the sky, one she can crawl over, where the sun shines and birds sing and pain does not exist.

Each day a brick. Heavy and solid. Each day she carries a brick to the wall and puts it in place.

"Good morning," Jen says.

Kat and Mad mutter back, dressing quickly.

Cyn throws the covers off and reaches for the stack on the floor. The undergarments are dingy and already reek of dead skin. The bottoms of her socks are black and damp. She peels them off and replaces them with another pair that are soiled but dry.

The girls walk past, asking how she's feeling, if she needs any help. Except Jen. She won't look at her.

Kat turns the block of wood nailed into the wall—a rudimentary lock cobbled together from parts in the barn—and opens the door. They brace for the weather and start the morning trek to the dinner house.

The girls run. Cyn walks.

The sleet stings like frozen sand.

The dinner house is warm.

The table is pulled away from the stove. Miranda's bed—the one she was sleeping on before retreating to the brick house—is in front of the roaring stove. Mr. Williams is sitting on it, fully dressed, hair slicked back.

"Good morning," he says.

Sid is curled up on the floor, a blanket serving as his mattress.

Cyn goes to the footstool to dress her wounds. She folds a piece of paper until it's thick and narrow, wedging it between her teeth like a bit, and begins to unwind the grimy wrappings. The bandage is soaked with watery discharge and slimy pus.

She bites harder.

Pills.

The time has come. The wounds aren't healing. She reaches for the cabinet—

She jerks her hand back like the cabinet is hot, slowly looking at the smudges on her first two fingers. She didn't touch the ink trap yesterday, hadn't gone near the cabinet... It can't be.

The dirty socks. The sore feet.

"I don't like the way those look." Mad starts up the griddle, looking down at Cyn.

Cyn quickly opens the cabinet, hiding the blue smudges. She pops the lid on one of the bottles and shakes out two white pills.

"You sure?" Mad asks.

She pops them in her mouth, dry swallowing. They stick in her throat. Mad hands her a cup of water. The kitchen door opens. Kat carries four eggs in one hand and puts them on the counter.

"That's it?" Mad asks.

"Feed's almost gone. Surprised we're getting any eggs at all." She blows into her cupped hands. "Need to think about eating those chickens before they go to waste."

Mad shakes her head, cracking the eggs on the griddle.

"Can you give them horse feed?" Cyn asks.

"Not much of that, either. Can't imagine they'll make it through winter in the pasture—grass'll be gone. Maybe it's best to let them go, fend for themselves."

They'd been preparing wood and food for winter, but what if nothing else survived?

Cyn smears ointment on her heels and dresses them up for another day. Ink smudges the wrappings.

<hr>

"No breakfast for them," Cyn says.

Mr. Williams and Sid sit at the far end of the table near the door. The old man looks at Cyn at the other end, next to the stove.

"No, you won't do that!" Jen slams the table. "You're not going to take away their food!"

"This ain't a camping trip, Jen! Mom and Dad won't pick us up before it's over, so let's get clear. We *will* run out of food; we will get sick."

Jen keeps her fists balled on the table.

"There's no room for manners, Jen. Unless something changes, we die. All of us."

"I hardly think we're a threat, Ms. Cyn," Mr. Williams says. "We've agreed to sleep in separate quarters, but it's not fair to deny us food when we've offered to help."

"You didn't agree to anything. We made you leave the bunkhouse at night. You're lucky we let you sleep in the dinner house."

"You did, Cyn," Jen says. "You made them leave."

"And you'll get food when you talk. You arrive like tourists and haven't told us anything. I've got a feeling you know plenty. Begin with him." Cyn nods at the kid with the blank stare, the wet lip. "What's his problem?"

"It's complicated," Mr. Williams growls.

"Start talking or start starving."

"You going to starve me, too?" Jen says.

"You threaten us, damn right I will."

"Or if I just threaten you."

Kat and Mad have already finished eating. Jen's plate is still full. She'll sneak them food later.

Not if I can help it.

"Well, Mr. Williams?" Cyn says. "You hungry yet?"

He stands up. Sid gets up automatically. Mr. Williams looks out the window at the brick house still battened down tight as a tank.

"Okay." No gold cap glittering this morning. "In private, Ms. Cyn. We'll talk in private. I'll leave you to finish your breakfast."

They go out the front door.

Jen looks at her plate, the food completely untouched.

"Eat your breakfast." Cyn forks eggs into her mouth. "If not, the rest of us will. But they won't, Jen."

She eats.

—
34
—

Cyn limps towards the barn, trying to keep the crutches from chafing her underarms. The sleet is sticking to the walls, wet on her face. Kat waits in the open breezeway. Mr. Williams is at the other end, looking at the mountains.

"Want me to stay?" Kat asks.

"No. Watch the boy, he's in the bunkhouse."

Kat steps aside. Cyn slows, careful not to slip. She leans the crutches against the stall. One of the horses pokes his head out, nibbling on the end of the crutch; his eyes are large in his skull.

Cyn takes a moment, then slow, limited steps down the middle of the breezeway.

"You did the right thing," Kat says.

Cyn stops and looks back.

"He's up to something and we ain't got time," Kat adds. "Hunger'll make anyone talk. You did the right thing."

She leaves her to go alone. Cyn doesn't want to admit it, but she's relieved someone understands.

"Quite a sight." Mr. Williams doesn't turn around. "Rich and detailed, not a thing missing. It's beautiful."

Cyn refuses to sit on the bench. She stands next to him. She's already sweating.

"You're cold and hungry." He looks at her, nostrils flaring. "You have an infection; you'll have a fever. It's all very convincing."

"No more games."

"I wanted to see the brick house before having this talk. It'll make more sense once I see the inside."

"I get the feeling you won't come out."

He looks across the pasture again. A gust of wind hits the wind harvesters.

"None of this is real." His expression is flat. He's no longer enamored with the view.

"I thought you would take this seriously." She turns around, wishing the crutches were closer. "Let me know when you're hungry."

She makes it to the first stall.

"You dream about the gray world at night."

She stops, hand on the wall.

"You dream of static, of fog and haze. You dream that something is out there in that nothingness, but then you wake up. You realize it's just a dream."

His voice is stronger.

"But then you went to the edge and discovered it wasn't a dream. You stepped out of the cold, out of this world, and saw the nothingness that is in your dreams. You went there, you peered into the gaping gray sky, the world of the Nowhere."

Cyn scratches the old wood. Not finding something to grab, she collapses on a bench, leaning back.

Exhaling.

"Where did you go?" he asks. "Where did you find the edge of this world?"

"Two miles out, straight south," she mutters. "There's another fence."

"That's not a fence, not like what's around the brick house. That is the limit of this world. You stepped out of it and into the Nowhere."

She turns her distant gaze to him. He's a fuzzy silhouette, the snowcapped mountain a bright, white backdrop. Her stomach turns.

"That gray void of nothing used to be another illusory world like this one, only it was tropical and lustrous and exotic. You won't remember this, but you and the girls would come visit it, but that was a long time ago, before it collapsed and Sid and I became homeless souls."

He steps closer.

"Our...*identities*...if that's what you want to call them—our true Selves—are frayed and dissolving. I don't think there's any way to truly express what it's like to be lost in the gray, Cyn."

She twitches. He smiles.

"You only came for a visit; we live out there. Imagine what it feels like to be pulled apart, piece by piece, and set loose on the wind, randomly mixed with so many other disintegrated souls. Sid and I were doomed to waste away, becoming thinner. Becoming less. Our souls bleached lifeless."

He laughs without mirth.

"But then you peeked into the Nowhere, you shone like a beacon. Suddenly, I knew this world still existed, that there was something out there besides the Nowhere. We were able to draw out of the miasma of despair."

He looks at his hands, turning them over like he still can't believe it.

"Sid, my boy, didn't transition as well as I did. Part of him is still out there."

"The world doesn't end, Mr. Williams. You don't walk two miles and drop off the edge."

"In this one you do."

"No, but someone did insert something in our necks that gets triggered by an electrical fence. I ain't saying I know how they do it, but it's possible. It ain't magic."

"No. It's a dream."

She chuckles, turning her head. "It's not magic, it's a dream—that's what you're saying?"

"You're asleep, Cyn, but this isn't your dream. Someone else is dreaming this world. And you're in it. We're *all* in it." He waves his arms, gesturing at the grand view beyond. "Your *real self*, whoever *you* are, is real, Cyn. You're somewhere, just not here. You think you're real, but you're asleep. You need to wake up."

"And you?"

"Me too. Sid, the girls...we're all real."

"But asleep?"

"We're part of an...experiment, so to speak. It's hard to explain, you'll have to trust me."

"Whose dream world is this? I mean, if it ain't mine, whose is it?"

"That's irrelevant. The point is, we can escape. We can wake up in our bodies, wake up in reality where the world exists beyond the edge, where there is no Nowhere. Where we can escape the suffering, get back to living."

"And you expect me to believe this?"

"No." What little joy had filled his eyes quickly drains. "You don't realize this is a dream, so you'll hang on to it to the very end. Only you can discover it's false. This is not how I wanted to tell you."

"Why are you still here? If you know this is a dream, wake up, then. Go ahead, disappear or say the magic word, whatever you've got to do, you do it and I'm a believer."

"Knowing the truth isn't enough, child. It's hard work to escape."

Cyn throws her head back, thumping the weathered wood. There are old nests and white streaks on the rafters, holes in the roof and cobwebs in the corner. These are not the details of dreams.

And she's never had a dream she couldn't wake up from.

Sweat forms on her forehead. She swallows the nervous swelling in her throat. "We're out here starving and freezing and you say just wake up."

"It was summer where we were." He holds his arms out. "That's why we arrived in those clothes. We're lucky we survived."

Her laughter is as empty as his. She rolls her head on the wall, eyeing him with a shallow smile. "You're a liar—you're up to something. And you can starve, for all I care."

She throws her weight forward. Her steps are small. Her heels are cracking.

"What's your plan?" Mr. Williams calls. "To survive long enough to see your feet rot off?"

"If it's a dream, I'll get new ones."

"Just because it's an illusion doesn't mean you won't suffer. You're invested in the dream, child. You don't want to give it up, no matter how much it hurts."

Cyn uses the wall to slowly turn around.

"What happens when I die, Mr. Williams? If this is a dream, won't I wake up?"

He sinks his hands in his coat pockets. "You already died; you have the marks on the wall to prove it."

The end of the breezeway tilts. She blinks the world back into focus, but the floor wobbles. She needs to get out, get some air, get away from the nonsense.

"You're saying we start over? We wake up in a cabin without memories?"

He nods. *Isn't it obvious?*

Cyn doesn't want to believe it. He's convincing, but that doesn't mean he's right. The squeeze of hunger will bring him back to his senses. He'll talk.

He'll tell the truth.

She just wants her crutches, wants to go lie down.

"We need to find the gate," Mr. Williams says. "It's the center of the dream. In our world, it was a sundial. If we find the gate in this world, we can use it to wake up."

Cyn reaches the other end. The crutches stab beneath her arms. She's panting and sweating. Nausea swirls inside her stomach, reaching for her throat.

"Tell me." Her voice echoes in the stalls. "What was your tropical world called?"

She feels him smiling. "Foreverland," he says.

"Foreverland is dead. If you don't tell me what you're up to, so are you."

She starts for the bunkhouse, where she can rest. Her mouth begins to water. She gets a few steps before vomiting. On her hands and knees, she throws up her breakfast onto the ground, melting the sleet.

This is not a dream, she thinks, heaving again. *Dreams don't hurt.*

$$35$$

"I can do it." Cyn tries to prop herself up on her pillow.

"Just lie down and shut up." Mad wipes Cyn's forehead with a damp cloth. "Eat the soup and take those."

Cyn looks at the oblong pills. "I'm not taking these."

"Those are from a bottle," Mad says. "The other pills must be old or you're allergic to the medicine. That's why you puked. Girl, you've got a fever and your wounds smell like road kill. You're going to take every medicine in that cabinet if you got to."

Cyn can't get warm. Can't stop sweating. This could be it. It's all over. *If the old man isn't lying, then I'll just wake up wondering what all those lines on the wall are for.*

She puts the pills on her tongue, chasing them with chicken broth. Mad brings another spoonful to her lips and sneaks a look toward the back where Roc is sleeping. "More of those clear bags are gone," she whispers. "I started a count."

"What bags?" Kat asks.

Mad tells her about the plastic bags in the cabinet. Chills storm Cyn's body with renewed force. Now she wants to forget about them, wants to forget the ink. *I'm stealing them. I'm the one who's been going to the little house in the woods, taking those bags with me. And I don't remember doing it.*

The dead woman on the path—she'd had one in her hand. Was she the one taking them before they awoke? What's in the cabin? What could make Cyn sleepwalk almost two miles through the night until the flesh wore off of her feet?

I wish this would end.

"Is the old man crazy?" Mad tips the bowl for the last couple spoonfuls. "He thinks this is all a dream and you believe him?"

"You ever go hungry in a dream?" Cyn says.

"He said we were part of an experiment," Kat says.

Kat admits she went around the barn and listened, and heard all the nonsense. Cyn wishes she didn't do that; now she's got to explain everything when all she wants to do is sleep.

"This ain't a dream—we'd know it," Cyn says. "He's just saying things, Kat. He's crazy."

"Maybe we're crazy," Roc says. "We just don't know it."

"Shut up," Kat snaps.

"You'd better hope I don't get loose, horse girl." The bed creaks. "You're the first one I'll break in half."

Kat shakes her head, arms crossed.

Cyn rests with her eyes closed. At first, she'd wanted to punch the old man in the throat for such a lie. Their days are numbered and he thought they'd believe anything, like children. But she's sleepwalking plastic bags to a little cabin, so he could say anything and it might be true.

"I'll talk to him," Kat says. "Figure out what he's up to."

"You do that," Roc says. "I feel better already."

"Get some sleep, Cyn." Mad runs her finger around the bowl and licks it. "More medicine later if you don't puke those pills up. There's plenty more soup, too. Miranda probably has more."

"Miranda?" Roc chuckles. "Proof you are dreaming."

The girls go to the door, ready to get away from Roc, whose only enjoyment is getting under their skin. She's good at it.

"Mad." Cyn, already half-buried in sleep, croaks out her name. She holds out her keycard. "Take this. I don't need it."

"I'll give it to Kat."

"No. Just...for now, hang on to it. Keep it safe. All right?"

Mad puts it around her neck, tucking it under her shirt. She puts her hand on Cyn's forehead, her palm clammy and cold.

Cyn fades into a soft haze. *I can't steal the bags if I don't have a key.* The front door closes. The bunkhouse is quiet except for the creaks and pops as the wind pushes against it.

"You asleep?" Roc says.

Cyn couldn't care less if Roc talks. They're just words. Besides, stampeding elephants couldn't keep her from sleeping.

"I lied to Kat," Roc whispers, cackling like she's lost her mind. "If I get loose, you're the first one I break in half."

"You'd better kill me if you escape," Cyn mutters. "You're a dead body if you don't."

The dark laughter follows Cyn into the gray.

$$—$$

36

$$—$$

The dream is endless.

Feverish.

As always, she's on the ledge, staring into the abyss of eternal fog. Where the memories are. Memories of the lost boys from Foreverland, dissolved in misty gray. Reduced to thoughts scattered in space.

But how did my memories get into the gray?

She feels them coming for her. She runs every time. She turns, racing from the chasm into the trees. She'd rather suffer in the dream than face life.

Rather than have those memories inside her.

Sometimes she wakes long enough to feel someone put dry pills onto her lips, cool water washing them down.

Feels the sweat on her pillow.

And then it's back to the ledge.

Back to running.

Wondering, who's the dreamer?

Who am I?

37

Cyn sits up. "How many days have I been in bed?"

"Seven," Kat says.

"A week?"

"Ain't lying."

Kat points at the wall. New scratches are on the wall. The girls kept track of the days while she dozed. The days blend together. *Those pills are sledgehammers.*

The shivers are gone. The sheets are dry.

She throws the covers off, the stench of dead skin and infection wafting out, and gently puts her feet on the floor. The wounds are oozy, but the swelling is down.

Kat rattles the bottle. "Last of this bottle. Hope you don't relapse or we've got to experiment with another bottle and hope we get lucky."

Cyn works up enough spit to swallow them. There's fresh snow on the ground, about six inches on the dinner house. The old man and Sid are visible through the window. Jen, too.

"You want to eat?" Kat asks. "Mad's almost got supper ready."

"No. I think I'll go for a little walk. I need to get out of this nasty bed. If I don't make it over to eat, tell the old man I want to talk in the morning."

"Why not now?"

"Got to think about some things."

Not a lot made sense in the delirium, but maybe Cyn needs to hear more about this dream experiment. She doesn't want to even think about listening to that crap, but unless a helicopter drops into the meadow, Prince Charming isn't coming.

It can't hurt to hear more about this gate.

"Jen's feeding the old man and the kid," Kat says. "They wait in the barn and she takes food out when she thinks we ain't looking."

"Figured she would," Cyn says.

"That's what I said. Now we're just letting them eat with us, Cyn. Hard to watch them starve, you know."

Cyn doesn't answer. Kat leaves her at the window.

She watches them through the windows. They eat supper, but it's not much. The old man looks up from the table and sees her. Cyn moves a little too quickly, pain lancing her hamstrings. She probably shouldn't be walking, but she's got to get out of the bunkhouse, even for a little bit. Her body is sore.

She moves slowly, walking out to the barn. The horses are anxious, their hide pulled between their ribs. She sits on a bench, admiring the mountains, recalling what he'd said.

Rich and detailed. Not a thing missing.

Can this really be a dream? She turns her hands over and rubs them on her thighs. Her pulse bounces in the backs of her feet.

She comes back to the bunkhouse when she's shivering and climbs into bed as her fever rises. She throws the covers over her head, pretending to be asleep when the girls come back. The stove crackles with heat. The last person in fastens the homemade deadbolt on the door, knowing that even the old man could kick it open if he wanted.

They wouldn't wake up if he did.

In the morning, Cyn's feet ache.

Her socks are wet.

Fresh ink on her fingers.

She gives up. *Please, let this be a dream.*

If the old man is right, there's hope that they can wake up. And maybe waking up is their only hope. If not, she's doomed. They all are.

Cyn struggles to get out of bed, wincing while getting dressed, but she sweats through the agony. The crutches creak under her weight. She opens the door without waking anyone, which is good. She wants to talk with the old man alone, still not convinced that he's sane. If there's a gate out of here, they can find it.

She limps through the snow and stops on the front porch, catching her breath. It's completely dark inside the dinner house.

The stove is cold.

The brick house is lit up.

The shutters are open, lights illuminating every window both upstairs and down. She holds on to the post and knows, before even opening the door, that the old man and Sid aren't inside the dinner house.

38

She's seen enough. Heard enough.

Miranda waits until dark. She turns on the cameras, watches their eyes grow heavy, and checks each of them twice before rolling the chair to the keyboard.

She punches a button. YES or NO.

Miranda takes a deep breath.

Clicks the mouse.

A rumble rides through the house. She flinches each time a shutter slides across a window, snapping inside the brick wall. Like dominoes, they clack one by one until it's quiet. Dust floats down from the ceiling. String instruments bellow from the front room.

The girls haven't moved, eyes dancing in REM. Floodlights illuminate the dead garden. Nothing moves but the wind.

Miranda shuffles through the hallway, exposed and alone. She looks out the window. The moon and stars are crisp. The glass is cold. A light flickers inside the dinner house. A hunched figure looks out the window.

Miranda has the urge to duck.

Too late.

A minute later, the candle appears at the front door, quickly blown out by the wind. The floodlights, though, show him the way. Miranda watches the old man plod through the snow, followed by a gangly figure. They pass through the fence, unflinching.

Their footsteps on the porch.

A knock at the door.

<hr>

Mr. Williams stands in the front room, hands behind his back, looking around. Sid is behind him with shaggy dark hair and a slack lower lip, waiting while the old man drinks in the details of the home.

The old man breathes deep, closing his eyes. Miranda isn't sure if the house still stinks, her senses long dulled to the odor.

"Who are you?" She holds out the photograph like a gun.

Mr. Williams cranes his neck, squinting. He slides his feet toward her, reaching out, plucking it from her hand. He caresses the photo. His eyes are glassy.

"I can explain," he says meekly. "Perhaps some food first?"

Miranda taps her foot, her stomach clenching. Cans of food are stashed all over the house, enough to last her a year. He'll know she's lying if she says she's out.

And she can't starve him. That's what the girls were doing.

Miranda goes to the kitchen and returns with two plates. They're sitting on the couch. Sid attacks the food like a dog, smacking with his mouth open. *Can't he do anything with his mouth closed?*

She fetches a teapot and pours cups for all three of them. The old man has more self-control, but he leaves little room for talking, keeping his mouth full until the plate is nearly empty.

"What's wrong with him?" Miranda asks.

Mr. Williams pushes his plate toward Sid and sits back on the couch, crossing his legs. "He's incomplete."

"What does that mean?"

"It's like a file that hasn't completely downloaded. It's just not entirely there."

Sid nabs the remaining squares of cheese from Mr. Williams's plate and pushes them into his mouth, chewing with his lips open.

Wide open.

"It's safe in here." Mr. Williams lifts his cup of tea toward the spider-webbed glass.

"Roc doesn't like me. The others probably don't anymore, either."

He sips. "Don't apologize, Miranda. You belong here; they don't."

He tips his head like he's catching the notes floating out of the speakers. He hums along with the refrain, closing his eyes, savoring the moan of a viola, bouncing his chin along with the pluck of violin strings.

He slides the stack of photos across the table and leans over. "Barbados. We had our honeymoon there. Barbara loved the place so much we bought a condo."

He picks up a photo.

"She was always so white, she couldn't be out in the sun with her fair skin. She'd had skin cancer twice, but she never listened. Loved the sun, she did."

He drops it on the other photos.

"Not all blondes are ditzy. Some are tough as nails."

Miranda twitches. *Blondes?*

She grabs the pile, shuffling them like cards. There's the group of women. The one with black hair is up front, the same color as Roc's. "That's not her?"

"No." He chuckles. "Always a blonde. Of course, she grayed as she aged." He drops his finger on one of the other women. "Gracefully, I might add."

Barbara was talking about Cyn.

"Where did you find these?"

She points at the room while staring at the picture and hardly notices Mr. Williams get up. Miranda flips through the other pictures, looking for another group photo. Maybe the woman that sponsored her is in the group. *Will I recognize her?*

She goes to the bedroom. He's at the dresser, turning a glass Buddha figurine in his fingers.

"This was her favorite, had it when she was a kid, attached it to all her backpacks by a string. When she was nervous, she'd rub the belly."

Mr. Williams looks around the room, his thumb circling the glass belly.

"This place is perfect," he says.

"What's perfect?"

He opens the top drawer and picks through brightly colored scarves. Smells one and smiles.

"Mr. Williams? What's perfect?"

He closes the drawer. "Let me see the rest of the house and I'll tell you what I know."

Miranda backs into the hallway, crossing her arms. "That's what you told Cyn."

He smiles, turning his head slightly.

"I promise, Miranda. I just need to understand a bit more, get my mind around this place; then I'll tell you everything." He holds up his hand. "Swear."

She taps her foot. "Bedrooms upstairs. Some strange stuff in the back."

He palms the Buddha and goes upstairs, pulling his weight along the railing. Sid sits on the couch, mouth-breathing.

"I was scared of this room at first." Miranda ventures into the back room. "The smell was coming from here and the door was different, so I just ignored it. But when Roc broke the window, everything automatically closed up."

She turns around.

"And the door opened."

Mr. Williams steps inside tentatively. He looks left, leans over the batteries, and rubs dust off the stickers. He inspects the furnace and water filters.

"I notice you leave all the lights on. You need to start turning them off." He pushes a button on the furnace. "And turn the heat down, put on a sweater if you're cold."

"It's been fine so far."

"Winter's coming and the solar panels won't harvest as much power."

He seems satisfied with that side of the room and takes a moment to survey the monitors before sitting in front of the large one.

"Cameras are everywhere." Miranda wraps the blanket around her. "I figured out sound, too. I can see inside the buildings. Sometimes I feel a little guilty watching them."

"Don't. It's for your protection."

"I saw you walk into the woods, around that little house."

He's afraid to touch anything. She had felt that way at first, too. Instead, he looks from monitor to monitor. The girls are still asleep, some already snoring. She taps a few keys, advancing the views on the monitor to the little cabin in the woods. It rotates around the back and then inside.

The old woman lies peacefully.

Mr. Williams rolls the chair over and leans closer. "Patricia."

He touches the screen.

"The dreamer becomes the dream," he mutters.

"What's she doing in there?" she asks.

He sits back, gazing at the screen, as if seeing something else. He mutters something unintelligible.

"Is what you told Cyn true? That this is a dream?"

"There must be..." He pulls open a drawer beneath the desktop, rattling through the office debris. His thick fingers are bent, the skin spotted.

"Mr. Williams?"

He mutters again and goes to the next drawer.

"Mr. Williams!"

He snaps out of the trance, sits up, and looks around like he's forgotten where he is and how he got there. His gaze settles on the doorway. Sid blocks their exit, a hand on each side of the doorframe. His eyes are big, his breathing heavy. Chest heaving.

"It's all right, my boy. She's just getting my attention." Mr. Williams calmly waves him away. "Why don't you go lie down in Barbara's bedroom, get some sleep. Miranda and I have much to discuss."

Sid's hands slide down the doorjamb and fall against his legs. Mr.

Williams nods again. Sid saunters down the hallway and goes into the bedroom.

"Tell me. Is it true?"

He sighs. "We are in a dream, Miranda. But we're not dreaming."

"I don't understand."

He takes another deep breath, starts to say something, but changes his mind. The old woman is still motionless, still sleeping. *The dreamer becomes the dream.*

"Perhaps you could prepare more tea while I visit the men's room?"

"What are you looking for?"

He takes the cup and sips. "A key fob. One of those little black remote controls, only this has one button, a red one. Have you seen anything like that?"

She shakes her head. The teacup rattles on the saucer. "Tell me what's going on, Mr. Williams."

He leans his elbows on his knees, staring into the black tea like the future is hidden somewhere inside. A smile touches his lips. He's seeing a memory.

"Harold Ballard was a visionary," he starts. "If you ever met him, you'd be overwhelmed with his charisma, charmed by his love of life. His mind was a true gem."

He shakes his hands, as if he can't find the words to express something so large, so special.

"It contained a universe, another world, an alternate reality where anything was possible. The boys, like Sid, called it Foreverland. It was truly magical, an island in the ocean, warm as the tropics."

He pauses again. Contemplating.

"I suppose he could've just lived there, inside his mind, for the rest of his life. But he wasn't like that. He wanted to share it with others, for the good of mankind. So he conducted these...*experiments*. I was part of them."

"Sid, too?"

He nodded. "But something happened, I don't know what. Everything was as normal as possible. Sid and I reached a critical juncture in the process when the world collapsed. Just one second it was there, and the next..."

Snap.

"We were disembodied, lost in a soupy dream, the gray place the boys called the Nowhere. We were ghosts." Mr. Williams looks at her. "It's the place in your dream."

"I don't dream, not like them."

"I see."

She curls the teacup against her chest. "What does any of this have to do with us?"

"Patricia Ballard is Harold's mother."

"The old woman?"

"Yes. She ran a sister program, an experiment like Harold's Foreverland."

"What kind of experiment? What were you trying to discover?"

"It's hard to explain." He avoids looking at her. "Let's say we were exploring expanded consciousness, living life outside the physical body. My wife, Barbara, volunteered to participate in Patricia's experiment, which only allowed females." He chuckles. "I was on a tropical island, and she was in this place."

"So you're saying this place, right here and now, is like Foreverland?"

"In a way. You see, the girls in Patricia's program—"

"The Fountain of Youth."

"Um, yes," he stammers. "I believe that's what they called it. How did you know?"

"I saw it somewhere." She sips her tea. "Go on."

"Okay. Whatever happened to Foreverland also affected Patricia, only she didn't crash. She rebooted. Your experiment started over."

"Then where's your wife?"

"I don't know." He pauses with a grimace, although it looks forced. *Fake.* "Maybe they got out before it crashed."

"But why didn't we get out?"

"Look, Miranda, I don't know everything, just where we are. I do know this, we don't want to stay here."

She pulls her legs onto the chair, throws a blanket over her lap and sinks into the cushions. Mr. Williams sits back quietly.

The music soothes the moment.

"It's not fair." She holds the teacup with both hands below her chin. "Foreverland was nice."

"It was utopia, Miranda. Patricia's world is an exact replication of reality. This place is exactly where my Barbara lived, all the way down to the pictures. I don't know how Patricia did it. It's almost like she absorbed the details of reality around her and created this alternate reality in her mind. Patricia made this world exactly like the physical one. There's almost no difference."

She hides half her face behind the blanket. "I want to wake up."

"There's no waking up." His eyebrows shade his eyes. "She didn't create this world to last, there's only so much food, only so much time. The only way out is to escape."

"And then what? If we die, we wake up?"

"In Patricia's world, you start over, you wake up without memories."

"How do you know?"

He sighs. "This isn't the first time you've been through this." The corners of his mouth turn down grimly. "We have to escape."

"A gate." Miranda pulls the blanket down. "You told Cyn in the barn there was a gate."

"It's like a doorway between reality and this world, the epicenter of Patricia's mind."

"What does it look like?"

"I don't know. Maybe it's another sundial. We'll know when we get near it, feel reality begin to quiver. There are several square miles to search and the weather is getting worse. It should be in the middle, but I don't even know where that is."

He rubs his face, yawning. His eyes are red. His cheeks hang like dead skin.

"I'm old and tired, Miranda. Old and tired. I can't take much more of this."

"We've got plenty of food, Mr. Williams. There are elk in the countryside, I've seen them. It's not as bad—"

"No!" He launches to his feet. Miranda sinks into the chair. "We can't wait, this won't last. And I won't go into the Nowhere again, do you understand? I can't do it, Miranda."

He points at her, his finger knobby and hooked.

"We have to find the gate. And when we do, I have to be the first one out."

She pulls the blanket up higher.

He downs the remaining tea and puts the cup on the table. He rubs his face again. "I need some rest. Would you mind if I take one of the beds?"

She nods, cowering.

Without another word, he slips into the bedroom next to the stairwell. Miranda doesn't move from the chair, curled up and shivering. It's very late. She is scared and awake, but sleep eventually comes.

At some point, she hears drawers opening and closing.

—

39

—

The wind harvesters' blades are locked in place against the punishing wind. Mad stops in the kitchen. Cyn looks up from the footstool.

"It's me," Cyn says. "I'm the one."

"What?"

She holds her head like she's clamping it together, hair tufts sticking out between her inky fingers.

"In the mornings..." Cyn starts, trailing off. "In the mornings my feet are cold, my bandages wet and muddy. But I don't go to bed like that—I just wake up that way."

"What're you talking about?"

Cyn holds up her hand, exposing the ink stains. "I'm stealing the bags."

"You're not making any sense."

"I know!" She squeezes her head, rocking back and forth. "I'm sleepwalking in here, stealing the bags, but I don't remember. I don't know why."

"And doing what?"

"Taking them to that..." She waves her hand at the wall. "That cabin in the woods, I think."

She doesn't tell her how she ruined her feet, walking all the way back the night of the excursion, not remembering a thing.

"But you don't have a key." Mad holds two keycards, both around her neck. "How are you getting in here?"

Cyn's eyes sit in deep, dark pockets. "I don't know."

She stares at her feet. The toenails are cracked and caked with mud, her skin slightly off-color. Throbbing.

Mad's hand is cool on her forehead. "I think the fever is back. We need to try another bottle. And unwrap your feet—"

The outside kitchen door opens. The wind spits sleet inside. Kat backs into the room, hood over her face. She hugs herself, stomping her feet.

"The chickens are dead."

"What?" Mad says.

"Chickens. They're dead."

"All of them?" Mad says.

"Yeah, all of them. Something got inside, feathers everywhere."

Kat pushes the hood back, looking at Cyn, who is hunched over. "What's up with her?"

"Sleepwalker," Mad says.

Kat waits, rubbing warmth into her arms. The chill creeps into Cyn just under her sternum. She shakes all over and looks up, her face about to cave in.

"I walk at night," she says. "I get up, I steal one of the bags, and I take it to the cabin in the woods. That's what the old woman was doing when she died on the path—I saw the plastic bag in her hand."

"So you took her place?"

"How the hell should I know? Does anything make sense?"

Cyn shakes her head. No one has an answer. The more they know, the less they understand.

The front door slams; someone stomps their feet, humming a little tune and flapping their lips. Jen is dressed in enough clothes for two Eskimos. She turns her head left and right, aiming the long snorkel at each of them, her face deep inside the hood.

"Anyone come out of the brick house?"

No one answers.

When the long, fuzzy hood points at Cyn, a deep breath is sucked in. She pushes the hood off, kneeling in front of her.

"You don't look good," she says. "And the bandages are wet and nasty, why aren't you wearing the boots? Get those off. We need to start a new medicine. Right, Mad? She looks flushed. Someone get some water."

Jen opens the cabinet and grabs one of the three brown bottles still left. Kat reaches in before the door closes, snatching a clear bag.

"You're feeding someone," she says. "This ain't medicine, I bet. These are nutrients; you're feeding someone through the veins."

Cyn takes pills from Jen and water from Mad. She sits up and lets Jen begin unwrapping her right foot, trying to remember taking the bags. But it's the same, always the same, every night. Blank. Empty.

How would she know how to fix an IV? How could someone force her?

The dreamer.

She doesn't want to believe the old man, doesn't want to think about the dreamer hiding away in the woods, making her sleepwalk to care for her.

"Ooh." Mad turns away, covering her nose. "Don't look, Cyn."

The odor is obscene.

The wound is pitted, the edges inflamed, the center white with pus. Her ankle is stiff and achy.

"That's not good," Kat says. "Double up on the pills, I say."

"Okay." Jen backs away. "All right. Mad, get a bucket of water and a rag. We're going to clean this up, get it wrapped. Then we're taking you back to bed and bringing you some soup. You got more soup, Mad?"

Mad drops the bucket and rag next to Jen. They stare at it.

"Kat," Jen says, "get behind Cyn."

"Why?"

"You'll need to hold her."

Jen's gentle at first. But Kat does have to hold Cyn. She wraps her arms around Cyn's chest, each dab of the cloth like a hot poker knifing through her leg.

The room starts to turn.

They carry her out. She doesn't remember that.

The storm pelts her, but she doesn't take cover. Her face is numb before they reach the bunkhouse. They tuck her in her bed. Kat stokes the fire. Cyn feels Jen lean over and hears her scratch the wall.

Adding another day.

40

The showerhead drips.

Miranda backs away from the mirror, the edges fogged. She pulls her hair up and clips it into place with a small barrette in order to show off her ears and the dangling pearls. Mr. Williams found the earrings in Barbara's room and asked her to wear them.

Don't sink to their level, he said. *Don't be afraid to be who you are.*

They're going to hate her, think she's showing off, rubbing it in their faces. But she likes them. They complement her complexion.

So does the necklace.

She brushes her teeth and rubs a splash of perfume on her wrists. One last look.

She feels good, like herself. Who she is.

Mr. Williams is standing at the window in the front room, hands in his pockets, staring at the dinner house. His hair is slick with comb lines. He found a yellow collared shirt and white sweater vest. Gender neutral.

Sid is on the couch, doing the usual.

Mr. Williams turns. Smiles. "You are a beautiful young lady."

"Thank you." She straightens up despite the tension in her chest. "I don't think this is a good idea, though. I don't want to go with you."

"We cannot allow our *wants* to be the compass of our lives, my dear. Life demands. We answer, like it or not."

"That doesn't make me feel better."

"How you feel is irrelevant." He wraps a wool scarf around his neck and holds a coat out.

She can't move. "They hate me. They'll hurt me."

"Of course they hate you. But they can't hurt you."

He lays the coat over the arm of the chair and reaches into his pocket. He dangles a black key fob.

"What is it?"

"Stay near me."

He holds the coat up again. The gold cap twinkles. He looks from beneath shaggy eyebrows with cold blue—almost gray—eyes.

She's compelled to move.

Miranda slides her arms into the sleeves. Mr. Williams zips it up and hands her a scarf.

"It's cold out there."

Sid puts on a frilly coat over multiple sweatshirts, sliding leather gloves over his hands, his wrists still exposed. Mr. Williams pulls a thick stocking cap over his head and buttons up an overcoat. He slides his hand over the back of Miranda's neck, his palm soft with lotion. His thumb caresses her hairline.

"Sid," he says. "Lead the way, my boy."

The wind whistles through the doorway.

Miranda steps onto the front porch and turns her back to the west, losing her breath in the frigid gale. She gulps at the air. Painful as it is, the air feels clean and fresh. Purifying. Only then does she realize how bad it smells inside the house.

"Come along!" Mr. Williams holds out his hand.

They walk single file, Sid leading the way. His lean body is hardly a shield, but bears the majority of the weather. Miranda shuffles along, head down, plowing through their tracks. Snow falls into her shoes, packing against her socks. When they reach the dinner house, the path widens.

They stop outside the bunkhouse.

Snow is melting into puddles near the door.

Kat and Mad are gathered around the stove. Jen sits next to Cyn's bed. They look up, their cheeks sunken, their listless eyes dark. They don't look emaciated on the cameras.

In person, they look like refugees.

Miranda's legs threaten to buckle. Her skin is cold from the weather, but her insides are numb with fear. She stays behind Mr. Williams.

He looks around, observing the quarters. Hand in pocket.

"You bring food?" Kat stands.

Mr. Williams pulls a chair up next to Cyn's bed and sits with a groan. Miranda goes with him. The blanket is pulled up to Cyn's chin. He feels her forehead.

"She'll be dead in a week," he says. "Maybe less."

"We're giving her medicine," Jen says.

"It won't matter. What I have to say is more important."

"You said this is a dream." Kat stands over him.

Mr. Williams is unfazed. Miranda steps back. She never should've trusted that thing in his pocket. The girls might be starved, but desperation can be dangerous.

Sid stands near the door.

"It is a dream, Ms. Kat." He leans forward, using his momentum to stand. "And the dream is ending. We need to be out before it does."

He walks to the stove and warms his hands. Miranda follows him. Kat tells her she looks pretty. She doesn't mean it.

"There's an exit out there," Mr. Williams announces. "I don't know what it looks like. Where I came from it was a sundial, but it could be anything. Whatever it is, it'll be located in the center of this world."

"You mean *dream*," Kat says.

"I don't have time for this." Mr. Williams's eyebrows lower. "You can believe me or not; you can stay here when it all comes to a halt. I don't really care. But what you will do is help me find the gate. I would assume these cabins are in the center of this world, but I have my doubts. That means it's out there. Somewhere."

He sweeps his crooked finger around the room.

"We'll need to find it. All of us."

"Ain't going out in this weather," Kat says.

"Yes, in this weather, Ms. Kat. You will go out and so will the rest of you." He nods at Jen and Mad. "We'll also untie the young lady in the back; the more feet on the ground, the better."

Miranda grabs the back of his coat. "I don't...that's not a good idea," she whispers.

"There will be five of you searching. You will go in five directions, walk for an hour, and return."

"You're not going?" Kat asks.

"I'm far too old to be out there." A dangerous edge sharpens his tone.

"If it's a dream," Kat says, "why do you care how old you are?"

He stares at her until it's uncomfortable, his hand working inside his pocket.

"You'll look for something interesting, like a sculpture or waterfall. I don't know. More importantly, you will feel it when you get near it. It will vibrate inside you, a tingling sensation at the very core of your existence. Do *not* touch it."

He takes a long moment to look at each of them.

"If you encounter it, do not touch it. Come back for the rest of us and we'll all leave this dream together. That's how it works."

He walks to the back of the cabin, Miranda attached to his coat. His footsteps clop on the wood floor. Roc is a dark lump in the corner. Miranda closes her eyes, both hands grasping his coat. She wishes Sid was with them.

"Miranda and I will bring all the food out of the house," he says. "We'll eat until our bellies are full, give us strength."

Roc rolls over at the mention of food.

He nods at her. "Can you behave yourself?"

She doesn't answer.

"If you can't, you will never leave this place. Answer me."

She nods. Miranda isn't convinced.

"This isn't a dream," Jen whimpers. "I can feel and see and hear. I hurt. This is real, Mr. Williams."

He walks over.

Mr. Williams kneels next to her with much effort. He reaches out, runs his hand over Jen's black scrub of hair, and cups her cheek. Her eyes are big, imploring. And they roll back.

She slides out of the chair.

Mr. Williams places her on the floor.

"What'd you do?" Kat says.

"I'm in charge, girls." He looks down at Jen, brushing something off of her lips. "There is a device imbedded in your neck. It will deliver a jolt to your nervous system if I want. It will render you unconscious. I have this control."

He holds up a fob and hands it to Miranda. It fits nicely in her hand, her thumb snug in the button's indention.

"And so does Miranda."

He reaches up. Sid is there to help him.

Mr. Williams's knee has stiffened. He limps to the door and waves Sid and Miranda to his side.

"I'm trying to help all of you, you understand. Without me, you would rot inside this dream for eternity. I don't ask for thanks, just a little help so that we all can escape."

"Bastard," Kat mutters.

Mr. Williams doesn't hear it, or chooses not to acknowledge it.

"We'll eat in an hour," he says. "Be dressed and ready. We'll plan our search."

"What about me?" Roc says.

Mr. Williams doesn't bother smiling. "Sid will come for you."

She mutters something, too.

Miranda holds the fob. Both hands shaking.

Sid opens the door for Mr. Williams. She hurries after him.

41

She can hear the weather battering the windows.

Doors open and close. Logs pop in the stove.

Coughing.

Cyn swims through watery delirium, a spirit paddling against the current, rolling beneath the surface, attempting to keep her head above sanity.

And failing.

Often she finds herself landing on the ledge, fear screaming her name from the chasm. Turning—always turning to run. To get away.

And she always returns. Never escapes.

She's caught in the current of thoughts and tension and contraction. Back to the ledge. Toes hanging over.

Nothing she ever does works. She never gets away, always comes back.

So she stops.

She stays on the edge, staring into the abyss. Gray swirling like lost souls. Loneliness howls inside her, but she doesn't look away this time.

This time she doesn't run.

Doesn't resist the discomfort.

She remains there, on the edge, with the tension. The fear. Without pushing it away, without grasping. Just there.

Just there.

No more running.

This time, she finds home on the edge.

"No stealing tonight."

Cyn is jostled from slumber. She hears the voice, different from the ones that whisper from the gray. This one is over her, near her.

She opens her eyes.

"Here." Mad puts something against her lips. "Swallow."

Cyn lets the pills fall under her tongue and swallows the water poured in after them. Feels like she's drowning.

Her head falls onto the pillow. So hot. So achy.

Mad and Kat are dim outlines in the failing light. It must be late.

"We got rid of them," Kat says.

Kat dangles something. The plastic bag catches a little light coming through the window, clear nutrient solution dripping through a tear on the bottom. Tubes wrapped around her wrist.

"No more stealing."

—
42
—

Mr. Williams and Sid are waiting outside the brick house.

Miranda pulls on her gloves and tucks her scarf into the gap under her chin before stepping outside. The sun is rising. Fresh snow glitters like a blanket of diamond dust.

It smells so fresh, so clean.

Mr. Williams smiles, throws his arm over her shoulders, and draws her tightly against him. He inhales deeply, feeling the clean air, too.

His hand finds its way onto her neck, thumb circling on her flesh. Goosebumps flash down her back.

"If all the days were like this, I wouldn't mind staying."

Another deep breath.

"Sid," he calls.

It takes Sid a moment to process this. He slides his hand down the railing, scraping a two-inch layer of snow onto the ground. Mr. Williams keeps his hand on her neck. She's too afraid to move, wondering if he can make the fob work on her.

The garden looks like a graveyard of fallen soldiers, old stalks beneath lumps of snow. An arm here. A leg there.

He stops at the first solar panel, wiping off the snow. He uses his arm like a wiper, exposing the black glass to absorb the light once the sun is up.

Miranda watches.

"A good start, yesterday," he says. "We'll find it soon enough, Miranda."

"How long do we have?"

He goes to the next panel. Sid is working his way towards them. Mr. Williams winks. "Plenty of time. Don't tell them."

They finish cleaning the solar panels and plod their way through the snow, around the garden. The outside kitchen door is cracked open. Mr. Williams discovered he could unlock all the doors through the computers, except for the small cabin where Patricia sleeps.

"Plenty of food," he says. "We don't have to go hungry, it'll last us."

Again, arm around her.

She walks stiffly, head down. Funny how they're still hungry in a dream. Still breathing. They don't really need food or air.

Not in a dream.

Sid walks through pristine snow piled at the foot of the kitchen door. He pushes it open and steps aside. The shelves are full of food. Mr. Williams chuckles, in the best of moods. He kisses the top of Miranda's head, gives her a squeeze, and steps into the kitchen.

Stops.

She and Sid wait outside.

Nothing looks out of place. But his cheer dies. Mr. Williams's hand slips into his pocket. He lumbers through the small kitchen, poking at something in the sink.

Miranda's afraid to follow. She backs up a step, feeling her chest contract. It seems as if his posture swells, that he fills the room with anger.

He holds something up.

It's plastic and limp.

It slaps onto the floor.

Mr. Williams grasps the edge of the sink, hunched over. Head bowed. Sid doesn't move.

"Dammit!" He swings his arm.

A stack of bags scatter, each smacking against the wall. He kicks through the debris, stomping outside. His face a shade darker.

Miranda flips on the light. The clear plastic bags ooze on the floor.

43

The silence wakes her.

She's accustomed to the bunkhouse creaking, the wind pushing against the windows, through the cracks. Now there's not even the *whump, whump, whump* of the wind harvester.

Just the silence.

Cyn opens her eyes, staring at the rafters. Her pillow still wet from fever, but her forehead cool. Legs no longer on fire.

Such a wondrous moment.

She falls back to sleep.

She wakes to the rustle of coats, to boots hitting the floor. The stove is fully stoked, embers popping against the metal belly. Trays sit on chairs, a few on the floor. Food, uneaten.

The girls are pulling on winter gear.

Roc is cursing from her bed.

Cyn's lips are glued together with slime. She pulls them apart, smacking them to work up saliva.

"How you feeling?" Jen asks.

"Water." Cyn pokes her hand out.

Jen brings it. It's a cold rush down a hot pipe. She hands it back. "What's going on?"

The front door slams open.

A Russian bear fills the doorway. His nose is ruby red. Cheeks scuffed by winter. He steps inside. The bear transforms into an old man scuffling into the bunkhouse. A fur cap is forced onto his head, the fuzzy edge resting just above his eyebrows.

"Do you realize what you've done?" He shakes plastic at them. "Do you?"

Sid comes in. Miranda after him, wearing knee-high boots and a flawless white coat, plus pearls and new earrings. Jealous anger stirs inside Cyn. *She's a thief.*

"Untie the one in back." He points a hooked finger.

Sid marches to the back corner. The bedsprings creak.

"What are you doing?" Cyn sits up. "Wait, you can't untie her. Do you know what you're doing?"

"I ask the questions." He spikes the bags on the floorboards, droplets spraying in all directions.

He pulls the hat off, grinding his teeth. He walks toward the stove, thoughtful steps. Head down.

Hand in pocket.

Kat and Mad step aside.

"We had months to survive." He turns around, shaking his head. "All winter, probably. Now we might only have days!"

He finishes pacing to the door and swings around.

"Do you understand? *Days!* You don't know anything about this world, none of you. You stumble around in the dark like children. I am your light. I am the one who will lead you out of here. And you!"

He crosses the room with large steps, shaking his finger at Cyn.

"You had one purpose: you were chosen to keep the dreamer alive. She chose you to bring those bags to her, allowed you inside her sanctuary to feed her, and you destroyed it. This is your fault!"

He stands over her, balling his fist, restraining himself from striking her. Cyn is unmoved, unblinking. If he decides to cave in her skull, she can't stop him.

"Thought you said this was a dream," Kat says.

The rage dissipates. His eyes blink heavily. He straightens, looking down at Cyn, nodding.

And then the pulse, the electric prod ignites a thunderstorm in her neck, lightning flashing behind her eyes. A thunderbolt in her throat.

Her body is like a steel plank.

And blackness falls like a marble slab.

Consciousness lifts like a fuzzy shade.

Her body buzzing. Teeth numb.

"Listen to me," a disembodied voice calls. "And do what I say."

Footsteps echo.

Moans follow.

Forms creep from the hazy light. The girls are on the floor. Mr. Williams walks across the room, his shoes grind at a turn, stepping in the other direction.

"Patricia is the dreamer. We are inside her mind; she creates the rules. And the rules mirror reality. That means her body, back in the woods, needs to be cared for, needs to be fed. That old woman on the path was the caregiver. When she died, Patricia chose Cyn to take her place."

He picks up the limp plastic bag.

"When Patricia dies, so does this world."

The girls sit up.

"Get dressed," he says. "Meet me in the dinner house. We will eat and plan routes. You will explore this land until nightfall. I would leave you out there half the night if Patricia didn't put you in the dream."

The girls sleep like the dead. They all dream the same. *Patricia's doing that to us.*

"Why?" Cyn croaks.

He turns toward her.

"Why does she do that?" Cyn asks.

"You're her children. She wants to share the dream."

"And you?"

His head shakes. Perhaps he's contemplating the button.

"You," he says with stiff lips, "are useless. Stay in the bed and die there."

He punches the door open. Miranda flees behind him.

There's a scuffle in the back. Sid drags Roc by the arm, her coat open, bootlaces whipping around her feet. She yanks her arm out of his grasp. His reaction betrays his slack posture: a lightning-quick slap to the nose. He twists her arm behind her back, bending the wrist until her fingers tickle the back of her head.

He marches her through the doorway, slamming it shut. Roc's curses are heard through the closed door.

The girls get dressed. Cyn is just getting the feeling back in her fingers.

"We'll bring you something to eat," Jen whispers.

"Where are you going?" Cyn asks.

"He's got us searching for the gate," Kat sneers, not bothering to whisper.

Cyn throws the blanket off, squirming to move her legs. "I'll come with—"

"Stop her," Kat says. "He'll freak out. Besides, you won't make it to the door, not on those rotten-ass feet. Last thing we need to do is dig a hole for your body."

Mad inserts pills in Cyn's mouth. "Here's two more"—she pushes pills into her palm—"and take them if we don't come back."

"We'll be back," Jen says, wrapping her face in a scarf.

They leave Cyn with the silence and a medicinal haze.

Then the gray.

44

Miranda stays outside, where the air is brisk and renewing. The cold washes away feelings of heavy dread. She imagines she's a filter, the pores plugged with dust and grit and decay.

The air blows it out. Makes her new again.

She opens the front door, where the air is dry and warm and unwholesome. Somehow she dies a little every time she goes inside.

Mr. Williams stands at the window, a cup in hand. The smell of coffee mingles with the stagnant odor of the brick house. Miranda stomps the snow off of her boots and steps past a fully loaded backpack. He holds out his arm, beckoning. She pretends not to notice, unzipping her coat.

"Come," he says, wiggling his fingers.

She's frozen in place again. He knows she heard him. She's looking right at him.

It's easier to just go to him. He's old.

Miranda comes within reach. He pulls her against his body, squeezing tightly. Perfume emanates from his wrist.

Kat, Mad, and Jen exit from the outside kitchen door and begin their trek through the woods out back. Roc and Sid exit the front door, walking west. Together. Even though Miranda never lets the fob out of her grip, she's relieved Sid is staying near her.

And if he causes her pain, she enjoys that.

"Don't worry." He pulls her tighter. "We'll find the gate."

"Is it true?"

"Of course, it's out there."

"No, I mean about Patricia. Will she die?"

His grip stiffens. He pulls a sip from the cup, smacking his lips and letting go of Miranda. He pulls a sheet of paper from his back pocket, unfolding it.

Miranda moves away, not wanting to be near him if she doesn't have to. She goes to the rack next to the door, pulling the coat off her shoulder—

"No."

Mr. Williams holds the paper out while continuing to look out the window. Miranda reluctantly takes it. The letter N is at the top. There's a small square drawn in the middle labeled "camp". Five arrows point out from it in different directions.

Miranda's name is penciled over one of them.

"You go east," he says. "You go until the sun is high and then return. Write down everything you see."

He sips the coffee.

"You want me to go out?"

"You're young and able, darling. In this body, I wouldn't make it past the meadow. You can walk all day."

She stares at the paper. It starts quivering.

"We all have to pitch in, Miranda."

He looks over his shoulder. She still hasn't moved. He puts the cup on the windowsill and begins to slowly zip her coat up.

"There isn't much time."

He tucks her scarf around her neck, sliding his hands over her shoulders, pulls the hood over her head and ties it below her chin.

"I've prepared a pack for you with food and water."

He puts his hand on her cheeks, a slight smile. He reaches out with the other hand—

Miranda breaks the ice in her knees, jerking away.

She pulls open the door and slams it behind her. She stomps through the snow, leaving the food and water, keeping her face in the wind, hoping it will shear away the smell of perfume.

$$\overline{}$$

45

$$\overline{}$$

A gentle hand wakes Cyn.

Her eyes, slightly crusted, open with effort. Mad is there, her face scratched with red lines. Her hand is on Cyn's shoulder, pills pinched in her fingers. She doesn't ask, just puts them between Cyn's lips.

Cyn lifts her heavy head high enough to chase the pills without spilling water. Not that it matters; the pillow is damp with sweat.

It's light outside. There's a lump in Jen's bed. Roc is making noise in the back.

"What's going on?"

Mad puts the cup on the floor and hands her a bowl of cold grits. She pulls the covers off the foot of Cyn's bed, inspecting the bandages. They feel dry, but a stench rises.

Kat limps to the stove, poking the dying embers to life, throwing another stick inside. She begins undressing.

"Jen hit a fence," Kat says.

"What?" Cyn gets higher on her elbow. "Where?"

"Went through the woods, the three of us. Went to that small cabin and split up. Jen went straight north and I went northeast. Must've walked about twenty minutes but didn't get far. Trees are thick and there's no path. Mad went the other way, same thing."

Kat's face is scratched as bad as Mad's.

"Right about the time I saw the end of the forest, I started to feel the buzz," Kat continues, sitting on the edge of her bed to shuck her boots. "I slowed down, but kept going. It got more intense the closer I got to the end of the trees. I could see the clearing right where they stopped, like I could just step out and walk into another meadow. I got all the way to the edge and felt like I was going to drop."

She leans on her knees, rubbing her face.

"Then I heard screaming."

"Jen?"

"She was a long ways off, but it sounded like she was set on fire. Took about ten minutes to get to her. She was just outside the trees, squirming in the snow, wouldn't stop."

Mad pulls the covers over Cyn's feet, tucking them in. Won't look up.

"How'd you get her out?" Cyn asks.

"It took a while," Kat says. "We reached in and grabbed her foot, damn near blacked out doing it. Once we got her, though, she stopped screaming."

"She ain't talked since," Mad says.

What memories are in her now?

"It was a road, Cyn," Kat says.

"What do you mean?"

"There were tracks in the ground, just like you saw. Mad and I think she ignored the feeling in her neck, just walked out of the trees and right through the fence."

"And started remembering." Mad goes to the stove. "Ain't that right, Cyn?"

"It's like the road was taunting us," Kat says. "Pretending there's a way out, but then we just start remembering."

"I don't want to know," Mad says. "Not anymore."

Their eyes are cast downward.

Their spirits will starve long before their stomachs. There's no escape.

No hope.

They feel the cage, too. Sense the walls. The illusion of freedom is crushing them. There was a world beyond the mountains, but not anymore. *Hope is the dream.*

"How far did Jen get?" Cyn asks.

"What?" Kat looks up.

"She walked straight north, how far did she go from the bunkhouse before she reached the fence?"

"I don't know, three hundred yards or so. Hard to say with all the trees."

Cyn visualizes the bunkhouse from a bird's-eye view. She trekked due south about two miles, give or take. Jen went in the opposite direction only three hundred yards or so.

She reaches under the bed for her coat and searches the pockets. There's a pencil and a tattered square of paper in the pocket. She unfolds it, holding it up to the light.

If Jen walked three hundred yards to the north—she puts an X on the paper—and Cyn went two miles to the south, then she could identify the perimeter. And if the fence is an enormous circle—Cyn sketches an outline using the two points as a reference—that would mean that the center would be...

"Got it."

Kat and Mad are at the stove. "Got what?" Kat asks.

Cyn circles the tiny X in the center of her notes and holds it up.

"I know where the gate is."

46

Miranda's elbow wakes her at three o'clock in the morning.

She had slipped on an icy rock during her exploration. Every muscle in her body aches, the blisters on her feet throb. And the pain relievers are wearing off.

There's a light on somewhere in the back of the house.

Mr. Williams is adamant about conserving energy. Lights get turned off, the heat turned down. Even the music. She lies on the couch, beneath three heavy comforters, listening to the office chair creak.

He's up.

Miranda doesn't want to move; it took forever to get warm. Mr. Williams wouldn't let her take a hot shower—too much power to heat the water. Everything needed to be conserved for the back office.

But she has to pee.

She wraps one of the blankets around her and waddles down the hallway like a human burrito. Sid is snoring in Barbara's bed. She put the necklace and earrings back; she doesn't plan on wearing them again. She saw the jealousy in Cyn's eyes. Doesn't want to see that again.

She's forced to drop the wrapping to sit on the toilet, holding it on her lap while she does her business. She doesn't flush, and she stops when she sees the mirror. The night-light casts yellow light on her face, illuminating the long red line across her cheek. A branch had nearly poked her in the eye earlier.

Miranda heads back for the couch, but Mr. Williams is exiting the forbidden door, the eternally locked one at the very back. He doesn't notice her looking out from the bathroom.

The office chair creaks.

Miranda looks inside. The monitors are lit up. The inside of the bunkhouse is on the main one. The girls are unconscious.

"Still up?"

Mr. Williams slowly spins the chair around, hands laced behind his head. "Too excited to sleep."

"Something happen?"

"Tomorrow will be a good day, I believe."

"Did someone find it?"

A sly smile. "Don't worry. Go to sleep, get some rest."

He leans back, sinking into the chair's depths. He hasn't slept in a bed for days. The chair has molded to his bottom.

One of the monitors is focused on Cyn. No more midnight runs. She can hardly get out of bed. She lies there, rotting.

Dying.

Aren't we all?

Miranda yawns, turning to leave. The back door is cracked open. The odor is a bit more noticeable. Now that she's been outside, she notices it more.

Fear pushes her back a step, but she holds her ground.

Mr. Williams notices. He throws his weight forward to lean out of the chair. He gently pushes the door. It clicks.

"Nothing you want to see," he says. The smile is gone. "Get some sleep."

He's right. She doesn't want to see what's back there. She just wishes he didn't go back there, that the door would stay closed forever. Instinct tells her that she never wants to know what's back there.

Miranda lies awake on the couch, listening to the chair creak and pop for quite some time.

—

47

—

Spreading her arms,
She tips like a statue.
Over the edge she falls,
And lets the chasm take her.

A sharp point pierces the soft tissue beneath her chin.

Cyn opens her eyes. It's too dark to see the face in front of her, but she can feel someone's breath. Taste the stink.

"I promised to kill you," Roc hisses. "To stick this wire through the top of your brain, but I want out of here. I want the old man to kiss my ass."

Cyn pushes her head into the pillow, but the point just follows her. The sheets are too tight. The weapon will be in her sinuses before she gets free.

"What are you talking about?" she says without moving her lips.

"You know where the gate is."

"You believe that crap?"

"What else is there? If the old man gets to it, he'll screw us—you can count on that."

"And if it doesn't work?"

"Then we die in Hell."

Cyn struggles to move her head. The tip of Roc's weapon is breaking the skin. "Back that off."

Roc leans closer, pushing it deeper. It's about to go through when she puts it against Cyn's throat. She relaxes her head. The spot under her chin burns.

"It's too far to walk," Cyn says.

"We've got horses."

"Then we'll need Kat."

Roc plants her free hand on Cyn's face and presses her lips to her ear. "Mess with me and you die with a rusty twig in your eye. You don't stand a chance against me, not anymore. You smell like dead ass."

She's right. Cyn doesn't have the strength to fight.

Roc springs back. Despite Cyn's decrepit condition, she's still wary. It's hard to forget a thorough ass whipping. She backs into the dark, barely an outline. It's still night, but morning must be close or they wouldn't be awake.

"Surprise," Roc whispers.

Kat wakes, startled. A hand clamps over her mouth.

There's unintelligible whispering, all Roc.

"Cyn?" Kat calls.

A loud slap. "I'm not playing," Roc says.

"It's all right," Cyn says. "Just do what she says."

"Get dressed before the sun's up," Roc adds.

She's thinking about the fob. Maybe they get all the way out there and get knocked out. Maybe not. One thing's for sure: they'll get knocked out if the old man comes to the bunkhouse.

"Wake up the others." Cyn reaches under the bed.

"No." Roc stands in the middle of the room. "Just the three of us."

Cyn drops a sweater on the floor. "I'm not going, then."

"You can come back for them."

"I'm not moving."

Roc bounds across the room and slams Cyn's head into the pillow, squeezing her face with one hand. The point presses against her temple. Spittle flies with each angry breath, like a dragon contemplating the next move.

"We can ride double," Kat says. "Cyn's going to need help staying on the horse anyway."

Roc presses down, her breath hot and humid. Cyn sees the whites of her eyes.

She leaps off. "Hurry, then; go."

Kat scurries to the other beds. The girls moan. Roc yanks them up. They protest, but not for long.

Cyn slowly puts on clothes. Sluggish. Sore. Her body full of sand. The others scuffle to get dressed, whispering back and forth. Roc's anger wanes; there are fewer threats and more action.

Maybe Roc is saving us.

Cyn puts on three pair of socks and looks down at the last thing.

Boots.

Even with the backs cut out, they're tight.

"Here." Mad drops four pills into her hand. "Take all of these."

Cyn rolls them in her palm. She just wants the pain to go away. Dream or not, she wants it to end.

She swallows them dry.

And shoves her feet into boots of hot, broken glass.

Somehow, she chokes down the scream.

48

Miranda wakes every twenty minutes, spinning on the couch, searching for the comfort zone. Finding none. She wishes for a little music to mask the sounds of the house, the creaks of the office chair.

It's the door.

She can't stop thinking about it. She's positive she doesn't want to see what's back there, but now that it's been opened, her curiosity nibbles.

It's almost six o'clock.

The sun will be up very soon. She doesn't want to hike, not today. Not ever. If only she could run a fever, she could stay on the couch all day, listening to her favorite composers. Just her and the comforter and Mozart and Brahms. That would be a good day.

Mr. Williams won't be happy. *Can he work that thing to zap me?*

There's nowhere she can hide, not inside the house. He goes everywhere and knows how to work everything.

She goes down the hall, dragging the blanket, giving the thermostat a little bump. The air handler kicks on. Lifeless dry air blows from the vent. Miranda leans into the back room; the monitors are lit up.

Light snores rise and fall from the office chair. Mr. Williams is slumped out of view. The monitors flicker with green light, one of them focused on an empty pillow. The others pan around the bunkhouse. All the covers thrown back, beds empty.

All of them.

She steps into the room.

Mr. Williams snorts, jerking in the chair. He spins around, eyeballing the blanket-clad blonde standing in the doorway. It takes him a moment to process, and then he remembers where he is and why.

She's looking at something.

Mr. Williams attacks the keyboard, cycling the monitors around the buildings. They're not in the dinner house. The floodlights illuminate the area with white light. Not in the garden, not outside the brick house. Not in the woods or at the small cabin—

The barn door is open.

Horses gallop into the open, free at last. Their legs stretching out, clopping the ground, snow powder tossed in their wake. Kat's on the first one, gripping the mane with both hands, hunched over, bouncing with the horse's stride.

The other horses bear two riders each.

"Sid!" The office chair flies across the room.

Mr. Williams limps toward Miranda, almost losing his balance. He fumbles his way into the hallway.

"Sid!"

Their footsteps hammer the hardwood. The door slams.

Miranda watches the monitors. Watches the girls ride out of the floodlights and into the early morning, hugging each other.

Sid sprints past the garden in his socks. Mr. Williams isn't far behind, aiming the fob at the distant riders. They remain on the backs of the animals, not breaking stride.

Fading into the snow-laden meadow.

They left me. Her head knocks against the doorframe. *I deserve it.*

$$\text{—}$$

49

$$\text{—}$$

The horses run on instinct.

Cyn squeezes Mad from behind, pressing her head against her back. "Hold on to the mane like it's your life," Kat had told them.

Cyn told them which direction to run, and to run as fast as they could. They have to get out of sight, as far away as possible. She'll figure out the rest once they can't see the cabins. The horse's backbone slams into her each time the hooves hit, sending painful waves through her.

She holds on.

Closes her eyes.

They're in the trees within minutes. The horses work their way between the trunks, ducking beneath the limbs. The slow pace eases the pain, but Cyn doesn't look up until they're out of the trees.

It's still dark. And she doesn't know where they are.

The horses walk the easiest routes, going around rock outcroppings and steep hills. But they don't stop. Cyn wonders if Mr. Williams will send Sid after them, if he'll run until he drops from exhaustion.

The sun breaks the horizon. Cyn gets her bearings and has them turn more to the left, hoping this will put them back on track. They can go in circles all day to find it if they have to.

They're not going back.

They reach a shallow valley. The horses dig in and scale the steep slope. Cyn hangs on, almost sliding off the back of her horse. They gather on the ridge, the ground gently sloping down the other side. The horses paw at the snow, tossing their heads.

Snorting.

The girls slump over. Tired and hungry. Spirits bending.

Cyn recognizes nothing. It's just an endless stretch of trees and hills and rocks, all covered in snow. Immoveable mountains in the distance.

Something flashes further up the ridge.

She wipes the tears from her eyes. It's a beam, a mirror, or something reflective.

"There!"

The boulder and dead tree are too far to see with any clarity. Cyn taps the horse with her toes, the pain receding in the numbing cold.

The others follow.

"You feel that?"

Cyn holds up her hand. The others trot to a stop. The boulder and tree are still fifty yards away.

"It's a fence," Kat shouts.

"Not a fence, it's different."

Cyn rubs her stomach where the quivering has begun. She felt that last time and thought the same thing, but a fence starts in the neck. This begins somewhere in the core, at the center of her being.

The horses walk closer. The backpack is still there, tattered and sun-bleached. The strip of aluminum rattles in the breeze.

Kat pulls up next to Cyn and dismounts. The others do, too. Roc stomps to the front, clutching a rusty bedspring. The end is bent outward.

Mad slides off while Kat and Jen reach up for Cyn. She leans over, falling into their outstretched arms. When her feet touch the ground, fiery sparks lance her dead legs, spraying pins and needles throughout her body.

She collapses.

Kat and Jen carry her closer. The vibrations in her stomach increase, beating back the pain, filling her with warmth and goodness. They lie on the ground.

Together, they stare at the dead tree, its branches worn smooth by harsh weather. Beautiful and ancient.

"What now?" Roc says.

"I don't know," Cyn says.

"Start by putting that away." Kat points at the bedspring.

"Not until this is over."

The horses are restless, wandering over to the nearest trees, nibbling at shoots poking through the snow, lichens on the trunks. The girls stare at each other. Jen hasn't said a word.

"Touch it," Mad says.

"She already did that," Kat says. "The backpack is against the rock."

"Don't tell me we wasted our time." Roc waves the weapon. "And don't tell me we need the old man for some secret word."

"Not the tree." Cyn takes a few breaths, her chest shrinking. "I didn't touch the tree."

There's a moment where she doesn't hear anything, the pain too large to process. She breathes so small. When she opens her eyes, they're looking at her.

"Someone," she says, "touch it."

"You go." Roc points the bedspring at Kat.

"You wanted to ride out here, you go."

Roc starts at her—

"I'll go." Mad jumps between them. "I'll touch it."

Roc wipes the sweat from her forehead, exposing the skin between the glove and sleeve. Her wrist is ringed with raw flesh where the restraints cut into her.

"Go, then," she says.

The horses look up from the trees, grinding lichen in their mouths. Mad strips the gloves from her hands and tucks them in her pockets.

The snow is piled on the boulder.

On the branches.

And the wind hardly moves as she reaches out. Her hand pauses a moment and then grips the trunk.

She goes stiff.

Like electricity coursing through her. The branch is like a live wire.

Her eyes go wide. Her arm stiffens.

She's not convulsing, just staring into nothingness.

"Do something!" Jen shouts.

Kat runs up—

"Stop!" Cyn shouts. "Give it a second."

Kat's only a step away, hands out. Mad is a statue. Catatonic. Transported to another world.

"Maybe she's gone," Kats says. "Maybe the dream body stays here."

"I'm sick of this." Roc pulls off her glove. "I want out before that grisly bastard shows up."

Roc lumbers forward—

Mad collapses.

She draws a deep breath like she's been held under water, starving for air. Kat and Jen pull her away. Mad's eyes are crazy. She's gulping like a fish.

"It's all right," Jen says, stroking her head. "It's okay."

They wait, giving her time. Soon she calms. Sanity returns. She looks around, wondering where everyone came from, like she's been all alone.

"The dream." She clutches Kat's coat, pulling her close. "As soon as I touched it, I was in the dream, standing on the ledge...there were things out there, in the fog."

She inhales, squeaking. Eyes wide.

Mad points at Cyn, like she knows. "The memories are out there."

Jen scurries away, like she's infected. She turns over and crawls past Cyn. She gets to her feet, stumbling down the slope, spooking the horses. The horses gallop away from her mad scramble into the trees, and she collapses on the ground in a heap of sobs.

"I'll get her." Kat is on her feet, sprinting down the hill.

Cries echo through the valley.

Mad crawls away from the stone. Roc clutches her weapon, staring down the slope. She swings her hand at Cyn, shaking. "This ain't, this is just some…"

"This is what?" Cyn says. "It took her back to the dream, what do you think it is?"

"You go." She gestures at the monument. "Grab it, see what happens."

Cyn dips her head. She finally found a level of relief, the cold embracing her legs with numbing comfort. She doesn't want to move, doesn't believe this will be anything. She welcomes death.

Just lie down and go to sleep, let winter have me.

"Get up." Roc gets a handful of her coat, dragging her through the snow. "Get over there and grab it."

Cyn winces at the sudden feeling. She knocks Roc's hand away and gets to her hands and knees. She's drooling. Snow is packed inside her gloves.

She begins crawling.

Hand in front of hand.

Knee after knee.

Until she bumps into the boulder. She stares up at the dead branches; the undulating trunk ripples like muscle. Smooth like polished wood.

Kat is holding Jen.

Mad watches blankly.

Roc's knuckles are white around the weapon.

You can have me. All of me.

And Cyn reaches; her fingers crawl over the boulder, contact the trunk—

Gray.

The edge is there. Her toes hang over.

And the haze swirls in the Nowhere mist.

Beckoning.

Body ringing like a struck bell.

The girls behind her.

Watching through a tunnel.

The wind harvesters thump.

Cyn feels the coarse pillowcase on her neck. The embrace of the mattress. Smells the woodstove.

She feels pressure in her forehead.

Her eyelids crackle, tearing apart the crusted seal. The rafters are blurred. She blinks but can't focus. Her eyes aren't responding.

Something is between them.

There's waxy balm on her lips. And pressure in her arms. Arms she can't move. She licks her lips in slow motion, blinking heavily. Trying to will her hand to lift, to remove whatever is stuck between her eyes—

A face.

Her brown hair hangs down. She's leaning over Cyn, obstructing her view of the ceiling. Her lips move.

A sound comes out, slurred and long.

She looks to the side and says something. Looks back. Tries again.

Her lips move. A single word.

"Cynthia?"

She reaches for Cyn's forehead and takes hold of the object between her eyes. It slides out like a sliver, a cold metal sliver, sending a queer sensation between her ears, down her throat—

There's sound.

Objects.

She turns her head. There are people in the bunkhouse. Adults. They're all watching.

They've come.

We're saved.

The woman's hand touches Cyn's arm. There are needles in her arms, tubes running to IV bags on a stand over her head. Across the room, Kat is tucked into bed with IVs in her arm, too.

A needle protruding from her forehead.

"Can you tell me the password?" the woman asks.

Cyn has no idea what she means. She asks her the question twice. Cyn shakes her head, confused. Lost.

The woman squeezes her hand and smiles. "You made it out,

NOVEMBER

Peel an onion, layer by layer.
What's in the middle?

—

50

—

There's dull pain in her arm matched only by the sensation in her forehead. Both are persistent.

Nauseating.

She rises into consciousness against her will, harpooned by discomfort and dragged to the surface. Her eyes crack open, not really seeing anything. The lids are weighty, wanting to close, wanting to sleep.

Pain denies her, pushing them open.

The beige ceiling is low and curved. It appears to be canvas held up by hoops. It smells like new fabric. The wind breathes against the walls.

Somewhere, someone is tapping a keyboard.

Cyn's lying in a bed, a dark green blanket up to her chest. Just beyond her feet, a brown curtain is drawn for privacy. She turns her head. On the other side of the narrow room is another bed, the covers turned back, the pillow dented.

She lifts her arm, pain radiating from inside the elbow. There's a tube sticking out of her vein, the plastic port taped down. The skin around the insertion point is yellowish.

She tries to lift her head—

"Ooh."

She drops back into the pillow. Didn't expect that dull pain to bite. She takes several quick breaths, bracing to roll onto her side.

The curtain slides open.

A slender woman stands at the foot of the bed, holding the curtain. Her teeth are very straight. Cyn holds still, examining her, deciding whether to see what happens next or try to make an escape, despite the pain.

"Are you thirsty?" the woman asks.

Her throat is hot. She nods once.

The woman comes back with a water bottle, bending the plastic straw and putting it to Cyn's lips. She draws a few swallows. It puts her at ease.

"Take these if you can. They'll reduce the discomfort."

She puts two pills between her lips and follows it with water. Cyn swallows them, recalling someone giving her pills before, but not quite remembering whom.

Or why.

The woman's hair is straight, cut at the shoulders and graying. "I'm Dr. Mazyck. Call me Linda."

"Doctor?" The word scratches its way out.

"I'm a psychologist. I work for the military. Do you know where you are?"

Again, Cyn looks around. Nothing is familiar. A four-wheeler drives somewhere out there, changing gears and speeding off. A generator starts up. In the background, there's a thumping of propellers, steady and low.

I should know what that is.

"You've had a long journey." Linda gently squeezes her shoulder. "You're safe."

Cyn takes another drink. Her forehead has cooled. She touches it without considerable pain. Her back and legs ache terribly. She moves her arm.

"Do you want to sit up?"

Linda pulls off the covers, puts her arm beneath the pillow, and uses it to slowly lift her into a sitting position. Her clothes are beige and clean, like hospital scrubs. Cyn puts her feet on the ground, expecting it to hurt. When the nausea settles, she reaches halfway down her shin, her fingers walking the pant leg up to expose her feet.

Her clean, perfect feet.

"I don't understand," she half-whispers. "There was something wrong..."

"What do you remember?"

Confusion obscures a thousand thoughts. She can't pick one of them out of the mental storm, the memories swirling around and around.

"I was lost." She looks around. An empty bed across from her. "There were others."

Linda nods, her light blue eyes sympathetic, understanding. But it just doesn't seem real, just something she's imagining, not remembering.

"You have been dreaming."

Cyn touches her forehead, very tender around a circular bandage. Tubes dangle from her arm. "What's happening?" she whispers.

A door opens at the far end of the room, letting in a draft. Linda stands and walks briskly towards the man hustling inside.

"Not yet," Linda says in a semi-hushed tone. "She just woke up. It'll take a little time for her to understand what's happened."

"There's no time," the man says. "The others are still inside."

"Don't push it, Thomas."

"Now's not the time to be cautious, Linda."

"Now is *exactly* the time to be cautious!" She stops him from going around her. "Give me an hour, that's all. She needs time to adjust to reality. If you go too hard, she could lose her grip. She'll be no good then."

The man stares at Cyn, listening.

"Trust me, Thomas. I saw it happen on the island. Some of the boys were caught between two worlds and fell apart. You could destroy her."

He's thinking. Puts his hand on her shoulder. "I'll just talk."

"Let me—"

He's too quick this time. He snags the folding chair from a desk just past the curtain and plunks down in front of Cyn. No smile from him.

"I'm Agent Carlson. You hungry?"

Cyn looks at Linda.

"I wish there was more time for pleasantries, but time is very short. I'm a federal cyber-terrorism agent. What's happened in the last month is all new to us. Quite frankly, it's the stuff of science-fiction movies."

Blankness moves into her eyes. He pauses, giving her a moment to comprehend, holding up a hand when Linda takes a step.

"Cynthia," he says, touching her knee, "you're part of an identity-theft conspiracy. You were kidnapped months ago, brought out here, and inserted into a dream. We are very close to finding the people responsible, but we need your help. Tell me what you remember before waking up."

Cyn looks back and forth between the two. She tries to say something but keeps forgetting what it is.

"Thomas." Linda steps up.

He leans forward, holding Cyn's gaze. "Tell me," he whispers.

But she's stuck. She's got nothing.

Linda gives his shoulder a firm pull. He stands reluctantly, not looking away. Linda guides him with her hand on his arm, whispering as they go.

"What did you mean?" Cyn calls.

They stop halfway across the room.

"When you said I was adjusting to reality, what did you mean by that?"

Linda comes back and sits in the chair. Thomas stays back.

"You've been immersed in an alternate reality," Linda says. "We're not sure how long."

"Weeks, we think," Thomas says without moving any closer. "Maybe a month."

Cyn focuses on the sound of the distant thumping, like a slow-moving helicopter. She closes her eyes, imagining white blades churning at the end of a long post.

Three of them.

Next to a barn.

It was so cold. So white and cold.

And hungry.

There was pain and fear, a brutal fight, marks on a wall, other beds—

"Where are they?" She opens her eyes and notices that the bed behind Linda is empty. "Where are the girls?"

Linda takes her hands. They're soft and warm. She looks like she's going to say something just as soft, just as warm and supportive—

"They're still in the dream," Thomas says. "We need your help."

Linda's lips tighten, but her expression shifts to something pained, sorrowful.

"Is that true?" Cyn asks.

Linda nods.

Cyn tries to stand but feels too dizzy. Her legs, too weak.

She left them behind. She didn't mean to do that, didn't want to abandon them. Why didn't they follow her? Why didn't they do what she did?

I left them in Hell.

"We need to take this slow. Let's talk about where you are, right here and now, and get a good grip on physical reality before we start investigating the dream."

"No." Cyn grabs Linda's arm. "Take me to them. I want to see them."

"You heard her," Thomas says.

Linda sighs, searching for a reason to stop her. Cyn squeezes tighter, hoping to look strong and confident. Hoping to hide the fear and her fluttery grip on reality.

"Please," she says.

"Leave, Thomas," Linda says. "Let the young lady get dressed."

Thomas leaves as quickly as he entered. Linda remains seated for several seconds before retrieving clothes for Cyn, closing the curtain for privacy. She has to rest once she's dressed.

She's not accustomed to moving.

<hr>

Linda holds the door open.

Cyn is greeted by sunshine and warm air. The tent is set up near the woods, behind the garden that's full of blossoming vegetables and overgrown weeds. She expects to see Jen pop up from one of the rows, hauling out a bundle of green peppers or eggplants.

Beyond is the meadow, wildflowers swaying in a gentle breeze. There was snow out there before. They crossed it on horseback, the bitter cold bringing tears to her eyes and aches to her ears.

Now there's a helicopter nestled in the grass.

"Are you all right?" Linda asks.

"It was...colder." Her knees wobble. She licks her lips and swallows, her chest fluttering.

Linda carefully pauses, allowing Cyn to look around, before saying, "We believe time goes faster in the dream."

Two red ATVs are parked in front of the brick house. People are inside, passing by the windows. They look more like Thomas than Linda.

"You don't have to do this."

"Where are they?"

Linda holds her elbow lightly and lets Cyn take the first step before guiding her around the garden, toward the dinner house. The outside kitchen door is closed. Cyn watches as they pass, expecting Mad to open it and shout at Jen to fetch the eggs.

The chickens are dead.

Cyn allows Linda to steer her around the front of the dinner house. They approach the bunkhouse. Thomas is waiting by the door. White trucks are next to the barn. The horses trot around the corner, along the fence. Cyn's breath catches in her throat, waiting for Kat to call them into the barn for trimming.

The wind harvesters turn like ornaments.

Thomas opens the bunkhouse door.

Cyn slows her gait, her breath coming in short bursts. Linda allows her to go at her own pace, half steps that occasionally stutter.

She steadies herself on the doorway.

Steps inside. Her balance betrays her; she reaches back to find Linda's outstretched arm. Her heart slamming.

The beds. The rafters.

The girls.

They lie on their backs, blankets up to their chests, arms at their sides. A wire protrudes from each of their foreheads, extending to the black box on the small table where there used to be candles and matches. Metal stands are posted at the end of each bed, decorated with a clear plastic bag and tubes attached their arms.

"It's exactly the same," Cyn whispers.

Linda lifts a hand at Thomas, stopping whatever he's thinking about doing. He walks past an empty bed and stares out the window at the barn, arms crossed.

Cyn lets go of Linda and goes to her bed. The blankets are piled on the mattress. She pulls them back, revealing marks etched into the wall. She thought she scratched more than that, but then she realizes.

The dream days aren't there.

But there are scratches. She put those there before they were trapped in the dream.

The small table holds a black box like the others. A wire is coiled next to it, a needle submerged in a glass vial. Cyn holds it up to the light. The gel holds tiny bubbles around a needle that's almost two inches long.

She touches her head. Remembers the queer sensation when she awoke. When they slid the needle out.

The floor teeters. Linda is by her side.

Kat looks so peaceful, like a young girl waiting for Prince Charming. Her brown hair is only an inch long. Cyn runs her hand over her own head, her hair the same length.

"Kathryn Landon," Linda says.

Of course her name isn't Kat. Those tags were just abbreviations. Like property.

"Kathryn was born in New Mexico. Her family worked on a ranch.

Her mother died when she was young. Her father never reported her missing."

Mad is positioned in the same way as Kat, hands at her side, that disturbing wire protruding from the middle of her forehead.

"Madeline Foreman, born in Florida, lived with her grandmother. When the grandmother died, Madeline's whereabouts became unknown. And there's Jennifer. That's all we know about her. No last name. We suspect she was kidnapped in India, transported to the United States."

"She didn't have an accent."

Thomas scribbles something. A clue, perhaps.

Roc is lying on her side. Someone is massaging her legs with lotion.

"We have a nursing staff tending the bodies to prevent bedsores."

Cyn winces. *The bodies.*

"Every couple of hours, they'll get turned. Those beds are made of some special gel that helps reduce the risk, but lying for three weeks is a long time."

Roc's arms are like the others, her tattoo partially visible. She's bigger than Cyn recalls. Or maybe Cyn just feels smaller.

"Her name is Rochelle Dandoval, last known whereabouts Los Angeles. Her parents kicked her out of the house after she beat up her mother a few years ago."

The final bed is empty, the sheets tucked in and the wire coiled on the black box. Miranda woke up in the house, not the bunkhouse. She's probably still up there.

"Why'd you ask me for a password?" Cyn asks.

"Just to be sure it was you."

"But I didn't know the password."

"Exactly. But someone from someplace else would've given me one when I asked." She glances at Thomas. "The men used passwords to identify each other when they returned from the dream. We were just guessing you wouldn't know it if it was really you."

"Guessing?"

"We don't have much to go on, Cynthia."

"He said this was an experiment, what did that mean?"

"Who did?"

"The old man."

Linda and Thomas exchange looks. "There aren't any males here, Cynthia."

"He said he was from someplace *else*." She shakes her head, staring blankly at the floor. "I can't remember."

"Foreverland?"

"How'd you know?"

Thomas scribbles something in a notebook. "Did he tell you his name?"

She has to think about it. "Mr. Williams. He brought someone with him, a boy. About my age. I don't remember his name, though."

"That's all right," Linda says. "How are you feeling?"

"Why don't you just pull the needle out of their heads?"

Linda holds her arm, just above the elbow. Cyn's not sure if she looks as weak as she feels.

"Think of the body as a vehicle," Linda says. "You are not your body, Cyn. None of us are. Whoever we are—the soul, the identity, whatever you want to call it—resides in the body. Right now, the girls are there."

"If we pull the needle out," Thomas adds, "they'll end up like human vegetables. Empty bodies."

Suddenly, the girls look like machines wired to a small computer, these organic humanlike things used to power an alternate world. It's the motionlessness, the lack of expression, the lifeless repose that clearly illustrates whoever they are—whoever Jen is, Mad, and Kat, Roc—whatever or whoever they are is not the body.

They're not in there.

"Where are they?"

"You were transported somewhere else."

"Where?"

"How did you escape?" Thomas interjects.

Cyn looks at him, searching for an answer. Finding none. "Where did they go?" she repeats.

"If we know how you escaped," he says, "maybe we can help them."

Cyn yanks her arm away from Linda. "Tell me where they went."

Linda gives her space and doesn't try to force comfort on her. She pauses, considering whether Cyn really wants to know the answer. But she already does. She knows where they went.

The image of an old woman suddenly forms. "Patricia," Cyn says.

Linda nods.

Cyn wishes Linda was holding onto her, keeping her from falling. Or maybe she just wants someone touching her, to let her know this isn't a dream anymore. This time it's real.

Because she's just not sure.

51

The next morning is brisk.

Cyn sits on the front porch of the dinner house, watching the morning sun streak over the meadow. Dew glitters on the helicopter, the blades sagging.

She dreamed that night. She dreamed a normal dream, one with random images and illogical scenarios, the way dreams are supposed to be. No fog, no gray.

No cliff to perch upon.

It seems so obvious now.

This is real. This physical world feels different, feels real. The colors more vibrant, the air more fragrant. The sensations deeper. The experience denser.

Is that what defines reality? Is the human experience in the physical world the gold standard for truth? Do our five senses separate illusion from enlightenment?

She shivers, not from the cold but the questions.

She can't ask them, not now. Not yet. She has to be here, has to be present. Those thoughts make her doubt.

Maybe this is a dream, too.

Linda steps onto the porch, a thick beige coat to her knees, carrying two steaming mugs. She hands one to Cyn.

"I'm sorry, tea is all I have. Would you rather have coffee?"

Cyn shakes her head.

Linda takes the chair on the other side of the door, cupping the mug with both hands. She inhales.

"Beautiful morning," Linda says.

Birds are chirping. Cyn doesn't remember hearing birds inside the dream. Maybe they were there in the beginning. Not at the end. Not when it was so cold.

"Oh, I almost forgot." Linda pulls an apple from her pocket. "If you're hungry. You haven't eaten much solid food, so it may take some time to adjust."

Cyn examines the apple. So red and firm. Shiny. She rubs the skin with her thumb and takes a bite.

The taste is explosive.

"We had fruit when we woke up."

Linda sips and listens. Cyn studies the apple after each bite, like each one is a new experience.

"I thought someone would come for us."

"We did," Linda says.

Another bite. Another look. "Not like I thought."

"Did you do that assignment?"

Cyn pretends like she doesn't hear, but Linda doesn't look away. Finally, she reaches in her pocket and hands her a folded piece of paper. Linda flips it over.

What do I remember? Nothing.

"You have lovely handwriting." Linda hands it back.

Cyn wads it up.

It's that question again. Over and over, they ask it. She's not pissed at Linda; it's just that the answer doesn't come to her—it only muddles her brain. Frustrates her. Like she doesn't want to remember.

And she does.

Suddenly, she's full. She puts the apple core on the porch railing and leans against it with the sudden urge to vomit.

She can't remember specific things. She just knows what they feel like. Heavy and thick and wet. Whatever memories she has, she doesn't remember them, but they weigh her down.

"No one cares," she says.

"I care."

Cyn spits. "No offense, but that's your job. You don't know me."

"I don't have to know you to care."

There's thumping in the distance, like wind harvesters coming down from the sky. A black dot approaches from the east, the chopper blades echoing off the trees.

"This might be a dream. Ever thought of that?"

"This is not a dream, Cynthia. You woke up, you're here and now. Trust me."

"Why should I trust anything?"

"You can trust me."

"Saying it don't make it true."

The mug hovers beneath Linda's chin. "No. It doesn't."

Cyn feels the helicopter in her chest, the percussion banging inside her, stirring up anxiety. She wants to run, but where would she go?

It hovers in the meadow, slowly dropping the landing skids into the grass, thrashing the wildflowers in the downdraft. A few people jog out to meet it, one of them Thomas. They help a man and woman out of the back door and shake hands, shouting to be heard. They half-duck until they're clear of the blades.

"More experts?" Cyn asks.

"There's a lot of evidence. This camp was abandoned when we arrived. The people who brought you out here had escaped, leaving you and the others behind. We need to know what's going on, how it works. Are there other places like this?"

A truck goes out to the helicopter; supplies are loaded into the back. Once that's finished, the pilot salutes and, when it's all clear, lifts off. Cyn feels the downdraft this time.

The new guests stand in front of the brick house. Two people come out to meet them. There's a meeting on the front step. Thomas gestures toward the dinner house and they all turn.

Pretty soon, he's walking toward them.

"How did you escape?" Linda asks. "They're going to want to know."

Thomas doesn't wave them over. He's going to make the trip all the way to the porch.

"You don't have to go, Cynthia. If you're not ready, you don't have to see everything, not yet. You can rest, get yourself grounded. I'd prefer you remember more so that you know who you are."

The helicopter is far above the trees.

The girls still have needles in their heads. Still in the dream. Cyn's not going to sit on the front porch sipping tea while they starve.

"Remembering doesn't make me who I am," Cyn says distantly. "My soul ain't memories."

Linda sips. They watch Thomas approach.

"Some people want to talk to you." He puts his hands on his hips.

Cyn steps off the porch. He leads the way.

Linda puts her mug down and follows.

—
52
—

Cyn stops at the tall grass.

There's a faint line, a subtle difference in how the grass grows, that crosses in front of the house, circling around it. Not one these people would notice.

Cyn stands at the line, the end of her boots almost touching.

"You okay?" Linda is almost to the steps.

She rubs her neck, wondering. When she woke up, she was the first one to hit the fence, like a cattle prod to the back of the head.

"Cynthia?" Linda's next to her. "We don't have to go inside."

She shakes her head. Takes a breath. "There's this thing in our neck."

"We know. They used it to track your location. It shouldn't be hard to remove, once you're back."

"It did other things."

Linda gives her space to sort through the thoughts.

"There were places we couldn't go or it would go off."

"How?"

"Like a jolt to the nervous system. If we crossed that line"—she points at the soft line, following it around the corner—"we were knocked unconscious. We called it a fence."

Linda's nodding. "I'm sorry, Cynthia. The boys from the island had something similar, but it wasn't activated by a fence. Are there other fences in the dream?"

She shakes her head, remembering something else that ignited the lump. Something the old man had, like a remote control. "I'm not sure. I don't remember."

She doesn't remember other fences. It seems like there was another place around there that initiated the lump and knocked her out. She's sure there is. And she doesn't want to go back there.

"Do you want to go back to the tent?"

"No. I don't think this is on." She rubs her neck again. There's no tingling, no sensitivity. "There was always a warning when we got near one, I'm not feeling it."

Still, she has trouble breaking the hold on her knees. She puts a hand on Linda's shoulder. She doesn't mean to close her eyes—it's more like a long blink during that first step.

And then she's on the other side.

"Nothing?" Linda asks.

Cyn shakes her head. *Nothing.*

Dead things are inside.

Cyn stands at the front door, impulsively sniffing the foul air. The hairs on her arms bristle. "Where is it?"

"In the very back," Linda says.

"Old woman?"

"Yes. The body was removed weeks ago. The smell probably won't ever go away."

They look around the front room. The couches are spotless; the tables clean. The front window is intact. The stone that Roc threw was in another dimension.

In the dream, she reminds herself.

"We're still trying to determine how they built this?" Linda says. "It's a gorgeous house."

Cyn cringes. *Gorgeous.*

She can see the paltry shelter through the window. She feels left out, ignored. Banished.

"It's built like a fortress," Linda adds. "Retractable shutters, security cameras. Quite an architectural feat."

"What were they doing in here?"

"Well, it's mostly living quarters. The upstairs is all bedrooms and a bathroom. There are a few bedrooms on the first floor, a kitchen down the hall."

There are voices in the back of the house.

They stop at the first bedroom on the left. Cyn is filled with the odd sense of comfort, peeking into someone else's bedroom without their permission. She's not supposed to be in here, but no one can stop her.

The bed is large enough for three people. Probably only slept one. Plastic containers are stacked on the bedspread. The desk drawers are open and empty. So are the dresser drawers. The closet still has a few items.

Cyn walks past the desk. The perfume smells expensive.

"Her name was Barbara Graham." Linda's voice sounds more distant than it should. "She mostly lived in the San Francisco area but had houses all over the world. She was married to a man named Michael Graham."

Cyn is careful not to touch anything, afraid she'll never want to leave if she does. There's a set of crystal figurines gathered on the dresser. She leans in closely. The Buddha looks like it's made of ice.

"Michael went by another name," Linda says. "Mr. Williams."

Cyn looks back. Linda is still in the hall.

"The men from Foreverland used aliases. It was on a tropical island, and when it failed, we discovered this one."

"He said he was lost, that Foreverland collapsed."

"He was still plugged when it did. He's dead."

Cyn's chest contracts sharply. "No, he's not."

"Cynthia, we're still not sure what's going on. We were surprised when you mentioned him yesterday. What we do know is that his body is dead. And so is the body of a boy who was in the bed next to him."

"Sid."

"Yes." Linda's not shocked to hear the name. "Maybe their identities were in Foreverland when it failed and they couldn't get back to their bodies. We assumed that since the body was dead, so were they. But obviously there's more to this than we know. Somehow there was a connection between Foreverland and the world you were trapped inside."

They were lost in the gray for a long time. How long? There's no sense of time in the gray. Just eternity.

And suffering.

Files are stacked in one of the open containers on the bed. A leather spine sticks out among the manila folders. Cyn doesn't ask, just digs it out. Miranda gave that leather-bound journal to her in the dream.

But she remembers what she told her. She warned her that one of the girls is dangerous and to be careful. Miranda was sure it was Roc.

The Fountain of Youth... This is Hell.

Cyn almost laughs. Even surrounded by this posh palace, she has the nerve to comment on suffering. This book will burn nicely in one of the woodstoves.

"How did she do it?" Cyn asks. "How did Patricia recreate a world exactly like this?"

Linda shakes her head. "We don't know. Her brain activity is nothing like we've ever seen. Maybe she's triggered something in the human mind that can just absorb the details around her."

"Miranda gave this to me." Cyn shakes the book.

"Who?"

"The girl with blonde hair—she's upstairs, I'm guessing."

Linda nods slowly. "And she gave you that book?"

"One exactly like it. I never read it, though."

"Why?"

She had lost it, but where?

Cyn thinks, overcome with foggy blankness. That's where those memories are: lost in some inaccessible part of her mind where it's rainy and cloudy.

Gray.

Photos slip out from between the pages. Oceans and boats,

beaches and homes. Old people smiling at the camera, having the time of their life. The photos are glossy, developed from film long ago. One of the photos is older than the others. The woman is younger, her hair not so gray.

Blonde.

"She brought me here."

Linda doesn't answer.

"Do you know where she is?"

"There are some leads."

Cyn traces the outline of Barbara Graham's face, wondering if she ever spoke with her. Of course she did. Her face is so familiar; they probably became friends, probably rode horses and hiked trails. She likes to think that she and Barbara ate dinner together.

She thinks she'd like to meet her again one of these days. And she hates herself for having that thought. But she can't stop. She drops the book and photos in the box, all except the one that shows her blonde hair. That one ends up in her back pocket. If she ever sees her, she's not sure if she'll hug her or knock her out.

Or both.

If she ever sees Mr. Williams, she knows exactly what she'll do. Tell him that he's dead.

Laughter in the back of the house.

They walk past the kitchen, the cabinets open and empty. Boxes on the counter. Everything bagged and tagged for analysis, as if the old women were hiding in coffee cans.

Linda passes Cyn and looks into the back room. "Gentlemen."

The laughter fades off.

There's muttering.

Linda glances back down the hall. The foul odor is stronger, mixed with the fumes of a scented candle. Cinnamon. It doesn't do much to mask death. She breathes through her mouth, but then she can taste it.

Cyn steps inside slowly. *The body is gone.* She wonders if it was back here, sitting in a chair, dead from a heart attack or a guilty conscience. There's another door in the back wall, this one closed.

Monitors wrap around the right side of the room, the largest in the corner. Two men sit in chairs, keyboards on the counter. Thomas is next to them.

Thomas slaps their seats. "Give us five minutes."

The techs tap a few keys, shutting down their work before leaving without looking at Cyn.

"What is this?"

"Headquarters," Thomas says. "These computers monitor the entire camp. It's a lot smaller than the island; that's why the old women only managed half a dozen girls at a time. Still, it may have cost a billion dollars to set it up and maintain its secrecy. Cameras are everywhere, constantly recording and backing up."

Thomas taps on the keyboard. The monitors begin cycling through views. She sees the tents on one monitor, the inside of the bunkhouse on another. She remembers the floodlights but never thought there were cameras. That means Miranda could see them. Before that, the old women had watched them.

They knew everything.

He points at the batteries and generators on the other side of the room.

"That's why there are so many power generators. If you think about it, one wind harvester would be enough for normal living. Their demand was much more than that."

"Patricia," Cyn mutters. Something tugs at her stomach.

Thomas looks at the big monitor. An old woman lies in a very small room with electrodes taped to her head, face, and chest; wires are bundled and connected to machines in the corner, where there's barely enough room to stand.

He looks at Linda, then Cyn. "Yes," he says slowly. "How do you know that?"

"Mr. Williams said she was in that cabin in the woods. We couldn't get inside, though."

And I took her IVs. And now they're gone.

"He said she was the dreamer," she says. "Are the girls inside her? Is that what he meant?"

"We don't really know," Thomas says. "Her brain activity is remarkable. Based on what we've learned about Foreverland and what you said, we're assuming that she's operating like a host computer—an organic server, so to speak. I don't know if you know what that means—"

"I know what that means."

Her emotions boil up. She's tired of this victim crap. She isn't a stupid kid.

"Instead of watching a movie, I was in it. She created a world in her mind and the old ladies sent me there."

"That's right."

"So that's where the girls are right now."

He's nodding. "We believe so, yes."

"Why?"

Thomas balks. Linda's hand is on her shoulder again. "Cynthia," she says in her softest, most supportive therapist voice, "we think they sent you there so you wouldn't come back."

"Come back where?"

Cyn knows, but she asks anyway. She doesn't hear Linda answer. Doesn't need to. The old women bring the destitute, the hopeless, the dregs of society out here to the middle of nowhere. Old women spend millions to sponsor a perfect young woman with a twisted mind in a healthy body.

They don't heal the mind. But they don't waste the body.

Old women unwilling to die.

Yeah, she gets it.

She knows why Barbara Graham brought her out here. And she hates herself even more for hoping that Barbara was nice, that maybe she was trying to help her.

That maybe she was good.

Not a murderer.

"Where is she?" Cyn asks. "Where's Patricia?"

$$—$$

53

$$—$$

The white truck is next to the helicopter. The men are loading boxes onto it this time, presumably full of evidence for analysis in a real lab.

The techs watch Cyn come out of the brick house. One of them smokes a cigarette. They stare. She looks right back at them, jonesing for a drag.

Do I smoke?

They call Thomas over. Maybe they're talking business. Maybe not. They watch Cyn and Linda walk toward the tents while chatting.

The wind harvesters are still turning, the solar panels following the sun as it peaks. All that energy going to the brick house, powering all that equipment, all those toys. Only a slice of it goes to the cabins, enough so that the girls don't die. They already had a miserable life, just more of the same out here.

That's the point. They made it miserable to be here, which made Foreverland even more inviting. Once the girls got a taste, they wouldn't want to leave.

Desire. Best drug there is.

Important people are in front of the tent on the far right, nearest the brick house. They watch Cyn and Linda approach. Popular for all the wrong reasons.

"Dr. Mazyck." A young lady wearing camouflage approaches. "Mr. Erickson would like to speak with you."

"Certainly."

They follow her to the third tent on the left, the one closest to the dinner house. Camouflage Lady opens the door.

"Wait here, Cynthia," Linda says. "I'll be right out. If you're hungry, you can go to the mess tent. There's a cooler in our tent, too. Help yourself."

Cyn's not hungry. Even if she was, she's not walking closer to the important people still outside the tent. Enough with the staring and wondering.

Cyn hears a deep voice from inside the tent. "How's she doing?"

A generator starts up, eating up the conversation before Linda responds. The important people point at the brick house. Thomas comes around the corner of the garden, shaking hands. They talk a bit, a few heads turning toward Cyn.

Dammit.

It feels like a bear is standing on her chest, a spotlight sizzling on her skin. She steps around the corner of the tent. The generator is too loud to hear anything inside. She's not sure she wants to hear it, anyway.

They're discussing what they're going to do with her—that's what they're doing. *How's she doing? What is she saying? What does she know? Does she remember? Does she remember?*

DOES SHE REMEMBER?

They should be talking about the girls. Not Cyn.

An ATV coasts out of the wood and parks behind the bunkhouse. The rider turns the key off and goes through the back door with an armful of IV bags. *Time for lunch, girls.*

The voices inside the tent rise above the hum of the generator.

"We can't keep her here," he says.

"You can't send her back," Linda says. "Not yet."

The voice fades into the background noise; perhaps they have realized that the walls are only fabric. They want to send her back...where?

Home?

The guys are finished loading the helicopter, sitting on the tailgate and talking to the pilot. It's too far away to know if they're looking at her, but she doesn't wait around.

The path to the little cabin is right around the corner.

She knows the way.

———

The trees soften the noise from the generators and all-terrain vehicles. Dried sticks break beneath her boots. Up ahead is the turn where the body had lain. Much of the undergrowth around that spot is trampled or uprooted.

The body was here, too.

They probably already know her name, where she came from. What she was doing. At least she's dead. *Good.*

A green tent extends over the front of the cabin, the flaps tied open. There are tables of equipment and computers with bundled cables running through the open door like black snakes. A skinny tech slouches on a folding chair, tapping on a keyboard.

A generator is grinding away behind the cabin, loud enough to mask her footsteps. He doesn't see her until she's in front of the tent.

"Whoa." He pops up, the chair falling over. "You're not allowed back here, not without permission."

He holds up his phone like somehow that's proof no one called to give her permission.

Cyn doesn't pay attention. She sees through the open door. She sees the body lying on an elevated platform. The hands are curled over the chest like dried claws. There's mild pressure building inside her head, the odd sensation that comes with bizarre and unlikely events. The impossible.

If what they say is true, there's a god in there. She contains a universe.

And the world slowly begins to turn. And tilt.

"Hey. You hear me?"

A shadow passes between her and the god.

A hand snatches her arm—

She pivots, raising her arm and twisting, kicking the back of his legs, using leverage to drop him. A fist glances off the side of her head, but she's on top of him. He bucks, but she hooks her heels behind his legs, limiting his range—

Footsteps.

Someone wrenches her arm behind her back. She loses her grip and the tech throws her off, scampering through leafy debris. A knee punches her between the shoulder blades, grinding her cheek into the earth.

"Stop!" Linda comes around the corner. "Get off her! Now!"

The man twists her other arm. Doesn't budge.

"She's all right, Henry." Linda kneels down next to them. "I promise, she won't do anything. Will you, Cynthia?"

She tries to nod, but her head is pressed into the ground.

"I'll take responsibility. Please, just let her up."

The knee eases a bit, testing her. Cyn holds her position and doesn't fight even though the strain on her shoulder aches. All at once Henry jumps back.

Linda helps her sit up. Cyn rubs her wrist, swinging her arm to relieve the pain. Linda rubs the mud off her cheek. "Are you okay?" she whispers.

Cyn nods.

"She didn't have to do that," the skinny tech says, rubbing the back of his head. "She's not supposed to be back here, and she wouldn't answer me. All I did was touch her and she went off."

"I understand, Jeff," Linda says. "We just came back to look at Patricia and she got ahead of me. It won't happen again. Will it?"

They wait for Cyn to respond.

She shakes her head.

Henry crosses his arms. Jeff continues rubbing his head where it was planted in the dirt. They're not moving. Linda places a call. A few seconds later, Jeff's phone buzzes. He answers the call from someone with more power than Linda.

The men stalk off.

Jeff explains how the hell a girl beat his ass.

The room smells like antiseptic.

Cyn stands on the threshold, listening to the hum of machines and the grind of the generator. There's enough room to slip between the wall and the platform.

Her wrinkled skin is like tissue paper wrapped around bones. It's hard to guess her age. A wire protrudes from her forehead, the needle completely embedded. A clear tube runs beneath her nose, her chest slowly rising and falling. Nothing else moves, not even the eyes beneath the lids.

So frail, so brittle and small. A dried-up body on the outside. A universe inside.

Are the girls still cold? Hungry?

Cyn abandoned them, left them to suffer alone. "She was in a vegetative state when her husband experimented on her decades ago. It's controversial technology, one that creates an alternate reality by directly connecting the brain to a computer, transporting the person's identity into a program. The technique is illegal."

"Why?"

Linda considers how much to say. "Too many side effects."

"Like what?"

Another pause. "Reality confusion, for one."

Sure. Which one is the dream?

"Patricia spent many years in a psychiatric ward before her son, Harold Ballard, took her. There are no records of where they went, but Harold is the one that created Foreverland. We can only guess that he used her to develop another alternate universe."

Linda strokes the blanket over the old woman's leg.

"She suffered from a split personality before her husband's experiment. He claims that he was attempting to heal her mind, to place her in a supportive alternate reality before waking her back up. Unfortunately, it locked her inside of her mind."

"You think she's a victim?"

"I don't know. Maybe she doesn't know what's happening; she's just trying to survive, trying to make sense out of her reality like the rest of us. Imagine being the only person in the universe."

Cyn feels like that now. She bends over the old woman's face. It smells like mold.

"We hope to begin interpreting what's inside her, to see her world, like pointing a camera inside her mind. If we can do that, we can communicate with her and the girls. Guide them out."

The wire is right in front of her. It would only take a second to rip it out, to end the girls' suffering. Would the universe turn off? She can't do that. As much as she wants the suffering to stop, she can't take the chance that she'll make it worse.

"How did you get out, Cynthia?" Linda says, sensing her thoughts.

Cyn shakes her head. What good would it do if she knew? They can't tell the girls. All they can do is wait.

And waiting helps nothing.

54

The generators cycle on and off all night. Cyn hardly notices them anymore. Like the rooster.

But there's no rooster here. No horses.

Just lots of people. Lots of food.

And guilt.

Linda's gone. Probably an early morning meeting. When she's not prodding Cyn to remember, she's talking to the important people. She hasn't said anything about home; maybe they were talking about sending her somewhere else. Like a lab for experimenting. For some reason, this place feels like home, not somewhere else. That should alarm her.

There's a chill this morning, enough to make her hurry getting dressed. She digs a yogurt out of the cooler and peels the foil off the top while stepping outside. Her breath is foggy.

The two helicopters are still in the field. The ATVs are lined up at the dinner house. She sees people sitting at the table through the windows, more of a meeting than a meal. Cyn dishes out the peach-infused yogurt and goes around the back. The back door to the bunkhouse is unlocked.

The inside smells clean.

The nurse isn't there. The door clicks behind her. Nothing moves. Clear bags hang on metal stands, empty tubes running inside skin. She rubs her arm where the stent was removed—still sore.

She's smothered by the silence. *Four bodies, but nobody here.*

The front door opens. A young man sets a box on the floor, washing his hands at the dispenser set up on a small table. He's smaller than Cyn by a few inches, maybe a few pounds, too. He pulls the blanket off of Kat's body, bunching it at her feet, and turns her onto her side, careful not to disturb the tubes and wires.

And needle.

He does the same to Jen and Mad.

"Oh good gracious!" He jumps back. "Have you been standing there the whole time, young lady?"

Cyn doesn't answer.

"Scared the hell out of me." He strips the blanket off of Roc. "Grab her feet."

He doesn't ask if she wants to help, just tells her. And that's enough to get her going. She approaches the foot of the bed, nervous to be that close to her. For some reason, touching her makes it real.

Feels like meat.

"Go wash your hands," he says. "I could use some help setting up bags and rubbing them down. Jackie is still taking care of Sandy and we're a little behind."

Sandy?

Cyn goes to the dispenser and rubs the sanitizing gel on her hands while he opens the box, pulling out five bags. Each contains separate packets that need to be mixed. He sets those aside.

Cyn hangs them on the stands. He connects them.

He shows her how to rub their legs, focusing on the pressure points where bedsores are likely to fester, including the buttocks. The beds, he says, are specifically designed to relieve pressure, but can't prevent sores indefinitely.

"If we weren't doing this, it'd get real smelly in here."

He lets her massage Mad's heels. Cyn rubs the lotion in a circular motion, her eyes following the wire from the girl's forehead to the black box on the table. Cyn's bed is on the other side, the needle still stuck in the tube.

When they're finished, he hands the extra IV bag to Cyn.

"I thought Jackie would be over here by now. Take this over there while I finish up."

"Where?"

"The big house, second floor. I assume she's taking care of Sandy still. I hope she is. The poor girl needs the IV changed."

"Who's Sandy?"

"The little Sleeping Beauty."

"You mean Miranda?"

"No." He flicks the IV bag hanging on Mad's hook. "I mean Sandy. She was in the brick house when we got here, second floor. Maybe she was in that empty bed before that, I don't know."

He points at Miranda's bed.

"All I know is that she's upstairs. Trust me, it'd be a lot easier if she was over here, but there's no way to move her. So if you'd be a dear and take that up to Jackie, I can get this finished."

Cyn stands there, holding the bag.

Miranda could be her middle name. She's just a kid; it wasn't her fault she woke up in the brick house.

But she did.

"You all right?" he asks.

Cyn's breathing loudly, exhaling through her nostrils like a bull pawing the dirt.

She can hear the techs talking in the back room, the keys tapping. The office chair popping. No one stops her from going upstairs.

All the doors are open. Boxes and folders are stacked, the beds stripped, the dressers empty. All except one.

She lies on top of the king-sized bed, hands folded over her stomach. Her blonde hair is splayed on the pillow, eyes closed. She's wearing loose-fitting clothing, rather plain. Probably not what they found her wearing when they discovered this place.

The IV bag is empty.

Cyn walks to the side of the bed. This piece of meat smells better than the others. Looks better.

She was so frail and timid when she woke up, curling up in the corner like a mouse. But she was the one who pulled her out of the fence that first morning. She was the one who sent out winter gear and warned her about Roc. Cyn wanted to protect her.

But then she went inside and never came out.

And neither did the food.

Not a mouse. A rat.

She was so different from the rest of them. It wasn't just her hair or the clothes; it was the way she spoke, the words she used. Once she was safely inside the fence, it was the way she looked at them. The way she wrinkled her nose when she was near, the way she turned her head. Kept her back straight; walked like what came out of her didn't stink.

And the thing in her neck didn't work.

"Miranda Myers is a seventy-seven-year-old woman." Linda is at the door. "She was diagnosed with cancer and was given about six months to live before she relocated out here. When we arrived, we found her body in the back room—the one behind the computer room. Sandy Bell's body was up here. At first, we couldn't understand why she wasn't in the bunkhouse."

Miranda's slender hand is limp. Cyn takes it, a lump rising in her throat. The heavy bracelet slides up her bony arm. *Miranda* is engraved on the gold plate. Before it looked like expensive jewelry. More of a dog collar now.

Cyn massages her hand, kneading the palm with her thumbs.

"We think Miranda was crossing into Sandy's body when Foreverland collapsed."

Sandy.

Is she as scared and meek as she looks right now? Or maybe she was scrappy, mean, and nasty like the rest of them. *I'll never know.*

"Did she introduce herself as Miranda?" Linda digs softly with the therapist voice.

Cyn brushes the blonde hair from the young face while rage and sadness tangle inside. She resists the urge to yank the hair from her pretty little head.

It's just a body. Sandy's body.

"She came out of the brick house when we woke up, like this innocent, scared little girl that didn't belong out here. Didn't belong with us."

"Do you belong here?"

"That's not what I mean. She didn't know anything about this. She was afraid of Roc. She was cold and hungry, like the rest of us. She went inside the brick house and sent out clothes for us to wear."

Linda takes the other hand, massaging it like Cyn.

"Her name is Miranda," Cyn says. "That's all I know."

"Where do you think Sandy went?"

Cyn shakes her head. "How am I supposed to know?"

"Right now, we think Sandy—her identity or soul, whatever you want to call that true nature—was pulled out of the body and replaced with Miranda's identity. It's a body swap, but we don't know where the girls go once they're pulled out of their bodies."

Where do you go when you don't need a body?

That's the question everyone wants answered. Just because you have an answer, though, doesn't mean it's right. Maybe Miranda knows. Maybe she knows where she sent Sandy once she pushed her out of her body for good.

Yeah, Miranda knows.

The sleeping girl's lips begin to quiver.

Linda doesn't notice; she doesn't see the wisp of smoke leak from the corner of Miranda's mouth. She doesn't feel the frigid grasp of misty fingers ooze from the young girl's lips, doesn't see the vapor slither up Cyn's arms, creeping around her neck. Doesn't see it seep into Cyn's vision.

Paralyzing her.

Dragging her into the eternal gray where her soul dissolves. Where she becomes thinner. Transparent. Yet she still feels the gut-dropping fall, the endless collapse of her identity.

The falling.

Always falling—forever and ever—in the Nowhere.

"Cyn?"

Cyn jerks away from the hand on her arm, her chest pumping air that's thick and stale. Linda takes both of Cyn's hands, cradling them gently.

Miranda is motionless. Lips sealed.

"We all had the same dream." Cyn's mouth is dry. "Every night."

Linda patiently squeezes, staying present. Giving her space to work through what's coming to light.

Cyn tries to swallow and says, "We would walk up to a cliff and look down. But there wasn't a bottom. There was just...it was just fog."

She hesitates, thoughts freezing.

"What's in the fog?"

Tendons spring from her wrists. Fingers clenching. Memories push through a thick veil. She remembers what's out there, remembers stepping through the fence at the edge of the trees, falling into the gray dream where memories pounced on her like demons.

Her stepfather is out there. Dope. Violence.

Desperation. Loneliness.

"Fear," Cyn says.

Linda squeezes, reassuring her. Cyn doesn't really see her, just feels her. But there's something else out there, too. They are out there. The girls that were shoved from their bodies. The boys from Foreverland, too.

And Sandy.

Everyone that was pushed from their body was thrown into the Nowhere like fistfuls of ash, where they would eternally dissolve. Forever fall.

She remembers that. She remembers the falling.

Arms out. Tipping into the abyss.

Merging with the gray. Embracing the fear.

And falling out of the dream.

Cyn clenches Linda like a ledge. Feet dangling. Linda allows her to squeeze as if her life depends on it. Cyn looks away from the bed, breaking the trance. Indentions remain on Linda's arm.

They remain next to the bed, holding hands. Cyn's breathing

returns to normal. The fear recedes. Nothing escapes Sandy's lips; her eyes remain motionless. *This is not the dream.*

Jackie arrives to connect an IV. They help her turn the body, rubbing her sore spots with lotion. Even though she doesn't know Sandy, Cyn cares for her body. She deserves that much.

They leave the brick house and stand on the porch. The weather is warming. Cyn doesn't tell Linda what she remembers.

I know how I escaped.

$$—$$

55

$$—$$

The sun is up.

Linda quietly walks through the tent and pulls the curtain aside. She watches Cyn's chest gently rise and fall then grabs a few things off her desk. The door closes.

Cyn opens her eyes.

That's the second time Linda has checked on her. And the second time Cyn was pretending to sleep. Linda knows she isn't sleeping well at night and tells her to sleep in as late as she wants. The morning will get along just fine without her.

At night, the bed feels like a cell.

Cyn wishes for the nights of falling into dead sleep, even misses the gray dreams, standing on the ledge. Better than the dreams she's having now, waking in the night like a pillow has been pushed over her face.

Linda woke her up sometime in the night and said she was making noise. Cyn doesn't remember the dream, only remembers drowning in a sea of emotions. Her pillow was damp.

She had waited there, listening to Linda fall asleep before sneaking through the tent and gently closing the door. The wind harvesters were still.

The moon full.

A couple of guys were on the front porch of the dinner house, a cigarette cherry streaking from lap to mouth. Their chatter easily carried across the garden. She went back inside, where sleep came in bite-sized pieces.

Now she dozes in and out to the lullabies of trucks and generators, wondering how far she can go in an ATV with a full tank of gas. There's a bag of clothes under her bed that Linda doesn't know about. Cyn has an urge to escape, to get away from people before they discover her secret. She keeps her memories tightly sealed, away from Linda's prying questions. There are more secrets inside her, and she'd be fine if they stayed hidden from her. She's had enough of the truth; she just wants some peace. If they're thinking of sending her home, then she'll have to steal a fully loaded ATV.

Home.

That word is supposed to feel warm and fuzzy. To Cyn, it feels like drowning. She doesn't have many memories of home. There are giant puddles of ink on the fabric of her mind, blotting memories out of existence, keeping much of what's inside her hidden. Maybe those ink spots were there before the old women punched her with the needle.

Doesn't matter. She's not going home. She's not going anywhere before she fixes things.

Cyn sits up slowly. She looks around the curtain just to make sure the tent's empty. There's a mirror under Linda's bed; she saw her fussing with it the other day. She finds it in a plastic bag. It fits in the palm of her hand.

Her forehead looks normal except for the tiny black hole. It's still sore, but at least it's not red and swollen. She can't move her head too quickly or it throbs. She frames the hole with two fingers, tender to the touch. The stent is a tiny knot embedded in her skull.

A going-away gift.

Her green eyes are sunk inside the sockets. She pulls at her blonde hair, barely finger length. She touches her reflection.

Was the dream just another layer of reality in the mirror that I've peeled away? Is this just another dream inside a dream? Is there another layer of reality below this? Will I wake up and realize that this, right here, right now, is a dream, too?

How many layers are there?

"It'll go away."

Cyn drops the mirror. Linda is holding the curtain back.

"Feeling rested?"

Cyn doesn't answer and wants to hide the mirror under her foot. Feels stupid for getting caught gazing at her reflection. It's not why she was looking in the mirror.

"I'll let you get dressed."

Cyn's sitting there in panties and a tank top, no bra.

"You hungry?" Linda calls from the other side while rummaging through stuff. "I saved you breakfast in the mess tent. If you're not feeling up to it, there's a can of Ensure in the cooler. Make sure you drink that. The doctor wants to see you this morning. If you're not eating, they're going to put an IV in your—*crap!*"

She drops something. A number of things get stacked. A drawer shuts. Linda mutters to herself.

"I've got a meeting in a few minutes, but I want us to go for a little hike across the meadow today, get a little fresh air. What do you say?"

The curtain pulls back.

Cyn hasn't moved. Still half-naked. "Hike sounds good."

"You all right?" Linda sits on her bed across from her. "You want to talk?"

"No. Just waking up."

She puts up her best smile. The smile sucks, but it's good by her standards. Linda hesitates, but she buys it. She knows things aren't easy. Cyn's tough. Right now she's just hanging in there.

Linda has no idea what Cyn's thinking.

"Breakfast, then?" Linda asks.

"I'll get it."

Linda pauses, looking inside her. She can't see the thoughts, but she's satisfied enough to stand. She reaches for the curtain.

"How much time do you think has passed in there?" Cyn asks. "It's been a week since I got out—how long do you think it's been inside the dream? A month?"

"We don't know. Why?"

"Just wondering." She stares into space.

Again, Linda tries to look inside her. She waits to hear more. She's not leaving until Cyn spills a thought or two.

"They could be dead," Cyn says.

"We don't know that."

"I left them."

"It's not your fault."

Cyn shakes her head. She's thinking. There are thoughts she wants to spit out. But if she does, Linda will know what she's thinking. She can't have that. She bites down, swallowing the words.

"Hey." Linda sits on the bed. "You sure you're all right?"

Cyn focuses on her, faking another smile. "Just a dream I had last night, that's all."

"The gray?"

"No. It's nothing. I'll get dressed, grab some breakfast."

Linda doesn't want to leave. If she didn't have a meeting, she wouldn't let her out of her sight. She'll probably call someone as soon as she leaves, have Thomas or someone keep an eye on the tent. Watch where Cyn goes.

That's why Cyn dresses quickly.

———

The nurse is sitting in the back of the bunkhouse, poking at the tablet in his lap. He looks up, smiling.

"You're a little late to help, darling." He goes back to his tablet and says, "Stick around, the girls need to be turned in half an hour."

Cyn stands quite still, looking at the walls, the rafters and beds, taking a mental snapshot of what it looks like, how it smells and feels. Memorizing this layer of reality.

She walks around, stopping at each bed. The bodies still uninhabited. Kat, Jen, Roc, and Mad. All of them still somewhere else. Miranda's bed still empty.

Sandy, she reminds herself.

Cyn's bed is still empty. The sheets tucked under the mattress, the wire coiled on the small table. She slows her breathing, swallows, and walks to the bed.

Walk. Don't run.

She sits on the edge, sinking into the gel-infused mattress. It molds to her bottom. There's an indention in the pillow, waiting to cradle her head. She reaches slowly and picks up the glass vial.

The surgical steel needle, suspended in the clear gel, gleams.

"Honey, don't touch that," he says. "That needs to stay sterile."

Her fingers shake. She pinches the wire at the base of the needle. Her pulse flutters in her fingertips.

"Sweetheart." The nurse stands. "You need to put that down."

It slides from the rubber stopper. The tip is blunt. She brackets the stent with two fingers—

"Don't." Linda's at the door, hand raised. "Please."

Cyn opens her eyes. The needle lowers.

No one moves.

"I can get them," she whispers.

"I can't let you."

"You know what they're going through? If they're alive, they're cold and hungry. And I can get them out."

"There's time, Cynthia. We'll figure out how to communicate. They'll learn how to escape, just like you."

"You've been real good to me."

"Don't do this."

Cyn grimly nods. Their eyes engage. Linda only makes it half a step, hand reaching—

An icicle slides between Cyn's eyes.

Her head goes numb.

DECEMBER

Meet me at the edge.
   Where we all fall down.

56

Cyn stumbles out of the trees, the white ground rushing towards her. She doesn't get her hands out, landing face-first in the white pluff. Doesn't bother clawing out of the drift, hunkering inside, protected from the wind.

Can't feel her legs.

Her hands.

Face.

The shivers are electric. She'll die out here, in the meadow, winter's hand wrapped around her throat. *No.*

She emerges from the snow dune, inhaling an icy breath dusted with crystals, chilling her from the inside. But there's something over there, across the meadow, over the barren white stretch. She wipes her eyes, but the world still sways like a storm-tossed ship.

She starts again.

Crawling. Eventually stumbling. Foot in front of foot.

Fall.

Up again.

The crossing is lost in time, but she emerges from a snowdrift. The cabins are there.

Her jaw chatters, her teeth chattering like frozen cubes. She wipes her eyes, trying to focus. *There are only two wind harvesters*, she thinks.

The bunkhouse...it's...*gone*. The blackened walls are sagging, spattered with icy white patches. The rafters poke through scorched holes. A white blade sticks out of the ground like a giant plastic knife.

The dinner house is on fire, too. Smoke blossoms from the roof. She's too late. It's all burning to the ground; the girls have nowhere to go.

I'm too late. This is my fault.

Her feet hit the ground like dead pegs. Four steps, maybe five, and she crashes into another puff of snow. Up again.

Little by little she crosses, she finds the other side. Discovers the dinner house isn't on fire; the chimney is belching a long white cloud. The bunkhouse, though, is still gutted, black and dead.

Cyn crawls onto the porch, fighting to breathe. She reaches up, hand shaking against the slick doorknob. Unable to feel the cold steel, unable to grasp and turn it. She collapses against the door, her head hitting the thick wood. She doesn't have the strength to raise her arm, afraid her hand will shatter if she knocks.

Thump, thump, thump. She bangs her head.

What if they're dead? What if everyone is gone? She may not make it out. She could be trapped here for eternity. And she was out, but she came back.

"I know you can hear me." Her lips hardly move. "Let us out, Patricia. Don't do this to us, please."

Thump, thump, thump.

"Please."

Thump.

"We don't deserve..."

Cyn closes her eyes. So tired.

So, so tired.

She doesn't feel the door move. Or the floor on the back of her head. But she hears the voices, feels the hardwood sliding beneath her.

And the warmth of a fire.

The ache begins in her legs.

Feeling is coming back. She still can't feel her fingers. Her tongue is a lump of meat.

She's leaning against the wall next to the stove.

Kat and Mad are knocking snowy crust from her legs and arms, rubbing her fingers, her cheeks. Their words are just sounds, no different than a dog barking or a brook babbling.

"Don't." Mad's voice. "Keep snow packed on that."

She's talking about the backs of her feet. Kat agrees.

"Mmmrggg." Cyn works her useless lips, her tongue not helping. She's met with a crushing embrace. Kat and Mad squeeze her at the same time.

"You came back," Mad says.

Cyn wipes her eyes, running her tongue over her gums. The girls come into focus. They're gaunt. Eyes set deeply. Open sores on Kat's cheeks. Mad's gums are receding. Roc is lying under the table behind them, wrapped in blankets, her bruised face peeking out. Blood caked on her bent nose.

They start asking questions. It becomes noise again. Cyn raises her hand.

"We've got to go. Now."

"It didn't work," Kat says. "When we grabbed the tree, it didn't work for us."

Pain is sneaking up Cyn's legs, spilling nausea into her stomach. She pulls her feet up so her heels aren't touching the floor. The snow on the back of her legs is pink. The shivering eases, lifting the veil on the cold fear hiding beneath.

"You saw the cliff," Cyn says, pushing the words out. "When you touched the tree, you went to dream."

"Yeah, but—"

"Don't run from it. You have to fall."

Kat and Mad don't answer. They know what's out there, what it feels like. They feel it every time they go to sleep.

"I know you're scared, there's fear in the unknown. Fear in the gray. Allow that. Fall into it."

Cyn shudders, biting back the urge to heave.

"Allow yourself to fall...and you'll wake up."

They're nodding. They don't mean it, but they're nodding.

"Trust me."

Roc throws the cover back and sits up. Her face is purplish, left eye swollen shut. But she's nodding. She knows.

We all fall.

Cyn looks around. "Where's Jen?"

The front door slams open. Winter howls inside.

Mad stifles a sob.

57

Miranda is no longer horrified.

Disgusted, sure.

She hides her face in her hands and pushes. The smell is of no consequence. Her olfactory senses have long been corrupted, the candles used up. Still, she closes her eyes and finishes her business, to get it over with. The lid snaps into place and she slides it next to the water heater.

She doesn't enjoy hovering bare-assed over a five-gallon bucket to move her bowels.

The furnace rarely turns on. The thermostat is in the hallway. Mr. Williams has control of that. He's conserving power. He also has a space heater out there to keep his bunions from freezing off.

Miranda has five layers of clothing. She only has to brave the elements when it's time to pull out the bucket.

Her food is stacked against the back door, the only room she still refuses to investigate. She cracks the lid on a bottle of water and takes a tiny sip. Not too much—just enough to keep from dehydrating. The food supply is dwindling.

And she's not leaving the back room.

Ever.

When the food is gone, she'll starve. She's sure of it.

She can't say she's accustomed to hunger. It's still there, twisting her stomach like a dishrag, wringing out every ounce of comfort. She thinks of it constantly, but still, it's not as bad as it used to be. Maybe when you see atrocity worse than hunger, it creates a sort of peaceful perspective.

Why are we still here? He said the dream would end when Patricia's food was gone.

That's when she stopped believing him, when she no longer thought this was a dream. Cyn is gone. They said she found her way out, just grabbed onto a branch and disappeared. All the rest tried, they grabbed it the same way and nothing happened. But Miranda is sure that something else went down. They killed her or something weird.

Mr. Williams did something.

Monster.

She saw what he did to Jen—she watched it on the security camera. Sid was right there with him, stood there like a lobotomized goon and watched, doing nothing.

Miranda did something.

She hauled food out of the pantry, as much as she could get before they returned. And then she locked the door. All it took was an override command on the computer. She'd been watching Mr. Williams operate the system, learning where to go and what to do. She acted stupid, like she didn't understand.

But he found out when he got back.

He and Sid banged on the door for hours. Mr. Williams begged and pleaded, promised he wouldn't hurt her. He just needs to use the computers, that's all. "Please, Miranda. This is hurting all of us."

Liar. *Monster.*

And when the promises didn't work, he proved it. He threw every name ever invented at her. Whore. Bitch. Murderer. A few others. None of them made sense.

He quit after a few days. But he left Sid to hammer the door with the back side of an ax. The clank of metal on metal drove deep inside her skull. It went on for weeks. If there were a button to end her life, she would've pressed it.

Finally, that stopped, too.

Miranda takes another sip and replaces the lid. She takes a package of ramen noodles out of a box and tears open a corner, saving the packet of seasoning for later. It will spice up the water and provide a dose of salt. The noodles are brittle, chalky.

She sits in the office chair, taps the keyboard, and leans back. The monitors come to life. The old man is in the kitchen, preparing tea, looking out the window at a bleak and angry world. Sid is vegetating on the couch. He probably wouldn't eat if Mr. Williams didn't put food in front of him.

The big monitor shows the view from the brick house across the garden, only hints of crops long since shriveled and buried beneath snowdrifts. Only one lump remains in the garden. It shouldn't be there.

She doesn't look at that.

Winter wind continues to scour the land, piling snow against the buildings and sides of trees. The charred remains of the bunkhouse are visible, skeletal and empty. Only two wind harvesters spin near the barn, the other a bladeless post pointing at the sky, rendered useless during a bitter storm.

Smoke puffs out the dinner house chimney. The girls are walking past the windows. They usually huddle around the stove, a stack of wood pilfered from the bunkhouse wreckage. The kitchen is nearly barren. They only move to keep the fire stoked. Or to do business in the corner.

They don't even have a bucket.

There are no footsteps in the snow. Winter wiped them out of existence. The sun went missing behind the steel clouds weeks ago. The forecast is easy.

Misery.

With one wind harvester down, power is limited. But that's not why it's so cold. Thankfully Mr. Williams can't shut the back room down from out there. He would if he could. And then Miranda would surely die.

Miranda learned the computer system. She could remotely lock and unlock all the doors, including the kitchen doors in the dinner house. That explained the electronic keycard locks.

In a fit of dreadful boredom, Miranda popped open the very back room once, her pulse bouncing in her throat, but when the smell oozed out, she kicked it closed with a definitive snap.

There are things worse than a bucket full of crap.

She even turned off the fence. It's a huge power hog. Roc isn't going anywhere near the brick house. Not anymore. And even if she did, she's not getting into the back room.

No one is.

Miranda nibbles on the block of noodles, stopping when it's half gone, wrapping up the remains for later. She chases it with a swallow of water and sits back to watch the cameras, the scenes rarely changing. Patricia looks like a dried apple, her lips puckered with radial lines. *Why won't she die?*

She puts her head back, closing her eyes.

Sleeping is hard. She tried to do push-ups and sit-ups to wear herself out, but got too weak. There's just not enough food to burn calories. But she's tired and figures she can get a couple hours of uninterrupted sleep. She crawls under the counter next to the computers where it's warmest, where there's a bed of coats to curl up in.

She drifts off. No dreams. Never a dream. Just sweet, sweet slumber. The only joy to be found in this dreadful world.

Bang.

She lifts her head, not sure if she heard that. Sometimes she hears voices when she's falling asleep, like someone is right next to her, whispering in her ear. Did she imagine it?

BANG.

The front door.

Miranda scurries out from under the counters and, getting down on her knees, taps the monitors awake. She cycles through the cameras...

Sid is running alongside the garden, forcing his way through the dinner house front door. Mr. Williams trudges along the path Sid left in the snow, walking as fast as a shrinking old man can walk.

Miranda punches a key.

The dinner house interior flickers on one of the smaller monitors. The girls are gathered around the stove. One is leaning against the wall. Her face is agony.

It can't be.

58

Sid's mouth hangs open. A tooth is missing.

Kat and Mad scramble to the corner and come up wielding broken table legs like crude swords. Each takes a side of the table, ready to cut him off. Roc stays put.

He doesn't come after them, instead acting more like a roadblock, letting the bitter chill steal warmth from the stove. Cyn chatters, looking for an extra club, something she can swing. Nothing's within reach, not that she could grip it.

Sid steps aside.

The old man climbs the porch, limping inside.

A ball of anger erupts in Cyn's belly, burning through the fear and hypothermia, a hearth trapped inside, artificially warming her will. If only she had the strength to stand.

He's weathered, like the sky leached gray into his flesh. A withering leaf. A decaying soul.

Sid closes the door behind him.

Mr. Williams rubs his hands, surveying the room. His dead gaze falls on Cyn. "Your stupidity is my good fortune."

"I know who you are," Cyn says.

"Your moronic friends could not find their way back to the gate. You will take me there now." He flicks his hand. "Pick her up."

Sid comes around Mad's side of the table. The club glances off his forearm. He snatches her by the coat and slams her into the wall. The club clatters on the floor. Kat comes over the table, but Sid wields Mad like a shield.

"Stop!" Cyn tries to shout. "Stop it!"

Sid charges Kat, using Mad as a battering ram. Kat jumps on the table with a club.

"Stop." Mr. Williams raises his hand.

Sid freezes like he pushed a button.

"He killed her, Cyn!" Kat points at Mr. Williams without taking her eyes off of Sid. "He killed Jen!"

Cyn sits up, but all the anger in the world can't help her stand.

"He took her out back and killed her, dragged her into the garden. I saw it. I saw her body."

Mad sobs quietly, the coat bunched around her face, hiding her tears.

"This is a dream; she is not dead," Mr. Williams says to Cyn. "You know that to be true now."

"She still suffered."

"And suffering will continue unless *you take me to the gate!*"

Blood vessels emerge on the old man's gray complexion. He paces at the front of the room.

"I am out of patience, girls. Your suffering ends when you get me to the gate. I will leave this world and you'll be relieved of your suffering."

"Kill me," Cyn says. "I'm not taking you."

"There's a problem with that, young lady. Death will not relieve you of suffering—you will simply be reborn in the dream to suffer again. You will forget, I will find you, and then here you'll be in the cabin again. But you have a choice. Take me to the gate and you will never see me again. It's your choice to suffer."

Cyn shakes her head. "Liar."

"*Use your head!*" He thumps his scalp with a single finger. "Why do you think there are so many marks on your wall? Our worlds were linked. You came to Foreverland, you interacted with the boys, but now Foreverland is dead and this godforsaken place cycles over and over and over. You wake up with no memories and I am sent back to the Nowhere, into the gray, lost until I can find my way back. I will not go back there, not again. This time it ends. I am leaving this world."

"Where will you go?"

He stops pacing. They share a knowing glance. *His body is dead. Where will he go?*

She knows.

He'll take one of their bodies. He'll wake in the bunkhouse in Cyn's body or Kat's or Roc's. Linda will be there and Thomas will ask him to remember how he got out and how the girls are doing...

And they'll have no idea.

"Sid," the old man says, "push her face against the stove."

"No!" Kat grabs the back of Mad's coat. Sid lets go with one hand and pops her in the forehead. Kat grabs Mad with both arms, pulling her back.

Roc grabs the table and stands.

"Stop it!" Cyn says.

"Where is it?" The old man holds up the fob, thumb on the button. "*Where is the gate?*"

"Call him off!"

"Tell me! Now!"

"Make him stop!"

Roc starts around the table. Mr. Williams points the fob at her—

"I'll tell you," Cyn says. "Make him stop."

Mr. Williams raises his hand. "This is your last chance. If not, I put all of you asleep. You will wake with half your faces melted to the stove. And I will continue experimenting with you until you do."

"It's due south—"

"No!" Kat shouts. "Don't tell him—he'll kill us once he knows."

Mr. Williams aims the fob at her like a weapon. The button clicks. Kat cringes.

Click. Click, click, click.

She opens her eyes. Still awake. Still standing.

Mr. Williams looks at the ceiling. "You little bitch."

"It doesn't work," Kat says.

"Sid, get over here."

Sid throws Mad and runs to his master's side. The girls pick up their weapons. Roc, too. The old man pockets the fob and lifts his chin, masking the doubt and fear quivering just beneath the surface.

"Girls," he says, "if you do not drop those sticks, I will have Sid beat them out of your hands. You know what he is capable of doing."

He nods at Roc.

"Stalemate," Cyn manages to say. Her legs are coming alive, waking in pain. "If that animal comes, girls, break his legs. Both of them. Without Sid, the old man is helpless. He'll never reach the gate."

The girls lift the clubs, each big enough to snap a bone, shatter a knee. He can't take all of them. They'll lose, sure. But so will the old man.

Stalemate.

The old man blinks heavily.

"I'm taking the girls to the gate," Cyn says. "I can't stop you from following, but if you interfere with us, then I'll stop and you'll never find it. We all die. We start over and you go back out to the Nowhere."

Mr. Williams's lips stretch over his perfect teeth. He calculates the offer. Without the fob, without Sid...there is no counter.

"Do we have a deal?" she asks.

He opens the door and says with his back turned, "If you attempt to lose us, someone will suffer greatly."

He goes outside, waiting on the porch. Arms folded. Sid follows.

———

"Can you walk?" Kat squats down.

No way she can walk. She closes her eyes, putting her arms up. Kat and Mad pick her up. Her skin burns with fever. The pressure on her legs is too much, like a thousand hot pins stabbing in and out.

The room dims. She loses a few moments of awareness, panting to stay alert. Yearning for the cold to take the pain back.

This body is almost done.

Just a mile, that's all. A mile and it's over. One way or another.

"Stop," she grunts, leaning against the table.

Mad gathers up the extra coats and sweaters they were using for bedding. The old man is still on the porch, huddled against the cold. He turns to see what the hell is taking so long. Roc is just inside the doorway, glaring back.

Her eyes are dead and buried in bruised flesh. She swapped out her club for a broken chair leg that's splintered and shaped like a blade.

"Don't," Cyn says.

Roc adjusts her grip, her knuckles white.

"Whatever happened, drop it. They're nothing. You understand, Roc? Nothing. You can escape."

"Here." Mad shoves gloves at them and wraps a scarf around Cyn's neck. Kat stretches another coat over the ones she's already wearing. Mad pulls a hat over her head.

Roc stares.

"You need to say it," Cyn says. "I need to hear it."

Her jaw flexes. Nostrils flare.

Roc puts gloves on. Mad hands her a wad of scarves and hats. Those go on, too. She nods once.

Good enough.

Cyn throws her arms over Kat's and Mad's shoulders. They prop her onto her feet. She can't support her weight. Just moving steals her breath. They drag her to the door.

"We need to get Miranda," Mad adds.

"No," Cyn grits. "She's dead."

"I just saw her in the window this morning."

"Not what I mean. Miranda's dead, she just doesn't know it."

Mad pulls back. "You serious? You really going to leave her? Kat? We can't do that; we ain't like the old man, Kat. We got our differences, but we can't leave her, you heard what he said—"

"That's not Miranda!" Cyn grabs a handful of Mad's scarf and hisses through clenched teeth, "Trust me. She's dead."

She lets go, lunging forward. Kat keeps her from falling and hauls her through the door. Roc follows, weapon in hand.

Mad eventually comes out.

59

They march into the meadow, a desolate stretch of snowy dunes. The figures fade into the blizzard, icy wind swirling, scraping the land, enveloping the small band of girls in its cold grip. Disappear.

Miranda pushes buttons, zooming the camera's view to maximum, focusing on the two figures that straggle behind them. The old man leans heavily on the boy, pushing through the snowy mounds.

The men fade in the swirling snow, too.

And she's alone.

This time, she's really alone. They're not coming back. They're escaping. Or dying.

Her hand shaking, she clicks through multiple screens. The door clicks. Miranda yanks it open, rushing into the hallway and through the house, pulling on the front door. The storm throws it open, the hinges groaning.

Barefoot, Miranda runs down the steps, snow pushing up her pant legs, reaching her knees. The world of white blurs, her eyes filling with water.

The wintry blast snatches the air from her lungs.

The cruel world grinds her pursuit to a halt. Even if she got dressed, if she traipsed over the frozen meadow, she wouldn't find them. The wind has already scoured their tracks from existence.

If they don't escape, they'll die. Either way, they're not coming back.

Really alone.

She begins shivering, her chin rattling uncontrollably. She runs inside and closes the door, sliding to the floor. Melting snow puddles between her numb toes.

The smell of death fills the house.

Cyn abandoned her. Miranda was the one that saved them. She was the one that disabled the zapper. If it wasn't for her, Mr. Williams would have knocked them out; he'd be doing things to them right now, like the things he did to Jen. And they couldn't stop them.

Miranda saved them.

And they left her.

Miranda is dead.

She said it, she knows something. Miranda isn't dead; she's sitting on the floor, holding the panic at bay. Staring down the hall, the metal door swung open.

The back door in view.

Cyn said it like she knew Miranda would hear it. She wanted her to hear it, wanted her to know something. Miranda looks at her hands, turns them over, runs her fingers over the bracelet and the name engraved on the gold plate like they're proof she's alive.

I'm alive.

But even she knows something isn't right. She's always known. Miranda pushes herself up, wiggling her fingers and toes to bring back sensation, wishing the cold could snuff out the fear squirming in her stomach. Wishing she didn't have to do this.

Wishing she wasn't alone.

She pauses in the back room. There's nothing holding her back now. No reason to wait. A few clicks with the mouse, and the lock on the back door whirs.

Snick.

The door moves but doesn't open. Waiting for someone to pull, to make the decision to go back there, to look, to see what's been hiding in the back all this time. For someone to summon the courage to see the truth.

Her hand quivers on the knob, but not because it's cold.

This time, she grabs it.

This time, she pulls it.

The moist odor of death hits her, filling her sinuses, sticking to the back of her throat. She gags before covering her face, her eyes tearing up. She uses both hands to filter the foul air.

It's dark.

A small green light glows on a monitor somewhere in the back. She doesn't search for a light switch, letting her eyes adjust, letting the smell seep out like a tomb that's been steeped in death for far too long.

Two examination tables are in the center, side by side.

A large metal lamp hangs from the ceiling directly over them. One table is empty. There's a bag on the other, brown vinyl. A zipper bisects the center. The corners bulge with liquid.

There are no clear windows to see inside.

She wouldn't look anyway.

She knows what's in there.

A white tag is attached to the zipper dangling at the top. She pushes through the dense air, adjusting one hand over her face, pinching her nose. She flips the tag over, bending over to read it.

Miranda Myers. Dispose.

The room tilts. Begins to turn.

She uses both hands to cover her face again.

Because it can't be. Because Miranda is alive, she's standing next to the table.

Not in that bag.

Something touches her hair.

She jerks back. A coil of wire dangles on a hook suspended from the ceiling, a needle attached to the end, pointing at the table.

Pointing at the bag.

She shakes her head, backing away. The room is dusty. The counters are covered with open journals and stacks of books, scattered pens and paper clips. A chair lies on its side. The computers are dead.

Except for the one across from the tables.

The one with the green light.

Her heart thumps in her throat. Ears ringing.

She's hardly breathing when she reaches down and touches the green light. When the monitor flashes.

Two photos appear side by side, separated by a column of data. One is an image of an old woman, liver spots on her puffy cheeks; her eyes, saggy. The gray hair is thin.

The other is a young girl with blonde hair and a fair complexion. It's Miranda. But that's not what the name at the bottom indicates.

Sandy, it says. *Crossover complete.*

The young girl is Sandy. And the old woman has a name, but Miranda doesn't read it. She knows what it says. She knows who she is.

What she's done.

"This is the Fountain of Youth," Mr. Williams had said.

For Sandy, the place is the River of Death.

Suddenly, the house feels like a coffin. The walls are tighter and thicker. The world, heavier.

She drops her hands, willfully inhaling the scent of death. Accepting it. Gagging on it.

Staggers into the hall.

Into the front room.

Hand on the window. The glass is so cold.

The empty world is cloaked in eternal winter.

—
60
—

Time is erased by pain.

There were trees and rocks, hills and valleys. And snow.

Cyn is draped over Kat and Mad. At times she's limp, her feet dragging behind them, carving a line in the snow. Fever rages inside, making the shivering more violent. Her bladder swells with urine, but she resists the urge to let it go. *What does it matter now?*

Roc keeps an eye on the old man, who is following behind at a safe distance. Cyn guides them, but she's not sure. It's hard to think, her thoughts flowing like molasses. And everything is white.

The trees creak overhead, the branches waving, occasionally snapping. The storm batters the valley as they exit the forest. The girls sway like the trees but keep their balance. Cyn rests her chin on her chest, concentrating on each step, looking every so often.

She's just not sure.

"There." Mad says it. "Look at that."

They force Cyn to stand taller, pulling her arms across their shoulders. At first she only sees a canvas smudged with whites and grays. She blinks heavily, licking her lips.

A hill.

A tree.

The branches without needles. Without snow. An artifact, of sorts, resisting the winter storm, not of this world. A gate to another.

She tries to turn her head. The girls turn her to see the old man emerge from the trees, Sid at his side. Mr. Williams looks up.

He sees it, too.

He knows.

"Go," Cyn says. "Remember...to fall."

"We're not leaving you," Kat says.

"I can get out, don't worry." *Lie.*

The old man says something. Sid lets go of him.

And the girls are running, pulling Cyn up the hill. Roc plows ahead of them, hopping through the knee-deep snow. Kat shouts, but Roc doesn't slow down, bounding for the exit with a wolf at her heels.

The girls struggle to breathe.

Cyn's head bounces; the world falters.

She's slammed through the snow and into the ground beneath, the frigid fluff falling over her. The shouts are muffled. A dull thud of a boot on her back.

Her head cracks beneath another boot. Lights sparkle.

Pressure on top. Someone holding her beneath the surface.

Suffocating. Drowning.

The weight rolls off. She pushes up, her face in the wind, gulping air. The world is blurry. Spinning. An animal is devouring Kat and Mad.

Not an animal.

Sid.

His long arms are flailing. The girls covering up, screaming. They're too far away. Cyn crawls, but she can't reach them, can't help them, can't stop the animal thrashing—

Another crash.

Bodies tumble down the slope, slamming into her. Arms and legs, elbows and knees. Screaming. Roc growls like cornered prey, slashing at Sid's face. Sid rolls over to get leverage and falls into Cyn's lap.

She locks her arms around his waist.

She latches her hands together, clasping each wrist. She wills her arms to clamp her dead fingers down. Sid throws his weight backwards and they roll down the slope. She comes up for air.

"Gooooo!"

She can't see them.

But she feels them hesitate.

Feels them bolt for the top of the hill. For the gate.

And then she closes her eyes. She buries her head against Sid's back, avoids the wild elbows, resists the twisting and rolling. Her fingers slip but don't release.

Down the hill they go.

She only hopes that the girls fall.

All the way back to reality. To the truth.

Her arms are empty.

She doesn't remember letting go.

A shadow passes over her. She looks up, snow melting on her lips. Mr. Williams is looking down. Sid is holding him up, blood streaming from both nostrils and dripping from his chin.

Mr. Williams clutches his chest, leaning against the boy.

"Wait...until I'm gone," he wheezes. "Then finish her."

"You'll leave him here?" The words are long and slurred on her slow tongue. "He'll go back to the Nowhere."

He looks up the slope, trying to catch his breath. "He doesn't know any different. A blissful idiot."

The old man rustles the boy's hair, mouthing the words *good boy*. He starts the climb, falling twice. It takes great effort to get up, to find his balance. Cyn holds out hope he'll tumble down, that he'll lack the strength to reach up, that somehow he'll freeze to the ground like a stone.

He slips only two steps from the gate, resting on his knees. He looks up, a ghostly supplicant raising his head to a false idol, a dead tree, his only hope of escape.

One foot. Then the other.

He stands.

Grasps.

And becomes translucent. She sees the tree through his fading body. Sees sleet and snow blowing through him.

And then he's gone.

But so are the girls.

They made it. They're waking up. And so is the old man, but in whose body? His is dead.

She knows. "Finish her," he said.

Once again, a shadow passes over her. Sid kneels. His fingers are like cold steel on her throat. Her lungs burn, but she doesn't resist, even when all the oxygen is used up. She doesn't feel much as the world fades.

Warmth fills her.

And winter is gone.

Winter is gone.

61

Sleep so deep. Dreamless, beautiful sleep.

A place inside that's warm and cozy. Like an infant pressed to her mother's breast, curled up and safe. Melting in a loving embrace.

No boundaries.

No lies.

Everything exposed. Present.

Nothing rejected.

Mmmmmmm.

She's not aware she's sleeping. There is no "out there", no "me", and no "you".

No "this" or "that".

And she rests in that moment. That eternal moment.

Having been nowhere, there is nowhere to go. Just here.

She's not sure when she became this. There are no thoughts, no memories.

Images arise.

Nothing she sees; it's just pictures, like she is the dream. She is all of it. She is the hills and trees, the wind and snow.

There is beauty and joy, cold and pain. Warmth and pleasure. And great sadness fills the heavens, tears falling in great, salty drops, becoming snowflakes in the frigid loneliness.

It's all there, all contained in this perfect moment where it all makes sense. Where it's all perfectly flawed.

Nothing to be changed.

She is this. And she smiles.

She expands, feeling endless and eternal. But there are boundaries. There is a line at which she stops, a great circle that envelops the wondrous wilderness. There is a tree in the middle, one with barren branches, smooth and rippling, a tree splitting a granite boulder.

A boy sits on the hillside not far from it.

He's next to a girl. She lies so still, her vacant eyes staring into the gray sky.

Me.

She inhabited that body. She left it, became this...this...she became this. And the boy, he did it. He held her down, pressing his thumbs into her windpipe until her bladder released and her lungs contracted.

Her heart beat its last note.

This is all a dream.

The scenes shift, her focus turning to the north, soaring through the trees, beneath the hills, and emerging above the cabins.

Miranda sits in the brick house, one sock hanging from her foot. The other is bare. Music blares, but she doesn't hear it. She sits cross-legged, muttering nonsense.

The walls grow closer. The air thinner.

Outside, the snow ceaselessly piles atop the roofs, growing thicker and heavier. The remains of the bunkhouse topple beneath the weight. The dinner house door is wide open, winter's breath frosting the table, snow filling the corners.

The garden is summer's graveyard, the crops long dead and buried. It is the final resting place for another body, a lump in the middle, its brown skin hidden beneath winter's blanket along with the reprehensible things the old man did to it.

Where are you, Jen?

Safe.

It's a word. It doesn't echo. It's a thought permeating the land. Jen is safe, it says.

Jen is safe.

Deep in the woods there is a small cabin. Inside, an old woman is withered and dry. She won't die. She can't.

She is this world.

She is the one that holds them, the one that imprisons them.

Why won't you let us go?

There is no answer.

Only the slow rise and fall of the ancient woman's chest.

But images unfold.

She sees the old woman's life. She knows her past. Her life. She sees, she feels and knows what is Patricia Ballard.

She was not a happy child. She could not see the difference between thoughts and reality. She struggled with dense emotions, a contracted life, and tortured thoughts. She was diagnosed as mentally ill, her adult life immersed in the psychotropic haze, of dry mouth and dull eyes.

Numb emotions.

She cut herself to feel alive. She plucked her eyebrows to punish herself for being so broken. She cried and screamed. Laughed.

Her life frayed, the edges quickly coming undone.

In her sane moments, she demonstrated brilliance. She painted vivid portraits, wrote stunning poetry, and conducted tearful sonnets. But the malaise of insanity washed those moments of genius from her, leaving her empty.

Reality was harsh. She couldn't accept it.

She said no.

She was a vortex of emotions spiraling into itself.

Until her husband saved her. Her husband bent reality to fit her warped identity. He gave her a universe, made her a goddess. The memory of the needle piercing her frontal lobe is parched and faded. She hardly remembers it.

Patricia has resided within the confines of her own mind longer than the outside world. She created these landscapes, this world. She gave life to her own reality the way she wanted it to be. She developed stars, created Heaven and Hell, God and Devil, and all the entities in between.

She lived in a lush paradise, an endless beach with tepid waters. She savored the sun's kiss, the moon's caress. Eternity was hers, as she wished it to be.

But loneliness crept into her universe.

She craved another's voice, the touch of a stranger.

She created cities with buildings and streets, cars jamming intersections and cafés with coffee, bars with whiskey. She walked among the people who lived in the skyscrapers; she acted like them, talked to them. But no matter how many came to the city, she knew they were just illusions.

They were just thoughts.

And the loneliness howled like winter.

Until her son came for her. He took her away and linked her with his own mind. Her son! She was no longer alone. And soon there were others. Children came to play. They came to the island.

Foreverland.

There were boys on the island. And the girls went to see them, spending day and night with them, wanting so badly to escape the reality of the cabin, to go to Foreverland.

Forever.

Patricia's loneliness dissipated.

Joy reigned. Filled her like the sun.

But she knew what her son was doing to the children. She could feel their identities fraying into the gray void, coming apart at the seams torn from the fabric of their souls. They dissolved.

They never returned.

But there were always more. Always new children to experience. And she was so happy. She had never had this, not in the real world.

And when he disappeared, when her son blinked out of existence, the sadness, the loneliness returned like a scornful god. It struck her long and slow, a cold blade slinking deep into her soul, cutting her over and over.

Forever and ever.

Her universe became cold and isolated, absorbing the details of the real world. Her reality was as harsh as the outside world. There was nothing she could do to stop it. Patricia spiraled into madness once again.

Snow falls in frozen tears.

It piles onto the roofs. Buries the land.

Let us go, Cyn thinks.

And day follows night.

Day follows night.

The snow falls. The weight buckles the dinner house.

The wind harvesters fracture under the weight.

The solar panels become lumps in a frozen land.

Miranda is driven mad with loneliness and guilt. She no longer eats. No longer moves. Frost covers the windows. When the end arrives, she goes to the bedroom and dresses in shiny black shoes and a striped dress. Her foggy breath streams between her chattering lips as she applies eye shadow, smacking her lips with red lipstick.

She walks outside, into the bitter world.

No coat.

Just a wish for the end.

She's numb within minutes. Her skin blue. The snow up to her waist.

She makes it to the meadow, where she falls. Where the dimness creeps in.

She is the last of the girls, and she goes to sleep in death's eternal grip.

Let us go, Cyn asks again.

I'm sorry. Patricia's voice tearfully echoes. She answers, No.

Cyn experiences the warmness once again. The lovely embrace of eternity. Feels the old woman take her to her breast, their souls merging.

Loving.

And night falls on the world.

But she will live to see the sun rise again.

62

The rising sun on us, day beginning.
The sky collapses.
And consumes us all.

The rooster is crowing.

He pulls her from a deep sleep. She struggles to open her eyes, the trace of the terrible dream still glowing.

The sky collapsing on a gray world.

Something vibrates in her throat, a moan escapes her lips. She doesn't recognize it as her own. Her eyes flutter open, her heart matching the alarm. *Wake up!*

It's dark. She can't see. But she feels the bed, feels the pillow cradling her head. She stares ahead, wondering where she is and how she got there.

There are rafters. There are beds with smooth blankets and empty pillows.

The rooster beckons.

She pulls her sheets back and slowly sits up, eyes fully open, searching. The scuffed floor is gritty and cold. She stands up, wearing a long T-shirt that reaches to mid-thigh and reeks of hard labor.

There's a small table beneath a window, an empty bed on the other side of it. Her reflection in the glass looks like an apparition. It must be very early morning; a hint of light illuminates massive white posts with churning blades. Horse hooves thunder in the distance.

She stubs her toe on a pair of worn boots, the tongues pulled out. Her feet fit snugly, the creases stiff and biting. They clop on the wood floor—

"Who's there?" someone says.

The girl freezes.

Something bangs the table. "Ow."

The girl stares into the back corner and sees a small figure bend over to rub her knee. She reaches out. The tip of a match flares, tossing shadows into the rafters. A candle holds the flame.

"Who are you?" the girl in back asks.

The girl in boots doesn't answer. The candlelight is reflecting inside a tin shield, directing it away from the girl holding it. The girl in boots lights a candle on the table in front of her.

The cabin glows warmly.

The girl in the back steps back. Her hair is black and shaved; her T-shirt down to her knees and smudged with dirt. Her skin is dark.

"Who are you?" the girl asks again.

"I don't know," the girl in boots answers.

She swings the candle around. There are boxes under the bed and slashes carved into the wall. She steps closer and leans over the bed. The marks are gouged into the wood, bundled in fives. The last several marks are thin and weak, like they were scratched with a fingernail or a butter knife.

There are voices outside.

"Dammit," someone says. "Hold still before I box you one in the ear." Long pause. "You said this ain't real."

The girl in back blows out her candle and shrinks into the dark. The girl in boots holds her ground, pointing the light at the door. She looks around for a club or something sharp. She can throw the candle at them if she has to, charge them.

The door flies open.

She steps back and crouches. Ready to defend herself.

Two girls look inside. They're wearing designer clothes that were dragged through the mud and tattered from long days. The white girl's hair is matted and knotty.

"Cyn?"

The girl in boots doesn't know what that means. *Sin?*

The smaller one steps inside, her skin black. She smiles and points at the back of the bunkhouse.

"Jen," she says.

Jen cowers slightly. The strangers approach her slowly, gently. They wrap their arms around her. She doesn't try to stop them.

The smaller one begins weeping. "We're so sorry, Jen," she says. "We couldn't stop him..."

The girl lets them hug her, lets them weep and apologize. Not that she can do anything about it; they've got her locked between them and aren't letting go.

"What the hell is going on?" the girl in boots says.

They wipe their eyes, laughing and crying, putting their arms around Jen and guiding her around the stove.

"We'd hug you," one of the girls says, "but you're dangerous when you don't know what's going on."

"Then tell me." She holds the candle up.

They shield their eyes.

"I'm Kat and this is Mad. We came to get you out."

"Where am I?"

"Later." Kat reaches out and squeezes her arm. "I'm so glad to see you, Cyn. We were afraid..."

She chokes on rising emotion.

Mad comes over and, despite her reservations, puts a hug on Cyn. They both do. Cyn stands there stiffly and lets them.

"You saved our lives," Mad says, squeezing tightly. "All of us."

Cyn doesn't know what any of this means. Neither does Jen. They watch the strangers go through another round of laughing and weeping. Mad stands back, wiping her eyes.

Kat reaches under one of the empty beds, blows her nose in a T-shirt, and throws it back under.

"Why can't I remember my name?" Cyn asks.

"You will, pretty soon," Kat says. "We need to get going. It's a little chilly outside. There are clothes under your beds—you should get dressed. We've got to walk a bit to reach the gate."

"What gate? What's going on?"

"Just trust us."

Cyn isn't trusting. She sure as hell isn't moving.

Kat keeps an eye on her as she pulls a box out from beneath the bed and gets out a few sweatshirts and some jeans. Mad does the same for Jen, and Jen goes along with it.

"Look, you got no reason to trust me, I know. But you're going to have to make that leap."

"I don't know you."

"You don't know yourself."

Kat holds the clothes in one hand, reeking of body odor. Cyn isn't reaching for those rags. But Kat's right: she doesn't know anything. These girls seem to know something.

"We know you, Cyn," Mad says. "I can prove it. Check those pants, the ones from under your bed. You read the tag on the inside of the waist, see what it says."

Kat throws them at her feet. Cyn bends down and picks them up without looking away from her. She flips the waistband and finds a white tag sewn to the inside.

Cyn.

"I know that don't prove anything." Kat holds up her hands. "But we're telling you the truth. You don't have to be near us, you just need to follow. And if you don't like what you see, you just go on your own way."

Mad starts to protest. Kat stops her.

"We got a deal?"

Cyn looks at the pants.

"You ain't got nowhere else to be, nothing else to do. And no one else to trust. You just got to fall with us, Cyn."

Jen is dressed and ready.

Cyn stares at the tag. She puts the candle down and slides the jeans on one damp, moldy leg at a time. Kat throws the sweatshirts at her feet, and she puts those on, too.

Fall with us.

Kat goes to the door, putting her hand on the knob. She takes a breath and opens it.

Cyn steps back. Alarms go off in her head.

An old man lies on the ground, his hands and feet tied with strips of clothing. He groans through a dirty rag tied around his mouth. His angry words are distorted, his eyebrows pinched. His scalp is red and ridged.

"We brought him with us," Kat says. "We didn't hurt him, Cyn. He was just taking up space he didn't need to be taking up."

"I don't understand."

"Don't matter. We'll leave him here."

The old man growls a string of words muffled by the gag.

"Why?" Cyn asks.

Kat looks at Jen. "He's a real bad man, Cyn. This is where he belongs."

Kat checks the bindings, making sure they'll hold long enough for them to reach the gate. Mad guides Jen outside, staying between her and the old man. Cyn comes out next, the old man cursing nonsense at each of them. But cursing for sure.

The morning chill slips down her neck. Cyn crosses her arms, shivering while staring at the helpless old man. He bites the cloth like a muzzled dog.

"Is that his house?" Jen asks.

There's a large brick house to the east where the sky is glowing, the sun still below the trees. A lamp lights up one of the front windows.

"Yeah," Kat says. "He lives there with his daughter. They helped build this place. We're going to let them have it all to themselves."

Kat, Mad, and Jen start walking towards a meadow. The old man begins another round of guttural, angry protests. A window lights up on the second floor of the brick house. The curtains part, and the outline of a girl appears, her hand on the glass. Maybe she'll come out for him when the girls are gone and untie him. He looks hungry.

The old man rolls into Cyn's leg. His eyes plead. The growls turn to whines.

"Come on!" Kat shouts.

Cyn walks around him. The grunts and cries fade behind her. Grass brushes her waist, the flowers tickling her outstretched hands. Mountains are on the horizon to her right. The brick house recedes in the distance, only the lit windows visible.

"Where you taking us?" Cyn asks.

"A mile due south." Kat says. "We're going to fall out of here, Cyn. I just need you to remember one thing."

Kat leans in and whispers in her ear.

———

Pain radiates between her eyes. A face hovers over her. Short brown hair drapes like curtains, framing an angular face and green eyes.

"Password?" Linda says.

Cyn's arms are pinned at her sides. Jackie stands at the IV, a syringe inserted in the tube, her thumb on the plunger.

"Password?" she asks again. "What is it? You know it—tell me."

Cyn shakes her head. She hasn't a clue what she's talking about. There's no password. She knows that, but maybe something has changed. She thinks, trying to remember where she was a second ago. She just woke up in the bed. But before that, she was...she was...

"Last time," Linda says. "Password?"

She closes her eyes, holding her breath. There was a tree and a rock. The sun was rising when she grabbed onto it.

When she fell.

When Kat told her to say—

"Sandy sent me." She opens her eyes.

"What's your name?"

"Cyn."

"Full name?"

She hesitates. "Cynthia."

Linda nods at Jackie. She pulls the syringe out of the tube.

Someone reaches over Cyn's head, her finger and thumb on the wire stuck between her eyes. A needle slides out of her head, a cold sliver that's been in far too long.

A drop of clear liquid streams across her forehead. The pressure between her eyes eases. Linda embraces her tightly.

"Welcome back, Cynthia."

And there's applause.

The bunkhouse is full of people. The youngest of them fall on her. Cyn is trapped by three girls and a grown woman.

Home.

63

The grass is knee-high. Wildflowers sway here and there, but few are left as the mornings have gotten colder. Mad, Kat, and Jen wander up the slope, Jen with a fistful of white flowers from the meadow.

Jennifer. And Madeline and Kathryn.

"Those are their names," Linda reminded Cyn. The three-letter versions are the names inside the dream.

We're not in the dream anymore.

It's been weeks since she woke up. Weeks since Kat and Mad were brave enough to come back for her and Jen. It took a lot of work, though. Linda and Thomas wouldn't get duped again. There was a close watch on those needles. They weren't planning on the girls going back inside. Cyn had done it, and look what happened to her.

"She did it for us!" Kat had argued. "You ain't stopping us."

No good, though. They were just kids—they didn't know the risks. And Thomas and the important people did, and they weren't going to take them.

But then Kat and Mad got clever. They lied to Linda and Thomas, said that Patricia was about dead and that Cyn and Jen would be lost to the Nowhere forever. They had no idea the word "Nowhere" would sell it. Linda bought it and came to their rescue. She persuaded Thomas to let the girls go back inside the needle.

"We running out of time, Mr. Thomas," Kat had added. "We'll lose Cyn forever."

Besides, Cyn wasn't getting out until someone escorted Mr. Williams back inside the dream. Otherwise, she had no body.

Yeah, Cyn's body.

His body is dead.

He exited the dream into the one body he knew would be vacant. Cyn was still in the dream when he made his escape, opened his eyes as a sixteen-year-old female, which beat the hell out of spending eternity in the Nowhere. He could figure out bras and tampons. No one would know the difference.

But Thomas and the important people had done their research—they knew how things worked on the island. They knew there was a password. When an old man transferred into a young man's body, they were asked for it in order to confirm the identity, to make sure the right person was in the body.

Linda asked for a password the first time and Cyn didn't know one. The girls were asked, too. They had no idea.

But Mr. Williams had said, with a smile, "Foreverland."

After that, he was easy pickings.

They sent him back inside the dream to make room for Cyn to return. It was her body, after all.

She shivers at the thought of that old bastard sliding into her body. It was a good thing she couldn't remember him when Kat and Mad came back for her and Jen. She would've done something to him.

Something very bad.

Strangely, she feels sorry for him. A small part of her, deep inside, will miss him. She told Linda that. She decided it was time to start talking about things, to start digging through the memories and working them out. To start remembering.

When she said a part of her was fond of Mr. Williams, Linda called it Stockholm syndrome. Cyn doesn't like the way it feels—wanting to kill him and save him at the same time.

"Little by little," Linda had reminded her. "We heal little by little."

The girls climb the green slope toward a split boulder with a picturesque bristlecone pine nudging the fracture wider. The ancient-looking branches are loaded with seed-bearing cones and short needles.

Unlike the dream, it's full of life.

Why did Patricia choose this as the gate? Was it because it was so far from the cabins? Cyn doesn't think that's it. She couldn't keep them from leaving the dream, but used their fears to trap them. Ultimately, the girls could leave at any time. They chose to stay in the dream by refusing to face their fears.

In the dream, the tree was dead.

But it was so difficult to see through the illusion when they were immersed in it. Cyn hadn't slept more than an hour at a time since escaping, afraid she'd awake in the bunkhouse, marks on the wall. And how does she know this isn't a dream? What if dreams are endless layers, each another dimension of reality? Which one is real?

When they're all peeled away, what will be in the middle?

She looks at her hands, turning them over. Linda had said that will help to ground herself, remind her she's in the flesh. *In the dream, you doubt. Here, you know.*

But Linda wasn't there. She wasn't seduced by the sights and sounds. The suffering.

Cyn touches the sensitive hole in her forehead. The stent is still there. Maybe they can remove it one day, but she doubts it. It will be there forever, Patricia's parting gift, something to remember her by. Maybe that's not a bad thing. In the dream, there was no hole. She can always look at that instead of her hands.

The girls reach the top of the hill. Jen lays the bundle of flowers on the stone. The flowers from their earlier trips are still there, dry and crumbling, the seeds blowing on the ground, where they will bloom again. They'd done this several times over the last couple of weeks to honor all the girls that are lost in the Nowhere.

Sandy is out there.

Miranda forgot what she'd done. She woke up with no memories in a young body with blonde hair. Why would she believe that it wasn't her body? She brought Sandy out to the Fountain of Youth and destroyed her identity so she could take the body. Whatever they are—a soul, an identity, an essence—can be moved in and out of bodies.

Sandy was pushed out and Miranda moved in.

Maybe the Fountain of Youth program intentionally made her forget what she'd done. Maybe it was easier that way, to forget what she'd done to Sandy. To forget she's a murderer.

Miranda started fresh. Her essence, her soul, got a new body to make more memories. *We are not our memories, that's not who we are.* Cyn even suspects Miranda had some of Sandy's memories and convinced herself she was innocent. She was using the stolen memories to ease the guilt. How would she know? How would any of us know who we really are if we get someone else's memories?

Doesn't matter. Whatever Miranda is, it's in Sandy's body.

So she's a murderer. And a thief.

All the girls, all their souls, are lost in the Nowhere, and Thomas promised to find them and get them out. But how will they get out? They don't have bodies anymore.

The distant thumping gets louder.

The girls look up. A helicopter banks to the east. Jen waves. They can't see her, but that's not why she's doing it. The helicopter is carrying Patricia to a lab far away. A universe is inside her, a world that contains Sid, Miranda, and Mr. Williams.

Mr. Graham.

Somewhere in the real world his wife is hoping to find him. She'll be expecting to reunite with her husband, expecting him to be inside a young man's body, one that he sponsored.

She'll be disappointed. But at least she's not trapped in the Nowhere.

A utility vehicle putters out of the trees. Linda steers it around a dip in the ground. Roc sits in the passenger's seat.

Cyn avoids looking at her. They don't like each other any more in the skin than they did in the dream. Roc would've killed them, and Cyn can't forgive her for that. A part of her wants to send her back to the dream with the old man and Miranda, because she's a piece of garbage.

But that's how the old women saw all of them: girls that had wasted their lives. The old women were just taking a body that had already been abandoned by the mind. A body is a terrible thing to waste.

"Time to go," Linda says.

The girls come down the slope, their laughter ahead of them. Linda doesn't mean it's time to leave the hill. It's time to leave the camp. *Forever.*

Kat, Mad, and Jen have family. They have brothers or sisters, uncles, cousins...someone in the world who wants them. Roc, it turns out, is eighteen. She doesn't need family. She can go right back to her crappy life. They'll keep an eye on her for some time. Probably forever. Some government official had informed them that they would be compensated for their pain and suffering with funds confiscated from the Fountain of Youth operation.

We're talking millions.

Cyn's memories about her stepfather were legitimate. Evidently, she was removed from the home by Family Services and placed with a foster family. She didn't stay long, though; she was reported missing a month after she arrived. She doesn't remember much of that, and the memories are coming back slowly. She's not going back to Ohio, though. She'll go somewhere else that has the funds to support her.

For now, she's going back with Linda. Cyn hopes it's more than just temporary.

The girls climb into the back of the vehicle.

"Can we make a detour?" Cyn asks.

"Depends."

"It's not far." She points down the slope at a line of trees. "I just need to see something."

Linda checks her watch. "I think we can manage. Hop in."

The vehicle is weighted in the back, but they're going over smooth terrain, straight downhill. She taps Linda on the shoulder and points at the gap in the trees.

Cyn climbs out.

The short hairs on the back of her neck tingle. She's afraid to move, afraid that it will mean that her worst fears are true. But she finds the courage to take a step toward the opening. She holds her hand out, reaching for a feeling she'll recognize in the lump still in her neck.

Fear stiffens her arm.

She steps onto the road, the tracks still on the ground. The same road she encountered in the dream, where the world ends. She walks several feet down it and turns around.

Drops her arm.

The girls are watching her from the vehicle.

Cyn lets out a deep breath. Smiles. Nothing tingles, nothing stops her. And the gray is still in the dream. *And this is not the dream.*

She's ready to start a new life in the real world. She's convinced it really is out there. And she's in it. At least this layer.

"Looking for a dead body?" Kat shouts.

The girls don't get out of the vehicle. They stay in the back, chatting away. Cyn considers walking a little farther, wondering if she can stay out here a bit longer, maybe wander down the road and get lost for a while, just be with her thoughts and the promise of a brighter future. It just feels so good to be back in the flesh, in the real world.

"What was the name of the old lady that had the leather journal?" Kat asks. "The one that sponsored Cyn?"

There's discussion. Linda answers. "Her name was Barbara."

"Yes?" Cyn says.

But it wasn't that she was agreeing with her. It happened so fast, so naturally. No one heard her. Not even Linda. But Cyn knows what happened. She almost collapses with the realization that she answered to the name.

She answered to Barbara.

Oh, sweet Jesus.

WHAT TO READ NEXT?

Ashes of Foreverland (Book 3)

https://bertauski.com/foreverland/

Tyler Ballard was in prison when his son created a dreamworld called Foreverland, a place so boundless and spellbinding that no one ever wanted to leave. Or did. Now his son is dead, his wife is comatose and Tyler is still imprisoned.

But he planned it that way.

The final piece of his vision falls into place when Alessandra Diosa investigates the crimes of Foreverland. Tyler will use her to create a new dimension of reality beyond anything his son ever imagined—a Foreverland for the entire world.

Danny, living outside of Spain since escaping the very first Foreverland, begins receiving mysterious clues that lead him to Cyn. They are both Foreverland survivors, but they have more in common than survival. They become pieces of another grand plan, one designed to stop Tyler

Ballard. No one knows who is sending the clues, but some suspect Reed, another Foreverland survivor. Reed, however, is dead.

Everyone will make one last trip back to Foreverland to find out who sent them. And why.

https://bertauski.com/foreverland/